In the VALE

John Hamm

TATE PUBLISHING & *Enterprises*

In the Vale
Copyright © 2008 by John Hamm. All rights reserved.

This title is also available as a Tate Out Loud product. Visit www.tatepublishing.com for more information.

No part of this publication may be reproduced, stored in a retrieval system or transmitted in any way by any means, electronic, mechanical, photocopy, recording or otherwise without the prior permission of the author except as provided by USA copyright law.

Scripture quotations marked "KJV" are taken from the Holy Bible, *King James Version,* Cambridge, 1769. Used by permission. All rights reserved.

The opinions expressed by the author are not necessarily those of Tate Publishing, LLC.

Published by Tate Publishing & Enterprises, LLC
127 E. Trade Center Terrace | Mustang, Oklahoma 73064 USA
1.888.361.9473 | www.tatepublishing.com

Tate Publishing is committed to excellence in the publishing industry. The company reflects the philosophy established by the founders, based on Psalm 68:11,
"The Lord gave the word and great was the company of those who published it."

Book design copyright © 2008 by Tate Publishing, LLC. All rights reserved.
Cover design by Isaiah R. McKee
Interior design by Nathan Harmony

Published in the United States of America

ISBN: 978-1-60462-905-7
1. Fiction: Action & Adventure
2. Fiction: Visionary & Metaphysical
3. Philosophy: Metaphysics/Religious
08.06.24

Dedication

This book is dedicated to my stepmother
Vallie Scott Hamm
who wanted me to write it.

Acknowledgement

I owe much to Linda Richardson's incisive criticism and Ann Drum's cheerleading.

1

The armored personnel carrier would have been no more than a dark stain flowing slowly across the meadow, if not for the full moon, the bright reflection from the snow, and the patrol vehicle's jerky searchlights grazing along the margin of surrounding forest to find, if they could, what ought not to be there.

Two men lay at the forest's wooded border beneath panels of white parachute silk that threw back all light, as if from the snow. They had watched the snow-tracked APC arrive three successive times. It always entered along the far side of the meadow and turned in their direction to follow the riverbank. Then it swept their side of the meadow and moved away uphill over the snow-packed utility road by which it had come.

The vehicle's regular schedule and the absence of any other human activity during their vigil told the men it would be gone for at least twenty minutes. They would have plenty of time to cross the two hundred yards of open space that lay parallel to the river. The frequency of motorized patrol implied, they concluded, the absence of any fixed outpost from which their transit might be observed.

Before the patrol came back, they should be well into the opposing forest and nearing their goal.

Training, experience, and good sense told the two that crossing the meadow was an extreme risk. Rivers, roads, and wide-open spaces headed the list of things to avoid when trying to move undetected through a patrolled area. Professional watchers keep a close eye on waterways and roads for the same reasons that lazy or heedless penetrators are drawn to them—they offer drinking water and deceptively easy routes of entry and egress.

If looking for security forces near a border or some other prohibited area, just follow a road or a watercourse. Want to make things even worse? Cross an open place like this meadow. It is the easiest place to see and be seen, a sentinel's delight and a near-promise of capture or worse for would-be evaders.

Knowing the danger, the men were hard-pressed by circumstance and a sense of urgency to chance it. Time was now their enemy. They had come a long way with caution and skill, but bad weather had put them seriously behind plan. Going around the meadow in the darkened forest, the only sure and prudent way to go, would take more than four hours. That was much too long and now even more so, considering the hour they had wasted watching the meadow and the patrolling APC. The people they were supposed to meet would not wait. The rendezvous would abort. Their efforts and successes up to now would count for nothing unless they made a desperate dash across the snowy meadow. Anyway, that is what they thought and feared.

About two feet of fresh snow had been added to an existing six by the storm that delayed them. Recent vehicle movements in the fresh powder should render their snowshoe tracks unnoticeable even by daylight. All they had to do was get across quickly.

At a less rational level, they were impelled by growing impatience and the frustration of having their mission's end almost in view—moods that do not promote sound decision-making. Weighing risks against probable outcomes, they had selected an open run as the only acceptable option. When the patrol lights disappeared this time, they would cross the open space as rapidly as possible.

Barney, the leader, would go first. If Barney got twenty yards without incident, Paul would follow. Twenty yards on snowshoes takes a lot longer than running it on solid ground, and timing did not permit them to get too far apart. The full distance was not so great, but the impediments of parka, pack, and snowshoes would make their run a significant exertion.

They stood up, folded and stowed the parachute panels, and quickly checked each other to be sure that all their equipment was properly fastened and secured to their bodies. Then Barney struck out over the open snow. When he was well gone and nothing had happened, Paul set out behind him. Barney looked back just once to be sure Paul was on the way.

Walking in snowshoes is similar to a ballet movement. It requires a toe-forward thrust with the heel angled up, so that the webbed oval glides above the snow, while the narrow end that looks like a tennis-racquet handle trails with minimum resistance over the surface. Running in snowshoes is almost a contradiction. Doing it on fresh, dry powder under a full pack is even more awkward and exhausting to the runner. This was true even of the modified, lighter version of snowshoes with which they were equipped.

In the lead, Barney dared not take his eyes for long from the place toward which he had chosen to run. Failure to maintain that critical reference point near the tree line might cause him to lose his path and lengthen their exposure.

Paul, following in Barney's trail, could afford to be slightly less attentive. Barney's moving form, ahead in the clearing, was much easier to visually reacquire than an arbitrary landfall at the edge of a darkened forest.

Fatigue and concentration alone would probably have kept either man from hearing much along the way. Besides, both wore heavy pile caps with earflaps tied down against the mountain cold. The flaps also shut out external noise.

Halfway across the meadow, Paul was conscious only of Barney's bulky figure in front, the demands being made on his own body, and the roaring of blood and breath inside his cap. His thermal underwear and parka, former friends against the night chill, now coated his skin with a scalding layer of sweat as he executed a repetitious, careening dance across the snow. Toe down, heel up, kick, glide, drag, touch; toe down, heel up, kick, glide, drag, touch. Eyes ahead. Follow Barney. Keep moving. Toe down, heel up, kick, glide, drag, touch; toe down, heel up, kick, glide, drag, touch.

With no warning, the deep snow he landed on lost its density. He was falling through it with no more resistance than if he were jumping into a swimming pool. Yet, his penetration seemed to be smoothly self-retarding. Now he came to a gentle halt with his shoulders barely above the snowy surface. For the moment his descent was done. Everything was still, and he knew himself to be in great peril.

Paul had visited the threshold of death enough times to be skeptical of people who cited fear and courage as symptoms or outcomes of the event. Others might react that way, but he could relate neither motive to the process of facing his own mortality.

Certainly he could be afraid. He had been many times, but never during an actual life-threatening moment. Fear affected him only before a threat became critical. He might decline a hazardous venture or more commonly detour around it to avoid the fatal portal altogether. He believed fear was a healthy emotion that normally prompted sensible behavior.

Entering a potentially dangerous situation, after carefully planning and training to eliminate or minimize every threat, was as close as he regularly came to a deliberate act of courage. The adrenaline rush before action, like the inevitable letdown afterward, was strictly glandular and not to be confused with bravery or any other quality of action.

When chance, mistake, or preparatory failure brought him directly to confront death or great harm, fear and courage were never at issue. His immediate response was always simple curiosity.

Now that Paul was suddenly up to his armpits in snow, his gloved hands extended awkwardly on the flimsy surface before him, he was extremely curious. What was going on here? Time had a way of moving very slowly in circumstances like these; he felt no need to hurry. Barney was moving away from him, but slowly.

Since he had apparently fallen into a hole, Paul's intuitive reaction was to climb out. This, he found, he could not do, because his snowshoes were hanging up in the snow beneath him. That was not surprising. He became alarmed only after discovering that his snowshoes and lower legs were not just buried in snow with the rest of his body—they dangled in empty space. Unlike the rest of him, they moved freely, except when he tried to pull himself out. Then the snowshoes, long and broad, caught abruptly, as if against the ceiling in a lower room.

Now he had a clearer picture of his situation. It was something like stepping amiss in an unfinished attic, falling through the insulation and plaster, and being spared a full drop into the room below only by being caught, arms and elbows, on the ceiling beams. The grim difference was that the snow was not as sturdy as ceiling beams and his snowshoes would not let him climb out. The equal-and-opposite reaction to his failed effort to break loose had left him inches deeper still in the snow. Struggling against his entrapment only made things worse.

Paul had seen plenty of similar terrain in other seasons and could quickly assess his predicament. Year after year, torrential springtime mountain runoffs would have eroded a network of rugged ravines that grew wider and deeper as they neared the river. Thoroughly hidden by winter snow, these great trenches allowed partial thaws, gravity falls, and other natural events to create randomly shifting cavities—snow caves beneath the surface. Large and small envelopes might fill in or grow larger during the winter. Those that remained would cave in or be swept away as the surface receded with spring thaw.

Paul's free-hanging feet told him he had penetrated a cavity of indeterminate depth. Factoring his height and the distance to the river, he estimated that his feet could be anywhere between five and ten feet from the bottom of the ravine—not necessarily so far from the bottom of the cavity, but that was just one of many unknowns.

Lifting his snowshoe-bound feet would only hasten his descent and maybe bring in a ton-or-so of snow on top of him. This was the probable end of any scenario he could imagine for getting out by himself. Unable to reach them with his hands, he could jettison neither the snowshoes, nor the boots so securely fastened to them. If he moved around, he would go down. If he remained still, weight and gravity would take him down anyway. At best, he would be buried alive under more than five feet of snow. At least, he would die quickly. In the spring his body would be washed down the ravine and turn up floating in the river.

Paul's assessment, including a prayer, took no more than three seconds. By himself he could not affect the situation, except to make it worse. He was not going to survive on his own. Beyond his prayer, the only aid in sight was Barney's gradually disappearing back, now something more than twenty yards ahead. If Barney knew the trouble Paul was in, he would turn around and help. He could stand back from the hole and hold out something for Paul to grab, a snowshoe perhaps.

That would work. If Barney took off one of his snowshoes, and Paul got a good grip on it, Barney could pull him to safety. There was plenty of time to do that and still get into the woods before the patrol came back.

Would Barney turn around and see him? Chances were not good. Barney was concentrating on a point at the edge of the woods for his bearing and was not apt to take his eyes off it until it was fairly close. By then, he would be nearly a hundred yards away. He would no longer be able to see Paul, even if he knew where to look and Paul had not already tumbled into the snow pocket below. Given time, which he would not have, Barney would not even be able to calculate his reverse track.

Paul was so accustomed to maintaining silence in this kind of work that he almost failed to consider calling out. On thinking of it, he first examined the possible consequences. Nobody inside the relatively noisy patrol vehicle was likely to hear his shout, even if it were on top of him. Prior assumption that the meadow was free of in-place observers seemed to be supported by the absence of any response to their progress across the open snow. Calling for help might be a good idea.

Paul had begun to yell before he realized that no sound was likely to penetrate Barney's earflaps or the cardiopulmonary override of his ongoing exertion. He shouted anyway, but his apprehension was correct. Barney did not hear him.

After a moment, he quit calling. *Why die with a sore throat?*

Attempts to stabilize his descent by spreading his arms were becoming less effective. Paul was up to his shoulders, and the snow around him was moving slowly but perceptibly. More precisely, he was sinking into it faster and faster.

He looked curiously after Barney, but could no longer see him. That meant that Paul's head was now below Barney's line of sight. When Barney finally stopped and turned around, he would find no one behind him.

Paul knew his chances had run out, but there was still time for another prayer.

He prayed for Barney too.

2

Paul had been in jail more than once. He suspected he might be there again. To be caught entering falsely and moving around illegally in other people's countries is likely to produce imprisonment. Paul regularly ran those risks. Capture was a serious enough problem, but things could always turn worse. Any prisoner was still better off than a dead man, and that was the usual alternative in such cases. The latter could still happen to him, unless he were extremely careful and immoderately lucky.

Paul considered the alternative and wondered why he was not dead. He knew he was just about to be, when he last looked. His eyes were still closed, but he was quite sure he was not packed into freezing snow or entombed in a ravine by the river. He was not even out of doors. Wherever he was, the ambient temperature was far more agreeable than that of any jail cell he could remember.

Where was he? How did he get here? Who had him? Why? What about Barney? Had Barney turned back to the rescue? Now there was a happy thought. Was Paul actually in jail? Had Barney gotten away into the forest and gone on to the rendezvous? If so, how did Paul manage to survive? There were too many unanswered questions about himself and his situation.

Paul decided to see what answers he could find within before opening his eyes to a flood of new information that might overwhelm him. He would not try, like a child or the fabled ostrich, to avoid being seen by refusing to see. Still, he might be able to escape notice for a while by adopting that tactic. So long as he remained motionless, he might postpone the arrival of unwanted and possibly troublesome attention.

To begin with, he was alive; a given of prime importance considering the circumstances of his most recent memory.

Maybe he was not in prison. His unseen surroundings seemed to lean toward that welcome idea. Even with his eyes closed he could tell that he was comfortable. Beyond the accommodating temperature, he perceived that he was not hungry. Yet his last meal must have been at least twenty-four hours before he awakened. How long would it have taken to move him from the mountain snows to wherever he now was and to make him feel so fully rested? He reckoned no less than twelve hours.

The noise levels and aural input were totally incompatible with any past experiences of incarceration. In fact he could hear nothing. Now wasn't that odd? No sound whatsoever. Even hospitals and libraries have subtle, underlying hums and purrs that can be discerned with minor concentration. Listening with his eyes closed, he heard only silence. He heard nothing natural like wind, rain, speech, or the common movements of life. He could not even detect an artificial murmur from whatever machinery would be needed to maintain the ideal climatic conditions he seemed to sense around him.

Paul thought about the reputed stillness of the grave. *Too negative*, he decided, quashing that idea for the moment.

The sensations in his body seemed incongruous with his most recent exertions. He was unquestionably fit, but even the best-toned muscles would cry out against the physical demands he had forced upon his for days. Why were his own making no complaint? Why, in fact, did he feel so completely at ease? Analyzing his sensory input, he realized that what he felt was merely the absence of discomfort—or anything else.

How long had he been here? He could not be sure without looking, but he was reasonably certain he had been bathed. Moving on foot through rugged, wintry territory for a long while with minimal hygienic opportunities and no change of clothes gives a man a gamey reek that would drive him crazy if he smelled it while he was clean. Blessedly, he is immunized against this stench, because it is all he can smell at the time. It is his only olfactory point of reference. He discovers its true strength only after taking a good shower and trying to get back into the same room with his soiled clothing.

Sniffing with care, Paul could find none of the industrial-strength body odor and wood-smoke residue he had shared with his garments for so many days. This also suggested these items were no longer within smelling range.

Additionally, his nose registered none of those antiseptic aromas common to hospitals and some jails. Neither did he detect the stale-urine signature of every jail that had formerly housed him. He was reminded of his previous sensory assessment by the nagging awareness that he merely smelled the absence of any smell at all.

Paul was not ready to move anything yet. In the likely event that he was being watched, he wanted to preserve the appearance of someone still asleep. Without moving, he could not tell how he was dressed or even if he had clothes on.

What was his physical attitude? Was he lying down or in a partly reclining position? That seemed a logical probability, but the various receptors of his body told him nothing. He felt no weight-driven pressure from surfaces beneath or around him, and the microscopic hairs of his inner ear were sending no data to his brain. At least he was not in motion, or so he thought.

Paul searched for any memory of events taking place between his gradual descent into the snow and the current moment. He recalled a contradictory combination of panic and resignation as he submerged and felt himself falling. The space into which he dropped was instantly filled so tightly with so much snow that he could not move. His body was being crushed and a hideous spear of icy pain was forcing itself through and beyond his face to freeze the nerves at the core of his consciousness. He remembered feeling as if he were about to suffocate or drown. He had no other memory until he awakened here, wherever here was.

Was he suffering from amnesia, or had he just been unconscious for the whole period since his painful entombment? He felt so thoroughly refreshed that the latter conclusion seemed most likely. How long had he been out? His current feeling of well-being suggested quite a while. Was it hours, days, or weeks?

Could he learn anything else from introspection?

No.

Now Paul opened his eyes.

The scene revealed was completely foreign to any place or experience he could remember or even imagine.

Because of his work, Paul spent a large part of his life just waiting on remote military bases where the primary diversion was nightly movies. If four or five films a week were shown, he was there to see them. The quality of the picture made little difference to him. Its main purpose was to provide diversion and there was only one picture-show in town. In more recent years, when VCR libraries and players became available, he continued to prefer a B-grade western or a science-fiction epic on the big screen to a classic Oscar winner of any genre on a television set.

This fairly innocent pastime had left Paul well acquainted with the almost miraculous success of special effect techniques, lately augmented by computer enhancement, in bringing the strangest things to cinematic reality.

Such viewing experience did not prepare him in the least for the incredible activity he now saw.

As stunning as his perception was, Paul was not alarmed. He was excited in a breathtaking sort of way. Typically, his main reaction was one of fascinated curiosity about the display of confusing phenomena that instantly blossomed around him. His mind failed to produce any memory fit for comparison.

He was suddenly in the middle of every manifestation of shape, shadow, and light he could think of, plus some he could not. They were all moving and interacting in ways he could barely describe to himself. He had no point of reference from which to proceed, no definition for anything he saw, and only a slight ability to correlate this massive input of sensory stimuli. His mind was stymied, but not disabled.

Surely this was no jail. On the other hand, he was not at all certain when, if ever, he might be able to leave the place, whatever it was—wherever it was. He saw nothing that looked a bit like an exit.

A seemingly limitless distance stretched away from him on every line of azimuth in every plane of the compass. Suspended in space with no apparent support, he had no horizon and no real up or down. Had he been able to rotate equally on his vertical and horizontal axes, he might have sighted along any degree from any angle, but he could see no floor or solid ground on any of them.

Is this, he asked himself, *what it is like to look into infinity in every direction?*

Far from empty, these great spaces were filled with constantly changing fields of moving light and form, covering the entire spectrum of human vision. Somehow, Paul was aware of wavelengths here that he knew he had never seen before. Some fields seemed to be at great distances, while others appeared quite nearby.

Here and there, colors and bodies of light appeared and disappeared unpredictably. They traveled in straight lines and arcs, occasionally merging or separating, but never stopping or even pausing. Sometimes, they intersected at right or acute angles to create or reveal new shapes, colors, lines, and trajectories. All this stood out against a background of abundant light for which he could locate no source. If describing his situation, Paul might have said it was like being inside a spinning global prismatic mobile of light and fuzzy substance, except that all the elements within the model looked as if they were operating at random, rather than along predetermined paths.

Nothing there, wherever that might be, appeared to be still or fixed, other than Paul himself. He could not even be sure of that. What if he were the only component in motion, where everything else was fixed? On the other hand, maybe he was just one of many manifestations, moving erratically through a designless vacuum.

Paul seemed to be sitting in something similar to a large dentist's chair in a nearly upright position. In spite of the fact that everything around him appeared to be moving at great speed, with nothing steady in sight, he had no fear of falling or being in danger. He felt entirely secure in his position, but was not disposed to try walking around for the moment. He found himself dressed in a light, soft coverall of spotless white. This, he thought, was definitely too dreamlike to be real.

Amid all the chaos of light and motion, he sensed people around him near and far. He knew they were there, but he could not exactly see them. Those that were moving, the only ones he saw at all, seemed to pass in and out of view. Unlike somebody walking through a darkened space between two lighted areas, they abruptly disappeared from one point and instantaneously popped up somewhere else. They sometimes appeared or disappeared at several different places at the same time. Some of them were talking, but he could discern nothing of what was being said.

Wait a minute, Paul thought.

He was hearing sounds—sort of. They meant nothing to him and were not particularly intrusive. Still, he had heard no sound when his eyes were closed. He closed them again to test this observation.

He kept trying to close his eyes, but it did not work. They did not actually close, or if they did, he still saw everything around him. There was nothing uncomfortable or disturbing about this. He was not even annoyed. It was just strange.

Were the senses of hearing and seeing somehow tied together in this place?

What a peculiar idea, he thought. Might all his senses be mutually interactive here? That fit into what was happening. Oddly, it was consistent with his recent experience. His prior inspections for tactile and olfactory data may have produced accurate results, but they were based completely on negative evidence while his eyes were closed.

Had all his senses been disabled until he chose to use his eyesight? Maybe his full sensory capacity was activated only when he decided to exercise that single sense. Now he seemed unable to reverse any results of that choice. The only sensory impressions he found at the moment were visual and aural, but perhaps his other senses were merely waiting for data. How could that be?

But wait. What about his sense of touch? He was wearing a coverall he did not feel upon his skin and his body reported no physical contact with the chair in which he sat. Yet, he could feel the rough skin of his hand by rubbing his fingers across it. How did that add up?

Could he find out anything more by continuing an inventory of the senses? The air around him seemed fresh and pure, but was devoid of any distinctive aroma. Maybe there was just nothing to smell.

Where was this line of thought going, anyway? Was it leading somewhere he did not want to be taken?

Then don't go there.
    Face it, Paul, you are already there.
    Who's talking?
    You are. Have you forgotten about these internal dialogs we sometimes have when you get confused?
    That's right. You're from my more cynical side.

I would call myself more practical.

Have it your way.

I try to.

Okay. Tell me something I don't know about this situation, and that would be almost anything. What are the alternative possibilities here?

Don't you know?

Look around and ask that again, wiseguy.

Okay. So the territory looks a little bizarre. Think you might be dreaming, drugged, or insane?

I am definitely not dreaming. This is like no dream I ever had.

Who says? That memory could be part of the dream.

Good point. But if it is just a dream, I'll wake up, right?

Where, at the bottom of that ravine by the river?

Maybe I dreamed that part too.

Don't you wish? If the snow and the ravine were a dream, how did you turn up inside this giant, working kaleidoscope?

Maybe you're right. Let's say it's not a dream. What about hallucinogenics or just plain hallucinations? That might be consistent with the weird things I am seeing.

If it is drugs, they ought to wear off, unless whoever tripped you out in the first place wants to keep you there.

Drugs might fit a capture scenario, but they are not very professional. All those hallucinogenic interrogation experiments in the '60s went wrong.

Right. Some of the subjects turned into schizophrenic zombies—not very reliable sources of information.

Which comforting thought takes us to the case for insanity. Could I recover from a psychosis?

Possibly, if it were chemically induced. But yours might be homegrown.

What do you mean by that?

Look at your occupation. How far is that from psychotic behavior on any given day?

Get serious.

Well, maybe I shouldn't be the one to mention this, but you do talk to yourself sometimes.

Running out of alternatives, aren't we? Let's go back to that thing I really don't want to think about.

Yeah. You're dead.

3

I am dead, Paul thought. *What do I do now?*

His whole adult life had been associated with calculated risks that included the chance of sudden fatality. He had seen it happen to others, not frequently but too often. He had always been aware of the lethal side of some of the things he did. He had been most palpably conscious of it in those moments when the lives of others seemed to be in his hands. When he bore that weight, he became almost ignorant of this own mortality.

For some reason, adrift in his bizarre surroundings, Paul remembered the first time this had happened to him. Very early in his career, he had been sent to a small airfield in southern Germany to watch people risk their lives while a revolution in Hungary unfolded and fell apart.

Before World War II, Furstenfeldbruck Air Base had been a primary training ground for the future flying aces of Hitler's Luftwaffe. By 1956, it was home to the U.S. Air Force Weather Service in Europe and a base for U.S. and other NATO fighter aircraft. Fursty, as American airmen commonly called it, projected a quiet loveliness against a background of striking grandeur. It is tucked just west of Munich among the lakes and foothills that run up against the Bavarian Alps to the south. The irony of such natural beauty and serenity, set against a Cold War mission of constant readiness to fight, was not lost upon those who lived there. In the autumn of that year, clouds were forming only one country away to the east that threatened the peace of the continent—possibly the world.

During late October, a week before Paul arrived at Furstenfeldbruck, students had marched in Budapest to sympathize with an earlier workers' rebellion that failed in Poland. More significantly, perhaps, they were also protesting the austere, communist regime of current Hungarian Prime Minister Rakosi and demanding the withdrawal of Soviet military forces that occupied their country.

The initially peaceful demonstration rapidly grew beyond its early intent. Joined and emboldened by Hungarian worker groups and other citizens, the students allowed themselves the indulgence of demolishing a huge statue of the late Soviet dictator, Josef Stalin. Thus innervated, they converged with entirely new demands on the government-controlled Magyar Radio headquarters. There the despised AVO secret police foolishly fired on them and the riot that followed became inevitable.

The next day saw Soviet tanks and troops in the streets of Budapest, but they were mainly out for show. Thousands of people gathered, unimpeded, before the national parliament to hear former Prime Minister Imre Nagy announce that he was taking his old job back for the sake of the country. In a climax worthy of grand opera, the crowd joined in singing the stirring, patriotic words of a nineteenth-century, Hungarian-nationalist poet. This was not an encouraging sign for the Soviet Union and its proxies in Hungary.

By the end of October many Hungarians had armed themselves with weapons pillaged from police and military stocks. The public was increasingly impatient with Soviet military presence in its capital city. Nagy formed a new government, officially dissolved the AVO, and arranged a ceasefire with the Soviets, who then surprised everyone by pulling out of Budapest.

The world, especially Europe, held its breath. Could it be so easy, only three years after Stalin's death, for an East European puppet state to rid itself of Soviet control? Rebellion had not worked in East Germany or Poland. Would Khrushchev, Stalin's eventual successor, let Hungary get away with it? If he did not, what then? What would Eisenhower do? Might the continent, still suffering from the most destructive war in history, soon find itself again upon the bloody field of battle?

Set against the prospect of possible war in Europe, the late-October attack by Britain, France, and Israel on Egypt over control of the Suez Canal looked almost like a comedic diversion. It certainly appeared to distract the United States. In early November the United States exerted most of its power and influence to deter its valued allies from deposing Egyptian leader Gamel Abdul Nasser and bringing relative stability to that part of the Middle East. The Eisenhower administration could seem to think of little else. On the surface at least, the Hungarian problem was not to be accorded equal priority.

While this Suez preoccupation persisted, Soviet tanks and troops moved back into Budapest to crush Hungarian hopes for independence. The weeks and months that followed saw tens of thousands of Hungarians escaping into Austria through wintry cold and snow. The American government sympathized with the Hungarians and scolded the Soviets, but lacking credible alternatives, stood well back from the tragic fray.

In the last days of October, while Hungarian freedom-fighters still had hope, Paul was ordered to drop a rather pedestrian project in Zurich and proceed to Furstenfeldbruck Air Base in West Germany for briefing.

Paul was met at the Munich airport on the first of November by the organization's regional director, Karl Nevins, who drove him to the base in an Air Force Volkswagen van on loan from the base motor pool. Karl was a tall, red-faced man over forty, who blended perfectly into the Bavarian background. Appropriate to the culture and climate, he was wearing a black, peaked workman's cap and a dark-green, loden coat. He drove with the self-assured aggressiveness of a native German.

During their brief transit from the airport and a quick, driving tour of the relatively small air base, Karl brought Paul tersely up to date. The day before, Karl had come out from his office in Munich to set up equipment, facilities, and logistic connections for the operational team. With Paul's arrival, the team was fully in place. Setting up had been comparatively easy for Karl, because he was familiar with the base and had established working relations with some of the key personnel there. Karl would be leaving, he explained, as soon as he finished briefing Paul and showing him around.

"What's your hurry?" Paul asked.

"Don't you read the papers? Our masters in D.C. are going all silly over Northeast Africa right now. I just happen to know a little Arabic. That's why they're pulling me out and giving you the team here."

Paul was taken by surprise.

"I've never led a team before. I've only been in the field two years."

"If you've been out here that long, you know what it takes. Anyway, Grogan must think you can handle it. The job is not very complicated; I've already set it up for you. It's mostly a matter of oversight and communication."

So far, Paul could only guess at what the job was.

"Who is Grogan?" he asked.

"Phil Grogan is a man you will learn about if you stay with the organization. He's earned quite a reputation. I'll bet he knows plenty about you by now. He selected you to lead the team, and he's directing the operation from headquarters. You will be working for him." Saying this, Karl pulled into a tiny parking area in front of a small, white-painted, wooden building near the end of the flight line. The only other vehicles in the lot were an olive-drab military jeep and a black, boxy, pre-war Mercedes sedan.

"The Mercedes is mine," Karl told him cheerfully. "What do you think of her?"

"It's a classic all right," Paul said, getting out of the van. He really knew very little about old German cars.

"But a pain to keep running these days," Karl observed, guiding Paul into the building. "This hut will be home until you're done."

The basically one-room structure was quite old, but sturdy enough to keep out the pre-winter winds that whistled around it. The sky was depressingly gray, and prophetic signs of premature, blowing snow bordered the road, forming blotchy patches over the nearly frozen ground.

Paul could easily imagine the hut in a pre-war and wartime role as some kind of fighter-pilots' ready room. Now, main-base activities seemed to have grown away from its isolated, barely used corner of the airfield. Inside, the only source of heat was a centrally located, barrel-shaped oil stove. Vented through the ceiling, this apparently makeshift device threatened to scorch anyone who remained for long within four feet or so, but provided no comfort at all to those who stood beyond that range. This probably explained why all four men in the room were wearing sweaters or coats and generally seemed to be avoiding any proximity to the stove. Paul silently gave thanks for the main sign of convenience and modernity, a small toilet and deep sink, visible through an open door in a rear corner.

Furnishings were limited. Besides six double-decked GI cots topped with sleeping bags, there were five wooden footlockers, a half-dozen metal folding chairs, and three mica-topped wooden tables. One of the tables was apparently dedicated to communications and supported two bulky, black, high-frequency (HF) radios. One set had a microphone for transmitting and both were connected to a small speaker. On the same table Paul saw what looked like a small very-high-frequency (VHF) transceiver with a built-in speaker. Another table was set up as a coffee mess that included a small hotplate. The last table held a nearly antique Underwood typewriter, two telephones, basic office supplies, a cheap white, plastic radio, tuned at low volume to the Armed Forces Network, and a small bookcase devoted to bound documents and several thick file folders. There were no windows. The only lighting in the place came from several large electric bulbs, screwed into circular, white-enameled, reflecting fixtures that hung from the ceiling by their electrical wiring.

Karl quickly introduced Paul to his team, most of whom looked to be not much younger than himself. All were in their early-to-mid twenties. George was his primary radio operator. Henry would be the administrator and reporter, which probably meant he could use the typewriter. Ted would handle the airborne radios, whatever that meant. The junior member of the group was Alan, who would act as communications courier and keep the team connected with on-base support activities.

When an organizational *ad hoc* team came together like this, first names were generally the order of the day. Each member carried a passport and other identification, but such credentials were often false. Within the team, first names were sufficient. Even those were apt to be phony.

Karl invited everyone to take seats around the table with the typewriter, which looked to be the center of administration. He briefed them standing up.

First, Karl called Paul's attention to a supply account folder, documenting all borrowed equipment and identifying to whom each item must be returned. At the same time, he explained that the HF radios were coupled with an air-base antenna system. He also noted that a gasoline-powered generator behind the building could be brought on line to provide more than adequate power for long-range HF transmission.

"Be sure everything gets turned in where it belongs," he said. "I have to come back here and live with these people."

Then he shifted his attention from Paul to the group.

"You will notice that I have arranged for you to have temporary meal cards. You can use them to eat in the mess hall by paying a reasonable surcharge for each meal. I've tried it myself and recommend it. Furstenfeldbruck gives the lie to all the bad things you have heard or said about military food, but there is an on-base snack bar, if you prefer. Stay away from the Officer and NCO clubs. It's a small base and you don't want to attract unnecessary attention. Does everyone have scrip?"

They all nodded. At the airport U.S. Military Travel Office, Karl had helped Paul convert some currency to the military payment certificates he would need for on-base commerce.

Now Karl placed a second folder, labeled Operation Plan, on the table.

"This will give you everything you need to know about the operation: radio frequencies, call signs, transmission windows, and the general order of action."

He paused.

"Have you been keeping up with what's going on in Hungary?"

Everyone nodded.

"Then you know that the Soviet Union, uncharacteristically, pulled back its military two days ago. Today they seem to be repenting that magnanimity. Prime Minister Nagy is begging the world for help. I wish him well, but he shouldn't hold his breath. If the forces there stay on their current path, this revolution will be broken in a matter of days. There will be determined resistance, of course, but lightly armed civilians will not hold up long against Soviet armor and regular troops.

"Before that happens, tomorrow night to be exact, you have a role to play in extracting about thirty Hungarian nationals. These are people we do not want to have swept up in the impending crackdown and roundup of suspected subversives. The operation will be quiet, sneaky, and over so fast that nobody will know it happened. At least that is how we hope it will go."

As he spoke, Karl steadily shifted his gaze from man to man and back again.

"Only one of you is actually going into Hungary." Karl gestured toward Ted.

"He already has a fair idea of what he will be doing. The rest of you should spend today and tomorrow familiarizing yourselves with the operation, testing your equipment, making the necessary contacts with air-base support functions," Karl now nodded at Paul, "and generally getting ready for the big night."

Paul made a slight hand gesture of acknowledgement.

"Paul, all preparations on the Hungarian end are out of your hands. The aircraft will stage from here and the pilot will contact you tomorrow when he arrives." Tapping his finger on the Operation Plan folder, Karl continued. "My notes provide all you'll need to know about arrangements for aircraft support and the right contacts on base. You'd better form a working relationship with Captain French in Air Weather Service. Her help might become essential."

"Ted, you will be recovering elsewhere after the mission, so take your personal gear on board with you when you go," Karl said to Ted, as an afterthought. "Any questions?"

"A few," Paul responded.

"Read the plan," Karl replied, sharply. "I'm out of here."

He was headed for the door as he said it.

With Karl gone, Paul spent the next half-hour telling the team about himself and getting acquainted with them. No one in the room had been with the organization more than three years, so their professional resumes were brief.

Ted was a bit older than Paul, but was comparatively new to the organization. Just graduated from the initial training course in the States, he had been sent directly to Furstenfeldbruck for this operation. That probably related to his prior experience as an Air Force airborne radio operator.

George had been in Europe over a year providing communications support for several delicate operations along the East German border.

Henry normally produced operational plans and reports for Karl in Munich. He was selected for the team because of his familiarity with the Operation Plan (OpPlan) they were executing.

Alan had been stuck for almost a year at a small logistics support office in nearby Augsburg; he had jumped at the chance to volunteer for a real operation.

Paul spent the next few hours skimming through the OpPlan and discussing certain parts of it with Henry and the rest. He did not mention that this was his first time as a team leader, but he was sure that fact was conspicuous. He was painfully conscious of it himself. He knew he would be up very late studying every aspect of the operation.

About three in the afternoon, after his first reading of the OpPlan, Paul telephoned Captain French and made an appointment to see her at four. Then he wrote up a daily activity report for Grogan and gave it to Henry. Henry would painstakingly convert the text, letter-by-letter, to an unbreakable, one-time code, type it onto a standard message form and have it ready for Paul to approve when he returned. Military communications centers employed sophisticated encryption devices and their technicians were, of necessity, cleared to the highest security levels, but operations like this required extra protection. More than lives would be at stake. At a basic level, the American people liked to think somebody was doing things like this when necessary, but they preferred not to know about it.

Paul was very happy with Karl's detailed thoroughness in setting things up. Among the many products of his diligence was a map of the base, clearly marked with every place Paul might want to go. This made it a simple matter to navigate his jeep from the flight-line hut to base operations, where he was expecting to meet the weather officer. Finding base operations would have been easy anyway. To

33

get there from the hut, all Paul had to do was drive parallel to the flight line in the direction from which he and Karl had arrived.

Susan French was about Paul's age. She had short, blonde hair and brought an attractive figure to her well-cut, Air Force-blue uniform. Paul could see, nonetheless, that the young meteorologist was a confident military officer who commanded the respect of the people working around her. He could also tell that she valued punctuality. She was waiting for him at the counter just inside the weather operations area, where departing pilots and aircrews came for final briefing before takeoff.

When Paul identified himself, she smiled and briskly led him through the map-walled main room into an enclosed area, which looked as if it might be used for small conferences or briefings. Paul guessed that this crisply capable professional probably had no office of her own, but worked instead from a desk in the open area outside. Inviting him to take a seat at a family-sized table surrounded by chairs, she seated herself across from him.

"I've been told you are interested in weather projections for Austria and western Hungary for tomorrow night," she said. Several air-navigation maps were already spread out on the table between them.

"That's right."

"What's your window?" she asked.

"The time frame?"

She nodded.

"I will not have a precise fix on that until tomorrow," Paul told her. "Right now, I'm pretty much stuck with dusk-to-dawn. By tomorrow afternoon, I should be able to narrow that for you.

"Tomorrow night is a long way off in terms of weather, but my best guesswork is that the whole area will look good through midnight. After that, some things might be coming together to affect visibility in eastern Hungary."

"The area including Budapest?" he asked.

"Yes, but for now it is only a remote possibility," she said, standing up to pass him a map of that area.

"Captain, I'm sure Karl told you this is a pretty touchy business. I would prefer you to be my only contact. No one else should know that anything unusual will be going on."

"My commander knows we have been asked to contribute to something sensitive. He's the one who told me to work with you after your friend spoke to him. He hasn't asked for any details, but I would have to tell him if he did."

"That's all right. Once I have a window, can you be on duty for the entire time?"

"You drive a hard bargain," she said, crossing her arms and making a wry face. "I'll have to work a double shift."

"Okay?"

"Okay."

On the way home Paul tested Karl's remarks about the base mess hall and found himself in full agreement. He noticed that the base theater was playing a western movie with Richard Widmark and Donna Reed. It looked like a good picture.

No, he thought. There was too much to do tonight, and the operation was set for tomorrow.

Back at the hut Paul went over the activity report, checked the encrypted version, thanked Henry for his diligence, signed the report, and sent Alan off with it to the base communications center. Based upon Paul's affirmation of Karl's comments, the other team members joined Alan in the Volkswagen to try out the mess hall.

The whole team spent the night in the hut, sleeping on the GI cots. That minor discomfort was the price of maintaining a low profile and keeping the team together. During the early evening, he had everyone but Ted practice turning on the power generator and bringing it on line in the dark. All of them performed transmission checks with the base radio-maintenance unit and studied the frequency and call sign assignments in the communications annex of the OpPlan. The main function of the team was simply to monitor the progress of tomorrow's operation. Paul wanted to be sure that anyone in the hut could effectively take that on.

He stayed up several hours after the rest were asleep, going back over every line of the plan. He had been through enough operations to know the routine, but this was the first time he had held leadership responsibility. That, he discovered, made a huge difference. Trivial details that might have been unimportant to him as a team member now took on critical significance. He found himself obsessed with the countless things that might go wrong, despite his most earnest effort to make everything work.

Those sections of the plan he had been given explained quite clearly what he needed to know, but that was all. Their pages were silent about how a military transport aircraft might penetrate hostile airspace, illegally take on over two dozen passengers, and come back safely with no one knowing it had been there. That remained a mystery for him until the following afternoon when he met the navigator.

4

Paul's remembrance of the Hungarian operation was interrupted by the sudden introduction of a startlingly different phenomenon into his curious, post-mortem surroundings.

Had he ever seen a more beautiful woman? She appeared instantaneously, like everything else he was able to see in this place. She just popped up about six feet in front of him. Then, unlike the other things around him, she did not immediately vanish, speed away, or change form and color. She was smiling at him.

At first he had an impression of long, reddish-golden hair, sparkling green eyes, and a figure that was softly statuesque. When he tried to look closely, however, he could not quite focus on her individual features. Even her hair and eye color became indeterminate from one instant to the next. Paul remembered this kind of effect from some of his dreams, usually nightmares, in which a successful outcome depended on being able to identify some detail that stubbornly refused to come into focus.

The visual results were similarly imprecise when he concentrated on her clothing. Brightly radiant as something out of a television bleach ad, it was either light green or dazzling white. The garment itself was something between a gown and a laboratory smock, but for all his effort, he could not say which style was dominant.

Her gender was undeniable. She was a complete statement in one person of all the physical qualities he had ever admired in a woman. Her stunning good looks brought him a simple surge of gratitude for what she was. Why, he wondered, did he feel no hint of concern for what her response to him might be? He was no Lothario, but even in his least conceited moments, such thoughts were not likely to be absent in the presence of such overwhelming attraction. Looking at the most perfectly appealing woman he had ever met, he was filled with admiration, but bereft of arousal. Odder still, this lack of erotic interest did not surprise him. Why was that? Like all the other paradoxes around him, it seemed almost normal.

"Do I know you?" he asked.

She chuckled and stepped gracefully toward him.

"Am I so easily forgotten?" she asked with a playfully reproachful look. "Perhaps I ought to be insulted." Her voice was low-pitched and strong, but thoroughly feminine.

From the moment of her appearance, Paul had detected a sweetly soothing aroma. He found no memory of the scent in his past. It was unlike perfume or cologne. Yet, it was somehow familiar and thoroughly comforting. It was also the first evidence that he possessed any sense of smell within this extraordinary locale. He could now account for every sense but taste. Did dead people eat?

"You must forgive me. I'm not used to being dead."

"Nonsense," she chided with a fond smile. "You've never been so alive."

"That depends on your point of view."

"Point of view has nothing to do with it. You are beyond that now." Her speech was almost melodic, but its delivery firm and direct. Her air of authority inspired Paul to accept what she said. Still, he was inclined to question any proposition that was contrary to the evidence of his senses or challenged the product of his intellect. He failed to consider what a ludicrous position that was for a dead man to take.

"What does that mean?"

"Look, Paul," she explained with the patient concern of an earnest friend. Her expression had changed from playful to serious.

"Up to now, your point of view has enormously influenced everything about you. You could not possibly have seen things the way others saw them. Neither could those others have seen anything quite the same way you or anyone else did. If you think about it, your point of view is just about the only unique thing you've ever owned. Nobody else ever grew up in exactly the same manner or went to exactly the same places in exactly the same order at exactly the same time. Nobody else did exactly the same things with exactly the same people in exactly the same way. Only you thought exactly the same thoughts, formed exactly the same opinions, made exactly the same mistakes…" She stopped in mid sentence.

"You see how this is going?" she asked. "We could be at it forever—well, not precisely of course. My point is that now, for the first time, you are about to start seeing things the same as everybody else who gets this far. The idea of having a different view of reality will soon become a quaint anachronism for you."

As she spoke, Paul experienced an increasingly overpowering impression of familiarity with this woman. What was it that kept tugging at a corner of his mind? It was not her appearance; he did not remember that. He could never have forgotten meeting someone of such complete loveliness. Still, something about her spoke to him from the past, something he clearly noticed but could not identify or define.

"Do I really know you?" he persisted.

"I told you that already," she said, impatiently. "Now can we finish with this point-of-view business first?"

"I suppose," he replied reluctantly. "You have the initiative."

He shrugged his shoulders and held out his palms in a gesture of submission.

Again she seemed to alter her approach.

"Paul," she asked, looking pensively into his face. "Have you ever thought of yourself as a seeker of truth?"

Seeker of truth? What an awkward term. He would be embarrassed to think about applying it to himself. Where was she going with this? Who was she, and why did she care what he thought about anything?

"Not since my junior year of college," he smiled, recalling his immature convictions in those days.

"Do you consider that identification pretentious?"

"Not by itself, perhaps. I just don't care much for people who think of themselves or like to be thought of that way."

"Really?" she asked in an amused, rising-glissando tone. He could tell she was about to demolish his position. This had happened before. Where and when had he known her? Why couldn't he place her?

"You disapprove of people who ask questions then?" she continued.

"No."

"What is a seeker of truth? Doesn't that imply someone who asks questions, really big ones?"

"That is not a definition I thought much about at the time. Let me see if I can tell you what happened. Around the middle of my junior year, I took an uncharitable look at some of the people I had devotedly believed in: thinkers from the past, academics of the day, and some of my student peers. I came to the conclusion that many of them were unimaginative fatheads. They spoke or wrote as if they had the answer to almost every question on earth. Their opinions, which had appeared sound to me in the beginning, wore thin and came apart when I looked beneath the surface. I felt cheated and became suspicious of any philosophy or theology that laid claim to having all, or even most, of the answers."

"I see," she said. "Did you stop asking questions?"

"No, but I stopped buying into other people's answers."

"So you did become one of them after all."

"One of whom?"

"Those fatheaded seekers of truth you so much despised." Her face lit up in amused satisfaction.

"Not exactly," he said hesitantly.

"Not exactly what?"

Paul was stunned into a few seconds of silence, not by her question, but by the way their exchange was going. He knew he had been on the receiving end of this kind of Socratic assault before. His intuition seemed outrageous, but all the clues had fallen decisively into place. His eyes told him he was wrong, but it had to be true.

"Miss Janet?" he gasped. Could he gasp in this place? Dead men, he observed to himself, seemed capable of much more than he ever imagined.

A thrilling quality came into her voice.

"Bingo, Paul. Well done. I thought the way you see me now would keep you in the dark, so to speak, much longer than this."

In Memphis, where Paul grew up and received his early education during the 1930s and '40s, most community institutions were seamlessly connected. The first-through-twelfth-grade schools, more than any other local establishment, held neighborhood people together whether or not they had children attending them. The local Memphis City School system transcended all boundaries but those imposed by racial segregation, which pervaded every aspect of life in that place and time.

With that egregious exception, social differences were of little importance. Most residents supported the local school in whatever way they could. Even older people, without children or with children then far away, were regular boosters of the many social, sporting, musical, and scholastic events sponsored by the schools to support extracurricular activities and educational programs not fully funded by the city.

Institutional lines connecting a city school to its neighborhood churches were hardly less clear and binding than the ties it maintained with the municipal school board. The Supreme Court had yet to instruct the nation on the Constitutional iniquity of such arrangements, so school and church resources were happily pooled or exchanged to the benefit, people thought, of the whole community.

Most of the churches promoted school activities, but of course the Southern Baptists abstained from endorsing dances. School groups like the band and the glee club readily participated in church functions throughout the area. A school's bandmaster and its vocal music director usually held leadership roles in the music programs of one or more of the nearby spiritual communities. Since the religious population of Memphis was overwhelmingly evangelical Protestant Christian, the children of Jews, Catholics, and openly professed atheists were a rarity in the public school system of that time. It never occurred to Paul to wonder how such denominational accommodations might affect people who held different beliefs from those of the majority. Neither did he pause to think about what other believers might be doing when they met in their own houses of worship.

In that comfortably incorrect day, some of the older, unmarried women who taught Sunday school at any of the neighborhood churches would be found teaching regular school children during the week. Thus, from Monday through Friday, many elementary, junior high, and high school students were likely to be taught math, English, history, geography, and the other staples of primary and secondary education by some of the same people they saw in church on Sunday morning. This happened to Paul several times in his school years. The most memorable of those times involved Miss Janet Thomas.

At that time in the South, it was still thought of as rude to call undue attention to an older woman's unmarried status. The term *spinster* was generally confined to discussions of nineteenth-century literature, and *old maid* merely identified a card game for children. The only polite description for such persons was *maiden lady* and that was a term used only outside the presence of anyone to whom it might apply.

Janet Thomas was a maiden lady of great refinement and substantial education. In an era when most women did not go to college, she had earned a graduate degree in the classics. When it was still thought highly improper for young ladies to travel alone, she had done a world tour by herself. While even homely women of good family and income were normally married by twenty-five, she had discouraged or rejected more than a few quite promising suitors before she was thirty. That was the year of the stock market crash that took away her family's fortune and brought on the Great Depression.

During a period when many well-educated and capable men could hardly get a job of any kind, she eventually found work in one of the very few occupational fields that normally employed women. Not trained for nursing, temperamentally unfit for clerical work, and physically unsuited to janitorial labor, she had little trouble qualifying for a high school position teaching Latin and world history.

Paul first saw her at the Baptist church and spent several years in her elementary-level Sunday school class. In the ninth grade she taught him first-year Latin and in the tenth he had her for world history.

In church or elsewhere she was carefully addressed as Miss Janet, but most of her students slurred the "Miss" so badly that it was indistinguishable from "Miz," the contemporary colloquial pronunciation for the honorific "Mrs." Decades later, Paul was mildly amused when passionate feminist advocates, having adopted "Ms." as a universal form of female address, decided to pronounce it "Miz." In Paul's school days, teachers were generally referred to by their last name, but Miss Janet accepted and encouraged an exception for herself. Even colleagues and school administrators rarely spoke of her as Miss Thomas. Only outsiders or mid-term transfer students made that mistake.

Miss Janet tried but failed to teach Paul very much Latin. Whether in church or at school, her efforts still always left him with something important. Merely knowing her brought him an education in decency and civility. Whatever he had learned of honor and integrity before the end of high school was greatly enhanced by her teaching and example. He knew that he could retain her respect, even while failing to accurately conjugate an infinitive or recall the date of some ancient battle. He was equally aware that he would lose that respect, and his own, if he cheated on a test or behaved in any other manner she deemed dishonorable. His private and professional life, since then, had often brought him to make difficult choices. The decisions he least liked to remember were those for which he had displaced Miss Janet's principles with the demands of expediency.

Whatever the curriculum, Miss Janet was a great teacher. Paul was never quite at home with Latin declensions and the precise chronology of historical events, but she ensnared his thinking by guiding him to novels like *Quo Vadis*, *A Friend of Caesar*, and *All Quiet on the Western Front*. However dry the topic, she captured student minds with imbedded commentary, questions, and debate on philosophy, civilization, law, politics, and the interests and fears that led nations to run the risks of war. She cleverly organized and conducted her lessons to provoke questions, which she invariably turned back on the inquiring student to generate discussion and promote active learning by the whole class.

Years later, Paul understood that these evocative excursions had been decisive in helping him identify lifelong interests and activities. They had led him to develop a critical methodology for approaching and dealing with the unknown, a habit of thought that had often made it possible for him to do his job and stay alive at the same time. Beyond any Latin or history he might have picked up along the way, they had taught him to think analytically and to synthesize from bits and pieces to a projection of the unseen whole. More than any other youthful experience, they had impelled him into the edgy kind of work he had spent his life doing. In no small measure, Miss Janet had influenced the manner and timing of his departure from the world to arrive in this very exceptional and, so far, baffling location.

People often spoke of Miss Janet as a wonderful, even inspiring person, but no one would ever have described her as handsome. She was taller than most women, so that her comparatively thin frame gave her a gawky appearance. She was careless about clothes and on her uncommonly large feet always wore the ugliest low-heeled, black sandals Paul thought he had ever seen. A large mouth and pronounced overbite would have disqualified her from any beauty competition. She was over fifty when he last knew her, but people of every age and type were still inordinately attracted to her perpetual expression of delighted interest in them and her fascination with almost everything that was going on anywhere.

Recognizing her identity, Paul knew that the incredibly beautiful person in front of him represented the way Miss Janet should have looked all along. He could have seen her this way before, he thought, if only people wore their souls inside out.

5

"Did you ever wonder, Paul, why there are so many different views in every religion, so many denominations, for example, in Christianity alone?" Greetings out of the way, Miss Janet was not going to let him escape the subject at hand. However beautiful she might have become, she remained thoroughly unchanged in demanding attention to the essentials.

"I thought we were talking about my point of view."

"We still are, so answer my question. Why so much bickering about God?" She made a dismissive, wiping gesture with her right hand, as if erasing a chalkboard. Her manner and tone were now relentlessly pedagogical.

"Don't people generally disagree about almost everything?" he asked. "Why should religion be different?"

"Isn't it?"

"What?"

"Different from anything else in one's life. More important, perhaps, or at least more intrusive."

"All right," Paul said, feeling like a teenage student in one of his favorite classes and enjoying it. Miss Janet always led conversations with a goal in mind; he had long ago learned to follow her lead.

"If you're in the mood for debate, I'll come along with you."

She smiled at him in silence, so he plunged into an extemporaneous answer.

"Religion is like philosophy or cosmology. It takes us back to the most basic questions we all have about ourselves and the universe. How did it get here? How did we get here? What are we doing here? Do we count for anything outside our birth, life, and death? Beyond our immediate, personal experience of earthly existence, does it matter how we live? How will the whole story end—or does it?

"Directly or indirectly, isn't all philosophical, theological, and scientific thought aimed at those kinds of questions?"

"I accept that," she said. "So what makes religion so much more important? Why do we care about and fight over it with such intensity? Why were so many people throughout history willing to sacrifice and die for it and others just as ready to kill for it?"

"You have me at a disadvantage. I don't know where you expect me to take this." Paul felt himself blushing. Did dead men blush? He could see her enjoying herself. She was not about to let him off the hook.

"Give me a minute to think," he said, while he tried to gather his wits and formulate an argument.

She waited quietly and patiently for him to resume. He was ready in less than a minute.

"Science is made up of our ideas about the way things are, whether humanity likes it or not. We may stumble along, finding bits of truth here and there, but we are constantly falling back. Most, if not all, of the scientific facts we think we've found turn out to be wrong or imperfectly understood."

"Wouldn't that make scientific research a senseless endeavor?"

"Not completely. We still make progress, because a residue of truth remains in most of the things we learn, even when we are compelled to abandon them. Say that a scientific certainty comes up false. In the late twentieth century that seems to happen almost every day, but it is never a total loss. We still have something left, if only the knowledge that we must look elsewhere for an answer. At least we know one place the answer is not."

"Where does that leave us?"

"Whatever we may think scientifically, the physical truth that operates the universe goes right ahead doing whatever it does. Our opinion does not count with natural laws. We may be ignorant about the laws of physics and chemistry, but we cannot disobey them without paying an inescapable, predetermined penalty."

"Can you explain that?"

"Sure. Make the sincerest of mistakes in a chemistry lab and the least consequence is likely to be a revolting smell. Even if we get careless with explosive stuff, the universe doesn't mind. We may blow things up and hurt ourselves or waste our planet by neglecting the environment, but that is only a manifestation of scientific truth. It changes nothing. Nothing in the arena of science ever changes. There is nothing moral about it. Good or bad, our intention is irrelevant."

"So much for science," she said. "Keep going."

"What's next?

"Philosophy, I believe." Paul remembered this as her typical method of instruction. Answering a question almost always produced another question.

"You're a hard teacher, Miss Janet, but I remember how it's done. Philosophy was the first of the sciences. It embraced almost everything that later emerged as a separate science. It planted the seeds of logic, analysis, and experimentation that made other science possible. Today we may see it a little closer to religion than science, because it considers ethics, morality, and even God, whom many modern-day scientists prefer to ignore."

"Aren't those more properly reserved to the province of religion?"

Paul knew her methods and avoided the trap of confusing philosophy and faith.

"Somewhat, but not exclusively. Like Thomas Aquinas, we can apply philosophical discipline to theological reasoning. Logic makes a reasonably good tool for that, but it may not work the other way around."

"What do you mean?"

"Aristotle could conceive a Prime Mover in the cosmos, but he did not think about raising a temple to its worship and glory. It was a force of history that had nothing to do with everyday life. To Aristotle the Prime Mover was more a matter of science than religion."

"Are you saying that philosophy is atheistic?"

"Not necessarily, but a true atheist is forced to base any concept of right behavior on pure philosophy. Atheism deprives him of any other approach. There is no God to look for, and he cannot turn to science because natural reality, the way things really work without God, just doesn't care how people behave."

Paul hesitated, mostly looking for reinforcement. Miss Janet nodded, but said nothing, so he proceeded to the final topic.

"Religion defines the way human beings apply theology in the real world. It is the only thing in our lives that tells us we matter. I am talking about spiritual reality, different and separate from the strictly demanding laws of nature. Spiritually, what we do and how we do it makes a difference. There are rules here too. We ignore them at great peril, but we have the privilege of doing that."

"I think you may definitely be ignoring a few facts at great peril," she said coyly. "What is your point?"

Paul was beginning to have fun. Miss Janet, he recalled, always pressed for clarity. No one ever got away with a half-formed thought.

"We cannot circumvent God's spiritual rules any more than we can defeat the laws of nature, but we can disobey him. We may choose a different path, insist on our independence, and try making it on our own. Isn't that what Adam and Eve were supposed to have done? There may be consequences, but they are of our own choosing. Ironically, when we reject God, we are exercising the freedom he gives us to do so. For better or worse, we are no longer helpless victims in a mindless, mechanical universe."

"What good is that?"

"Most religion says that what we believe and do makes a genuine difference in how our own narrative and the stories of humanity and the universe turn out. It tells us we can change things and shows us how to do it. Part of that includes the opportunity to follow God's will for our lives. Christianity, in particular, tells us that God cares what happens to us, even when we defy him."

"Aren't you glossing over the difference between breaking scientific law and breaking God's law?"

"Maybe I am. The most important difference, I suppose, is that when we ask God, he forgives us and lets us start over. By its very nature, scientific law never does that."

"Can you summarize everything you've been saying?"

"I'll try. Philosophy, taken by itself, offers us choices with mostly random outcomes that have no effect on the universe beyond ourselves."

"And?" she prompted.

"The mechanical laws that run the universe, the rules scientists are always trying to expose, exact absolute consequences with zero options. Take it or leave it, every cause is inextricably linked to an inevitable effect. We can predict some of those connections, but the rest are locked into rigid directives about which we remain mostly ignorant."

"'Mostly,' is right."

"Doesn't that make our choice of religion, or even the rejection of it, the most critical decision we are able to make? Isn't it the single most important thing in our lives, because it enables us to find and become ourselves? Doesn't that explain why we are at once so quarrelsome and so dedicated about our religious convictions?"

"I asked you first."

"Okay. It does."

"Very thoughtful, so far as it goes, but your reasoning is superficial. Not actually your fault. You have a lot to learn about how God does things in this life and the last. We are going to do something about that. Still, I am glad to see that you did not stop thinking about God when you grew up. Many people do, you know"

"How is that?"

"Really," she chided, "haven't you been looking for truth all your life, truth with a capital T, Truth that doesn't change just because you are looking at it from a different place, at a different time, or with a different set of facts in your head?"

"Yes."

"Didn't you meet a great many people with views that were drastically different from your own?"

"I did."

"Why was that, do you think? Were they all just insufferable fatheads for seeing things some other way?"

"No, indeed. Some of them, a lot of them in fact, were well informed and quite sincere in their beliefs."

"How could that be?" she snapped back. "Can the truth, the big-T kind or any other for that matter, ever change or be different than it is? Are you trying to tell me that truth is relative?"

"No," he drawled, seeing now where she had led him. "Everyone on earth is making a journey through life, but no two of us take exactly the same trip. We only know about what we are able to see at any given moment from our own very personal pathway. Others, separated by time, space, culture, and experience, are sure to see identical truths quite differently. As individuals, we are often unable or unwilling to see the same truth in the same way. The truth is not different. We are."

"Precisely! Didn't you just answer my questions about why there are so many different Christian denominations? Doesn't that tell you why your viewpoint of truth was, at least until now, unique? Aren't you still looking for that kind of big-T Truth at this very minute?"

"Certainly."

"Good news." She broke into a broad, warm smile. "Your journey is almost over. You're nearly there."

"Where? Is this heaven?"

"No, Paul." Her expression changed, and she seemed mildly offended. "Don't think that. How disappointing it would be if this were all there is to heaven."

"I don't know about that," he objected. "I am as rested as I have ever been. I have not eaten, but I am not hungry. My body suffers no pains or problems. I am as clean and comfortable as I remember ever being. I am locked in stimulating conversation with a wonderful mentor I never expected to see again. I am also delighted to find that her appearance now matches the beauty of the soul I always knew she had. What else could I want? What more could heaven offer?"

She smiled again when he spoke of her beauty, but showed neither pride nor modesty about it.

"I hope," she said, "you will understand the loveliness of souls a little better before you leave here. Still, the reality of the place you are bound for—you may call it heaven—will completely overwhelm and envelop you. It is an entirely spiritual dimension that cannot be described with the words and concepts you know from your life up to now. That is one of the reasons you are here."

"This is only the beginning?"

"More than that. Your life until now was the beginning. You have come through a difficult and confusing time on earth. Much of what you thought was true is not. Now you need a tutorial in reality. After that, you can safely proceed to the entirely real. You will see what is true, just as it is. For the first time, you and the great company of souls standing together before God will be able to see his complete truth from exactly the same place and time. Then you will know what is real, right, and permanent, because you will have become a part of it."

"Thanks. I may not know what heaven is, but I can't exactly define this place either—and for some of the same reasons. Isn't where and what we are right now an example of spiritual existence, too?"

"Yes, but not as fully as the other you will come to know. A complete transition from your grubby life on earth to spiritual totality in one leap could be too disorienting for your soul. You might not handle it well, if you handled it at all. Until now, you were like a caterpillar whose whole universe is bounded by the inside of its cocoon. When you leave here you will be, for lack of a better term, translated into what you truly are where you really belong."

"Where am I now?"

"Some call it the Vale."

"How do you spell that? There's a ski resort, a dip between hills, and something that conceals or separates. They are all pronounced the same way."

She laughed softly.

"Well, it is definitely not a ski resort. Your second meaning is the one I intended, but v-e-i-l also has a certain descriptive rightness about it."

"Purgatory?"

"We don't use that name here. It is much too negative. This is not a penitentiary. You have not come to pay for past sins before you can move on. That debt was paid in full before you were born."

"I see, but then what is the Vale?"

"The Vale is rather like a sanitarium, where you can be healed of past infirmities and strengthened for what is next. It is a way station between what you thought was life and the real life that waits. In a very true sense, you are already there in that other place, but that will take a little explaining. You will learn more about that soon."

Paul had begun to feel a little awed by her description.

"Can I flunk this course, Miss Janet?"

"I hardly think so. Some patients need more therapy than others, but I know of no case where one who came to here did not finally pass on through. I would describe any other outcome as impossible."

"'Came to,' as in woke up? How long have I been here?"

"That would be very difficult to explain right now. You will find that time here does not work quite the way you are accustomed to thinking about it. That is one of the reasons things look so peculiar to you now. We will sort out some of that while you are here, but I must tell you again that it will not be at all the same when you get to the next stop. What you'll find here is a very watered-down dose of what it is like to be in direct contact with God."

"You spoke of patients. Am I a patient here?"

"Yes, within the metaphor I was using of the Vale as a sanitarium."

"But you just alluded to patients who don't wake up."

"Regrettably true," she said, stonily serious for the first time since she had arrived. "It is the only sadness we have to see, but it does happen—all too often. They deliberately fight against regaining consciousness. Of course, that started long before they came here. There never was any hope, but it breaks your heart to see them that way. Our Lord himself grieves for them constantly, but even he cannot bring them back now. They have lapsed into a self-generated coma, from which there is no waking. They are aware, I think, but only of themselves. They resist coming to. They do not allow themselves to be revived. They do not want to return. We have a place for them."

"Hell?"

"We call it the terminal ward. No one has ever left it. The spirits who tend them there cannot leave either."

"I think I would rather not know much more about them," he said.

"The attending spirits?" she brightened. "The fact is you've met quite a few in the past. They are confined to their own spiritual realm, but they are able to visit the universe of earth and do so quite regularly. They were a danger to you then, but you no longer need to be protected from them. You did not see them then, and you could not see them now, even if you wanted to."

"I am glad for that."

"And I can think of a few hundred reasons why you should be. They are an ugly, voracious lot, indeed."

She paused for a few seconds, as if in thought.

"I need to check your vital signs before I go."

"Vital signs?" he asked. "What are you going to do—take my temperature or check my blood pressure?"

"Nothing like that," she said, "but I need to be certain that you can handle yourself here until I or someone else comes to help you."

"Someone else?"

"Probably. To tell the truth, I do not come here very often; only when somebody I know is passing through. Everyone who comes here is confused when they first wake up in such seemingly outrageous circumstances. Unlike you, some of them become rather frantic, so it is always a good thing to have them greeted by a familiar soul. They never recognize me at first, but most seem to sense the presence—forgive the pun—of a kindred spirit." She smiled, impishly, at her own joke.

"I must say," she added, "that I have never seen anyone take their awakening quite so calmly in the beginning as you have. You haven't seemed to be the least bit frightened or disoriented."

"It's part of the training," he told her with a grin.

"I don't understand," she said, looking puzzled for once.

"I'll explain it next time I see you," he smiled. "You were saying something about vital signs?"

"Yes, how are your senses doing?"

"My thinking processes or the touchy-feely-smelly stuff?"

"The latter, please."

"They all appear to be working, but I did notice something a bit strange earlier on. While my eyes were closed, I seemed to be in some kind of sensual bubble: no sight, no sound, no smell, no feel, and presumably no taste. When I opened them, there was a flood of sensory input. At least I could see and hear, and from the moment you appeared, I have been smelling an incredibly sweet aroma. The other senses I'm not quite sure of. I've had no occasion to test them fully, but they seem to be limited. Anyway, trying to close my eyes did not reverse the situation. I could not seem to close them, and I kept on seeing. Once my senses were turned on, I completely lost control of them."

"Good! As I told you, this is a spiritual place. Still, it was purposely designed to preserve some of the trappings of your former world and body until you are better prepared to deal with an absolute spiritual environment. In truth, you have only one sense here, but right now it is masquerading as some of those you formerly knew. It will seem to you at any given moment that you have all or none of them. When you first woke up here and opened your eyes, the initial shock sort of locked your sensory throttle in the open position. That was why you could not turn things back off. Blinking your eyes is not something you do around here. Just think how confusing that would be. By now, you should be able to manage things on your own. Try closing your eyes, and see what happens."

He did as she said and experienced utter sensory deprivation.

"It works," he said, reopening his eyes and restoring his senses.

"Fine," she went on. "You will no longer experience hunger or thirst. None of the physical appetites or functional needs of your body remain. Thus, you will find that sensations of taste, touch, and smell are subdued or absent altogether. You will not know pain of any kind. You will require no sleep, whether or not you close your eyes."

"And when I do close them?"

"That's the good part. When you want to meditate or think things through between sessions, you need only close your eyes. It will shut out every sensory distraction. Open them when you are ready for company, and your next therapist will be right there."

"Just like that?" He was a little surprised.

"Just like that," she smiled. "I told you. Time and space here are not what you are used to. Don't worry. You cannot possibly keep anybody waiting or be late for an appointment here."

"Could you tell me what I have been smelling, despite my diminished senses, since you showed up? It is delightful, but I cannot place it."

"Can't you?" she asked. "I suppose, when I came to you here, I brought a small sample from beyond of the prayers and praise that are everlastingly raised before God. Their sweetness and beauty is being translated for you now as the most wonderful incense you could possibly imagine. Let me tell you that what you sense now is the merest, infinitesimal trace of the glory you will find it to be when you discover its fullness."

She started to turn away, but seemed to remember something and stopped.

"One more thing before I go. For the moment, you should not be ambulatory. You do not yet understand spiritual mobility and wandering off would just disrupt your therapy. Eventually, when you have been prepared, you will have the run of the Vale. It is a fascinating place and very good exercise in getting ready for your final home."

At this point, she stepped slightly to one side and was instantly out of sight.

6

With Miss Janet gone, Paul looked around to see he was still adrift in the maelstrom of light, color, and shadow where he had been before she came. He was not actually getting used to the scene. He did not understand why it was the way it seemed. Yet, he was forced to accept it as a fact.

Comparing the place to heaven, Miss Janet had told him it was a modified form of spiritual reality. She had convinced him this was not some extravagantly staged production set up to deceive him. Neither was it a product of his own insanity; he had already faced and discarded that argument. Like it or not, what he saw from where he sat was reality where he was.

Miss Janet was definitely correct when she said he would experience no kind of pain. He had been sitting, or so it seemed, in the same position for an indefinite period without incurring aches, cramps, or discomfort of any sort. His body, or whatever had taken its place, reported no need to stretch or move around. Encouraged by what she had told him, he launched a thorough self-examination and was rewarded to find an unprecedented sense of euphoria and wellness in every part of him.

Had he ever felt so good all over and all at once?

Never.

Despite the narrow frame of his comfortable chair, he did not feel at all restrained. Under these circumstances, he was entirely content to follow Miss Janet's advice and remain as he was until called upon to do otherwise.

He decided to think about things with his eyes closed and turned off all the extraneous inputs from his pseudo senses. This business of being able to have his senses fully shut down had distinct advantages. At first, there seemed to be no downside. Imagine how many nights he might have gotten more easily to sleep, if merely closing his eyes had also cut out the distractions of noise, uncomfortable temperature levels, and nasty odors. On the other hand, he would not have awakened to the sound of an approaching menace, might have frozen to death in lethal comfort, or could have failed to respond to the telltale aroma of smoke. The idea of one all-purpose sense worked well enough here, but being able to shut down one sense without inhibiting the other four had been a matter of survival in his past life.

According to Miss Janet, this place would not be real where he came from or where he was eventually going, but it was much more like the latter than the former. She had also suggested that it was an intermediate environment, something like a decompression chamber. It was specifically designed to help newly transformed souls, like him, adapt gradually to the spiritual way of things before moving into the rarefied atmosphere of heaven.

She named it the Vale and did not approve of having it called purgatory. She likened it to a sanitarium that would heal him and build him up for his next big leap. He suspected it might also be similar to a decontamination station. Could he be carrying some worldly ticks and fleas that would not be acceptable in God's total realm of the spirit? That seemed entirely possible, if not probable.

What was it she had said after grilling him about viewpoint and looking for truth? She said she was glad he had not stopped thinking about God. That was it. What did she mean? How do you stop thinking about God, especially if you grew up Southern Baptist, going to church twice on Sunday and at least once in the middle of the week?

Of course, he had not always been a Baptist. There were long periods of no church involvement and other stretches with moderate church attendance of no particular denominational or spiritual significance. When he spent time around military installations, a fairly common occurrence, he began to think of himself as a General Protestant. That was what military chaplains called most services or programs that were not Catholic or Jewish.

He might have been a member of that great General Protestant non-denomination for a long time, but he had never forgotten about God, not the real God he had come to know. Perhaps getting to know God had taken Paul longer than it should have, but that was his own problem, not a divine one.

As a child, he had received conflicting visions of God. Unfortunately, the more authoritative version was God from the pulpit in the person of Dr. George Fathringill Trumbull. Dr. Trumbull's version of the deity was as scary as God gets. That God did not just hate sin. He hated sinners and he seemed to delight in seeing them burned eternally to an everlasting crisp. The pastor was a matchless oratorical painter, able to create a masterful panorama of human souls trapped in the never-ending torments of the devil.

Sunday after Sunday, Dr. Trumbull's fiery sermons registered in Paul's mind as a direct message from God.

"It's your choice, kid. Accept Christ as your Lord and Savior today, or go to hell and burn forever. Pick one, and be quick about it. You could die tomorrow, but don't count on that. You might not even make it through the night."

At last, Paul was caught up in the preacher's vivid portrayal of damnation and the fires of hell.

I give up, pastor! I'm no fool, he thought, rushing down the aisle in a terrified search for salvation.

After that, Paul, who was a persistently introspective youngster, found himself worrying day by day about more than the usual thought-crimes he was committing moment by moment against God. Now he lived with a dreadful uncertainty, even greater than the one from which he had sought to be saved.

Had his conversion been sincere? At the time he had thought God's Holy Spirit was moving him, but that overwhelming presence did not seem to come back afterward. Was God even hearing his end-to-end prayers of contrition and pleas for forgiveness? These were the petitions Paul felt compelled to mentally offer up with lightening speed after each thought-crime, lest he be struck down unexpectedly with some sin still on his soul?

Paul knew he had a very active imagination. Had he errantly invented his own conversion experience? Had he lied to God? He was not sure, but he knew that God was, and that really scared him.

Keeping him sane, Paul had a number of blessings to counterbalance the oppressive influence of Dr. Trumbull's sermons. All of them were people. He had supportive parents at home and Miss Janet in Sunday school. They and most of the adult Christians he knew, those who did not mount the pulpit every Sunday, said very little about God's punishment. When they talked of God, it was usually of his love, mercy, and forgiveness. They spoke often about God's mercy and heaven, but rarely of God's wrath and hell.

Paul was in mid-adolescence before he understood how very superior their vision of God was to that of the preacher. It took him at least that long to begin thinking that, perhaps, God did not want him to be in constant dread of hell. He at last realized that his prayers ought not be founded on the terrors of eternal torment. Hell there might be, but centering his belief in God on fear of punishment was superstition, not faith. Once he saw the difference between the two he was much more comfortable thinking and talking about God. He no longer expected to be damned for his thoughts. Aside from one dreadful period in his life, Paul was always thinking about God at some level. With the same exception, he never gave up talking to him either.

During college and for some time thereafter, Paul began to view most of his earlier life with scorn and skepticism. Whatever his parents and teachers had seemed to think important to his childhood education was—well, childish. He saw it all as a matter of axiom, *cliché*, or something only a child would think more about.

He would rush past things, a little embarrassed, that he had memorized as a child: Scripture like the twenty-third Psalm, the Lord's Prayer, and John 3:16, historic and patriotic bits from the Constitution, the Declaration of Independence, and speeches by Washington and Lincoln, uplifting passages from poets like Longfellow and Tennyson, and lines from some of Shakespeare's plays. Their eloquence, depth, and importance were lost upon him, because he did not find them worthy of adult reflection or study.

As a young man, Paul did not like being reminded that he had ever been a child. He would not concede that he had learned anything beyond the rudiments of language, science, and civility while he was one. His mental reaction when confronted with anything intellectual or spiritual from his childhood was, "Don't bother me. I know that." Stories and teachings from the Bible fit quite naturally into that category.

In pursuit of what he thought to be intellectual sophistication, he somehow failed to notice the inconsistency of such views with his respectful and affectionate memories of Miss Janet. Long after college, he discovered how much this kind of snobbery had retarded his earliest, adult quests for the real truth about God. Only then did he recognize what he had missed in that process and come to understand how badly he had failed God and himself

Here in the Vale Miss Janet had said something about big-T Truth. Evidently, she had access to Paul's prior thoughts and private vocabulary. Big-T was the name he had started to use when he returned, humbled by tragedy and personal failure, to the question of what he believed about God. Big-T Truth meant the way things really were, whether he knew it or not and whether or not he would like it if he did.

Big-T was how God made everything to be. It was non-debatable and non-negotiable. Paul's opinion, if he had one, did not matter. It was God-sized Truth beyond human comprehension. Yet, it was as universal as truth can get and Paul, along with the rest of humanity, was built into it. Nobody could possibly see all that was Big-T. Further, it would be preposterous to believe that anyone other than God might be able to understand it, even if God made it possible for them to see it.

All anyone could hope to identify were little-t chunks of God's complete everything in that great ocean of all-Truth, over which humanity perpetually drifted through an ever-present fog of ignorance. One could look—ought to look—peering through clouds of confusion and despair, but never hope to see it all. In truth, no one could ever see anything at all the way God does.

Paul had once heard a cosmologist talk about a Unified Theory of Physics. The idea was that, somehow, the entire operation of the universe might be reduced to a single theorem. It was something like a modern physicist's Holy Grail. For humankind, Paul decided it was a less practical search than that of medieval alchemists for the Philosopher's Stone they thought could turn lead into gold.

On the other hand, the concept of a Unified Theory of Physics might accurately describe the way God sees things. After all, he made them that way and knew how he did it. Perhaps little-t fragments of that great, creative moment could still provide quick peeps into the depths of God's universe, glimpses to inspire understanding and faith, however brief and dissociated those flashes might be.

Paul had almost abandoned regular Bible reading between the ages of twenty and forty. There was always a Bible around his apartment, the one his parents had given him at his high school graduation, but he rarely opened it except as a literary reference or to find a useful quotation. The idea of reading it seriously, as he once had, simply did not occur to him, except on occasions in the field when things were not going well.

Those were times when he faced the greatest fear he knew. That was the terrifying prospect that somebody else might die or be trapped because of his own mistake or incompetence. Such situations did not often allow for the availability of a Bible. They certainly did not provide the time or opportunity to read one.

That was when he remembered God automatically and prayed most fervently. Sometimes when his prayer seemed to have been answered, he would offer up a second or two of thanksgiving. Most often he had so much to do that he forgot about giving thanks—even about the prayer—and just went on.

After the action was over, its insistent urgency answered, he enjoyed periods of quiet. Then he would find someone with a Bible and browse through it. He had favorite Psalms and Gospel readings, but his most cherished passages were from the letters of his namesake, Paul of Tarsus. He could lose himself for hours in the other Paul's incisive teachings and logical arguments about God's love, redemption through Jesus, and living the Christian life. At those times, it never occurred to him that he was studying the Bible or doing anything particularly Christian. Neither did he stop to think about why the apostle's ancient writings resonated so purely and distinctly within him.

Paul did not calculate at the time that he was still thinking about God. He completely failed to recognize, or even consider, the obvious fact that God had not stopped thinking about him.

Mulling over these memories in the Vale, Paul recalled the first time he had lapsed into Bible reading in reaction to a crisis. It had been at Furstenfeldbruck during the Hungarian Revolution of 1956. Now, with his senses stilled, Paul thought again about that incident and some things it revealed about his character at the time.

7

Colonel Dawes was waiting outside base operations around two in the afternoon when Paul pulled up in the jeep. To Paul he looked like a living caricature of dashing aviators from bygone years. Age had brought gray into his black curly hair, but his brown eyes still sparkled with unconcealed vigor. His jaunty grin was only enhanced by the wrinkles in his tanned, leathery cheeks and the thin, slightly curled moustache above his lip. He was wearing a faded, classically baggy, flight suit with a World War II, leather bomber jacket in a style no longer issued by the Air Force. At his feet was a thick, brown-leather map case of a type Paul had seen only in old war movies.

This guy, Paul thought, *is a walking myth.*

"Tom Dawes," he shouted over the engine noise, tossing his case into the back of the jeep. "Thanks for coming to get me."

Paul caught the hint of a southern drawl beneath academically precise pronunciation.

"Want to see the airplane?" Dawes asked.

"Why not?" Paul replied, following the colonel's instructions to a ramp across from base operations. The aircraft was a 4-engine

C-54. An excellent but aging breed, it was more designed for passengers than for cargo. It had long been surpassed by modern carriers, capable of hauling greater payloads.

"Let's go on board," Dawes said, as Paul killed the jeep's engine.

Resting on its nose gear, the aircraft sat parallel to the ground. The colonel took his map case with him up a boarding ladder into the rear of the fuselage. Inside, Paul followed him forward between two narrowly separated rows of passenger seats into the flight-crew compartment in the nose. Entering the door to the flight deck, Paul saw what looked like a radio operator's position on the left.

Ted, he thought, *will sit there during the mission.*

In its more current airframes, Ted had mentioned to Paul the previous evening, the Air Force was rapidly eliminating any need for dedicated radio operators. Radio communications were more important than ever to aircraft control and safety, but simplified radios and improved communications design in the cockpit were allowing pilots and co-pilots to handle all their radios by themselves.

Reaching the front of the flight deck, Colonel Dawes dropped into the right-hand seat, so Paul sat down on the left, which he knew was normally the pilot's position. By lifting the inside seat arms, the two could turn to face each other.

"I figured this would be a good place to talk," Dawes said. "I know this plane is clean, because we just flew her in from Rhein Main this morning. Now you must have some questions. Let me have them."

"It may sound odd as the first question, but are you really an Air Force officer?"

"Yes, indeed I am. What was your first hint?" Dawes chuckled.

"The uniform and the fact that you are a pilot, I guess, but this seems a strange role for active-duty military to be taking on."

"To begin with, I am not the pilot this time. That's Joe Walsh, who is over at base operations right now. He's taking care of all the flight planning, fueling, and other support stuff that pilots have to do. I'm his co-pilot and navigator."

The colonel, Paul observed, was a very casual man who seemed to smile almost habitually.

"My current connection to the Air Force, I admit, is a little unusual, but no less genuine. Starting in the Army Air Corps, I have been pushing tin around the sky since before Pearl Harbor: single-seat fighters, multi-place bombers, and transports like this. I've done them all. Even took off once from an aircraft carrier. Never landed on one though and don't mean to try. People who do that are just plain crazy."

"But how do you happen to be here? This is not exactly an Air Force mission."

"I will agree that it is an unusual marriage. First, I am a real Air Force colonel. I command a small squadron north of here, but I have a very competent executive officer. He does everything that needs to be done and makes sure that the things I need to sign are there when I am around. Heaven knows what he thinks I am doing all the time I'm gone, but he is very judicious and never asks."

"What are you doing?"

"Things like this, although I'll say that this operation is a bit dicier than most."

"You are employed by my organization then?"

"Not precisely. You might classify me as an adjunct contributor to various projects that apply for my help. That only started after the Korean War. I really can't say much more about it." Dawes was starting to sound irritated, although his smile remained.

"Even to me?" Paul's organization was the deepest black of any he knew. The colonel's attitude suggested there was something deeper.

"Especially to you. Now, don't you have any another questions?"

Paul saw he was getting nowhere. Anyway, it was not material to the operation.

"You win. Can you tell me just how you are planning to pull this thing off?"

"That's one I can answer," Dawes' voice was cheerful again.

"It may help you to hold up your end. Here's how it goes." As he said this, he was pulling several air-navigation charts, like the ones Captain French had shown Paul and identical to others in the operation kit at the hut, out of his case. As he spoke, he pointed out places and routes on the map to illustrate what he was saying.

"Tonight at about twenty-one hundred local time we will launch out of here and head south over the mountains into Austria. We will have filed a flight plan to proceed via international airways through Austria to Belgrade, Yugoslavia to discharge and pick up cargo. It mirrors fairly routine routing for embassy support missions that do not require diplomatic clearance. We will also be cleared for a turnaround flight back through Austria into Germany.

"Going in, we will pass over Innsbruck, Austria, and enter an air corridor toward the Yugoslav border. We will make radio contact with the Vienna air authority and remain under that control while passing west to east over Austria. That track will consume most of our flight time going and returning.

"As we approach the Yugoslav border, we will call Vienna Control, tell them we have contact with Zagreb on the other side, and wish them goodnight. Believing our lie, Vienna will expect us to leave its frequency and go over to Zagreb Control. Although we will remain on Vienna's radar for a bit, I anticipate they will stop paying attention to us. Then we will lurch east out of the air corridor, drop our altitude to get below radar, and fly, not into Yugoslavia, but into southwest Hungary."

"What about Hungarian fighter planes? Won't you draw an air defense reaction from them?"

"Like I said, we plan to go in under the radar. Things are pretty confused in Hungary right now and I do not expect the air defense establishment to be at all prepared for what we're doing. The Hungarians will be looking to the east for Soviet military activity and the Soviets in Hungary will be focused inward, rather than out.

"We will have a few mountains to get over, but they are some of the lowest in the country. Once we get past them and out over the eastern plateau, we have a straight, low-level shot into an abandoned airfield east of Budapest. That is where we make the pickup. Ingress to egress, we should be in Hungary less than three hours."

Dawes paused for a question, but went on when Paul remained silent.

"Coming out, we fly back into Austria, pop up to the correct altitude, and enter the air corridor just north of Yugoslavia. Now we call Vienna Control to announce passing into their airspace and request control for the flight back into Germany. As I already said, we will have flight clearance for the return trip from Belgrade, so Vienna will be expecting us. Of course, we never actually checked in with the Yugoslavs, so they will just figure we canceled."

"That's very impressive, colonel, but how are you going to navigate your way into an abandoned airfield in the dark?"

"Thank you for asking. It is not only a very good question, but also the reason I am here. People on the ground will provide some makeshift runway lights once they hear us coming and see our landing lights come on, but getting to that point is the hard part. Have you heard of SHORAN?"

"Some kind of blind-bombing technique, isn't it?" Paul said.

"Yes. It uses radar against radio beacons at known locations to vector a bombing track onto a known target. That is not exactly what I will be doing this time, but the principle is the same. I will use radio direction-finding and distance-measuring equipment against known navigational beacons and other radio markers to chart our course into the airfield location. It's tricky and it takes a lot of concentration, but I have practice and some sophisticated equipment to help.

"While I'm doing that, the pilot will be fully occupied with altitude management. Neither of us will have time for monitoring radios. That is why we are taking your radio operator with us. He will not be transmitting while we are outside the air corridor, but he will monitor your HF frequency even while we are on the ground.

If you need to talk to us, he should hear you. You have the codes, frequencies, and call signs?"

"Yes, but I'll feel a lot better with your full track plotted on our maps."

"That's one of the things I'm here to do," the colonel said, stuffing his own maps back into his antique satchel. "Shall we start?"

Wind and engine noise in the mostly open jeep kept them from talking much until they were at the hut. Inside, Colonel Dawes dropped his bag beside the admin table and surveyed the room.

"You people don't care much for gracious living, do you," he said. The entire team was present and they all laughed.

Good to his word, the colonel spent almost two hours answering questions and helping them set up their maps for the operation. Then Paul took him and Ted back to base operations in the Volkswagen. He wanted to have a few more words with Captain French to confirm his window of concern before the operation began, but learned at the weather desk that she was not in yet. That was understandable, since he had asked her to work back-to-back night shifts. He left a message for her to call him.

Back at the hut, Paul suggested that everybody get some rest before the operation and set an example by crawling into his own sleeping bag. He deliberately gave the appearance of nodding off almost instantly. Actually, he continued to mentally review the operation for more than an hour before he dropped into a brief sleep.

"Port Hall, Port Hall, Port Hall, this is Court Pipe, Court Pipe, Court Pipe. How do you read? Over." The radio speaker was intentionally turned on so the whole team could hear Ted's strong voice booming through the normal crackling noise of open HF radio.

"Hello, Court Pipe. Hello, Court Pipe. This is Port Hall. I read you five by five. How me? Over." George's voice, transmitting on a different frequency, came equally strong from the speaker, although Paul, Henry, and Alan, standing near him, needed no amplification.

"Port Hall, this is Court Pipe. Copy you loud and clear. Test complete. Court Pipe out."

Through the VHF speaker, the team continued to monitor the Furstenfeldbruck VHF tower control frequency. Periodically, they could hear Colonel Dawes' voice using standard Air Force flight identification methods, as he obtained the necessary permissions and received instructions for movement to the active runway and takeoff. Later he reported reaching flight altitude on course to Innsbruck and was given permission to leave the frequency and go over to Austrian control. Tuning to the new frequency, they were able to hear him make contact, report passing over Innsbruck and acknowledge altitude and course instructions. They could not hear the ground controller and soon lost any ability to monitor the aircraft as it descended on the other side of the Alps.

From then on, only HF radio communications were possible between the team and the aircraft, and those were limited to a prearranged format. Soon after the last, audible VHF transmission, Ted's voice again came from the HF speaker.

"Port Hall, Port Hall, Port Hall, this is Court Pipe, Court Pipe, Court Pipe. One normal. I repeat. One normal."

This told the team that the aircraft had passed over Innsbruck, which was point one of four that would be reported on the outbound flight route. The word, normal, simply meant that everything was going according to plan.

George continued to monitor, but would not respond to position reports. He was prepared at any time to broadcast a prearranged recall code to turn the aircraft back.

Paul could anticipate no reason for such a broadcast, other than the development of weather conditions that rendered mission completion impossible or unreasonably dangerous. That was what made Captain French's contribution so important. She had called him during the first hour of her evening shift to confirm that she would be on duty for the remainder of the night. Other threats, should they develop, would lie beyond Paul's ability to know about or act upon, and that made him very uneasy.

The flight leg crossing Austria from west to east was the longest part of the outbound journey. As the evening stretched out, Paul felt rising frustration at being cast in a passive role, while the C-54 crew was taking all the risks. He would have preferred sharing their hazard to sitting safely on the ground, acting as their scorekeeper.

Eventually, the team heard Ted transmit a "four normal" message. That meant the aircraft was about to leave the international air corridor just north of the Yugoslavian border and dart low and unlighted into southwest Hungary. There would be no more point-normal reports until it returned to Austrian air space. Any radio transmissions before that time would not be a good sign. How much time the crew would be on the ground was uncertain, but their absolute maximum time in hostile territory, Colonel Dawes had said, should be under three hours. Paul was increasingly edgy, but he pretended to be calm.

"This will take a while," he said. "Anyone want to nap?" No one slept, but Alan and Henry played chess on a small, traveling board. George continued reading a paperback novel he had begun while the aircraft was over Innsbruck.

Waiting was agony for Paul, who tried to occupy himself with minutiae while the seconds crept by. As team chief, he carried the weight of responsibility. Yet, he had genuine control over nothing. Events far off would determine success or failure, but he would know the result only after the operation was history. He was supposedly in charge, but the outcome was completely beyond his influence. The answer would eventually be known, but he would have almost nothing to say about it. The operation's purpose was working itself out in the dark skies of Hungary, while Paul sat on the ground in West Germany feeling helpless. Practically speaking, he *was* helpless.

Paul hated the idea of helplessness. Even as a boy, he believed there was no real need for anything to ever go seriously wrong so long as one was careful enough. Mistakes did not just happen. They resulted from a lack of knowledge or forethought. If you prepared fully and thought through every step and consequence thoroughly, nothing should ever bring about disaster. Disaster came only when you failed to avoid it.

In some ways this attitude had helped him. When failure befell, he was often able to see how it could have been averted and learn from the experience. In his work with the organization he had quickly been recognized as a good planner and one with a talent for spotting flaws in schemes that looked foolproof.

A degree of predictability was one of the things Paul liked about his career choice. He knew that the operation in progress had been assembled, speedily but carefully, from hundreds of contingency scenarios about things that might go wrong in Eastern Europe. The plan had been put together, contentiously tested, and minutely adjusted by area experts, while people and resources were being organized and brought into place. During development, it was progressively adapted to conform and respond to a constantly shifting situation. The whole thing, from conception to execution, had taken only a few days. If necessary, it could have been done faster.

Paul believed in what he was doing and trusted the organization that sent him out to do it. Everything was based upon reason, purpose, order, and probability—except when the objective came near. Then he could see through the mists of doubt and know how treacherous the boggy swamps of certitude might become.

Helplessness was not compatible with Paul's understanding of the world. He did not sympathize easily with people who found themselves in that state. Finding it in himself was intolerable. Maybe that was why he prayed at times like this. He did not reason through what he was feeling or why. He simply knew that at such moments his life was only nominally under control. Nothing was safe or certain. Any one of a thousand variables might sweep his game pieces from the board and leave him powerless. Silently praying, *Dear Lord, help us,* was all he could think to do. At least that meant he was doing something.

Over an hour after the last position report, one of the telephones rang. Henry, finished with the chess game, was sitting at the admin table roughing in parts of the operation report to be sent later, so he answered it.

"For you," he said, gesturing to Paul with the handset. Paul grabbed it impatiently.

"Yes?" He said into the mouthpiece.

It was Captain French. Her voice was firm, but listening to it brought a slight tremor to Paul's hand. She enunciated so clearly and authoritatively that he sensed she was bringing him news he would rather not hear.

"I don't know what this will mean for you," she said, "but the area you are worried about will very soon be socked in like a London pea-souper."

"Fog?" he asked.

"One like you would not even want to be walking in. It will probably remain that way until well after sunup."

"When?" he asked.

"I told you. It is happening at this very moment, and some places will be going much faster than others."

"Budapest?"

"Plus-or-minus fifteen minutes. That's the best I can guess, and you should know what a crapshoot long distance forecasting is."

"Thanks. I owe you breakfast," he said and hung up.

The captain's information was cause for serious alarm. If the aircraft was about to land or was already on the ground, the crew members needed to know about the radical weather change that might trap them there. Ironically, Paul's initial feeling was one of gratitude. Now he had something to do besides wait. Glancing at his watch, he estimated that the crew had been in Hungary for about an hour-and-a-quarter.

Paul's end of the telephone conversation had attracted attention; the whole team was looking at him expectantly.

"George, get Ted on the horn."

"He's in radio silence."

"I know, but he'll be monitoring, even on the ground. He'll answer."

"If you say so."

"Court Pipe, Court Pipe, this is Port Hall, Port Hall. Do you copy? Over."

Only the static of HF dead air followed. It was louder than before, because George had boosted the volume.

Khaaaaaaaaaaaaaaaaaaaaaaaaaaaaaaaaaaaa…

George repeated the call several times to no effect, except for what seemed like heavier static still.

Khaaaaaaaaaaaaaaaaaaaaaaaaaaaaaaaaaaaa…

Paul watched as George unsuccessfully tried balancing the receiver volume and squelch controls to minimize interference and let a response get through.

"Any ideas, George?"

"Maybe they're on the ground."

"And?"

"They may have shut down some engines while they're loading passengers."

"So?"

"Not as much transmission power. Ted may be reading us and trying to answer, but he's sending at such low power that it's not getting through."

"Good thinking. Any ideas?"

George shrugged his shoulders.

"The only thing I can do is keep trying. I can always pass traffic in the blind and hope for the best."

"We'll have to, if it comes to that, but I want to be sure they've gotten the message. Give it a few more tries," Paul said.

Paul was worried and time was critical; it might already be too late. The warning had to be prompt or it would do no good. Sending in the blind meant just sending the message over the airwaves with no way of knowing whether or not Ted had heard it. That remained a last resort, but it would leave dreadful doubts if the mission failed to return. Still, the message had to be sent—soon. Was there anything else he could do? His thoughts and another prayer took only a second, but time was short and steadily running out. He had to decide very soon.

Paul, like every operator, was trained and experienced in radio communications, but what could he do when the problem was a lack of communication? In less than a second he knew, but could not imagine how or why. Was it his earlier prayer or mere coincidence? That made no difference; he must act now. No time remained for anything else.

"Let me have the microphone," Paul said. What was happening here? He had an overwhelming impression of *deja vu*? Where was he getting it? This was not a technique he would have been likely to think up on his own. Was it something he had seen in a movie, in reality, or in a dream? He could not tell, but that did not matter. Would it work? It had to. He pressed the transmit button and began speaking slowly.

"Court Pipe, Court Pipe, this is Port Hall. If you copy, give me a series of Roger's. I have traffic for you. I repeat. If you copy, give me a series of Roger's. Over."

Everyone gathered around the radio table was silent, listening to the crackling noise from the speaker. Then they could hear it, embedded within the flowing mass of noise. The signal had very little strength behind it, but its continuous stream of speech transmission was letting brief, running sub-syllables break through.

"Khaaaaurradkhaaaazhurkhaaaadzhkhaaaa..."

Paul could not recall any experience of hearing human speech, however garbled, that had left him in such a state of elation. He concluded that George had guessed right about the aircraft being on the ground. Had the fog already begun to envelop it?

"Uh-Roger, Court Pipe, this is Port Hall with traffic. Message follows. Fall Sky. I say again. Fall Sky. Over."

Once more, they heard anemic fragments rising above the static from a litany based upon the procedural word, Roger. That was enough.

Fall Sky was not the recall message. It was a prearranged, sort of obvious code for suddenly deteriorating weather. The rest of the team now understood what Paul had learned from the telephone call. For all Paul knew, Ted might be acknowledging something he could see for himself. Was it too late? Were they already stuck on the ground or being forced to attempt a takeoff in poor visibility?

"Keep the volume turned up," Paul told George. "If they can't get out, they may call us. Otherwise, we should hear from them within an hour-and-a-half."

Again Paul felt alone and powerless. Again he prayed internally, while trying to look totally unconcerned and at ease. His prayer also gave thanks for the method he had been given to confirm receipt of the message. That was when his memory produced a recollection, unbidden, about how he had known what to do.

More than two years before, during his initial field training at an organizational site in the remote reaches of West Texas, one of Paul's instructors had been a man called Arthur Dayton. Dayton, like Ted, had come to the organization from a background in military communications and enjoyed telling stories from his past. Now Paul recalled a class in radio procedures, when, almost as an aside, Dayton had described a technique like the one Paul had just used. He had said that it demonstrated one way of structuring transmitted speech in order to pierce heavy atmospheric interference. If he met Dayton again, Paul thought, he must be sure to tell him how well his illustration had worked in a pinch.

Whatever Paul now knew about the source of his successful technique, he could not predict the outcome of tonight's effort. All he could be sure of was that Ted had acknowledged receiving the message. Had Paul sent meaningless information to a crew that was already trapped and helpless?

Except for the crackle of static from the open loudspeaker, the hut grew silent. Each man waited apprehensively for a radio transmission that meant the difference between success and disaster. Minute dragged on after minute for more than an hour-and-a-half with no sign of hope. For Paul, time had become a long and empty tunnel, disappearing into endless darkness.

"It's been an hour and forty-five minutes since the last transmission," George said with a catch in his voice.

"We can't give up. We've got to keep hoping…and praying," Paul said, at last betraying his own mood.

At that instant, Ted's voice transcended the static.

"Port Hall, Port Hall, Port Hall, this is Court Pipe, Court Pipe. Five normal. I repeat. Five normal. Court Pipe Out."

The hut erupted in celebratory shouts and explosive applause. Paul was wildly happy and went between the tables shaking hands, pounding backs, and telling everyone what great work they had done. Actually, he thought at the time, the team had done very little, and their role may well have been irrelevant to the outcome. So what. Not failing in something like this counted just as much as succeeding.

Paul crossed paths with Ted several times after Furstenfeldbruck. On the first occasion, Ted told him he had recognized the method of calling for a series of Rogers as one he himself had learned from experienced Air Force radio operators. At the same time, he told Paul what had happened that night on his own end of their radio link.

According to Ted, the pilot had become concerned about some suspicious weather indicators prior to landing and was eager to load up and get back into the air as quickly as possible. George's first calls had come through while the aircraft was rolling on a taxiway toward a loading area with both outboard engines cut to conserve fuel. When Ted reported that the team was trying to make contact, the pilot began monitoring HF radio himself and eventually heard Paul's extreme weather message. That was all he needed to know. He immediately turned the aircraft around, taxied back onto the runway, lined up for takeoff, and insisted on boarding all passengers in place. His precaution delayed takeoff, which made the mission late getting out of the country, but saved the operation. People were still coming on board when the fog closed in and visibility dropped to zero, but the C-54 was already on the runway, aimed in the right direction, and able to launch on instruments in the absence of any visual reference.

"Henry," Paul said after a few minutes, "let's start polishing the report. I want to send it as soon as they get back into German airspace."

Soon afterward, Paul called Captain French to thank her, tell her that things were going well, and confirm his earlier offer of breakfast.

For the team in the hut, the return leg across Austria seemed to take no time at all, when compared with the flight out. Before it seemed possible, they heard Colonel Dawes' familiar drawl through the VHF receiver reporting a position over Innsbruck. Soon after, he contacted Munich Control for permission to enter Germany

"Nice ending, everybody," Paul said, when things quieted down and the aircraft had passed on north. "We can start packing up now."

"Say," he added, "Does anyone happen to have a Bible?"

No one did, but he was able to borrow one later that morning from Susan French.

8

Paul opened his eyes in the Vale. As forecast by Miss Janet, all his senses returned with a rush of newness and intensity. This phenomenon was still a bit of a jolt, but he had another reason for unease. Leaving his memory of the Hungarian Revolution behind, he did not find himself back where he had been when he closed his eyes. This was not what he remembered of the Vale.

He was now looking down on a wooded snowscape. He knew instantly that the vista was a bird's-eye view of the mountain meadow where he had so recently concluded his life. He clearly saw the snow-tracked APC he and Barney had been trying to elude. It was headed away from the utility road and down into the meadow.

"You do not see Barney down there, but you can barely pick out his snowshoe trail, going into the trees."

The raspy baritone voice, barely above a bass, was as unmistakable as it was long unheard. Paul broke off his examination of the meadow below to focus on the spot in front of him where Miss Janet had last stood. In this case, unlike his initial experience with Miss Janet, Paul was immediately able to identify his former colleague and friend, Matt Harriford. Maybe that was because in life Matt had been blessed with remarkably good looks. The swarthy, handsome face with its narrow, black mustache and wide-mouthed, perpetual grin would have stood out in a crowd of hundreds. Matt had a mouthful of perfectly arranged white teeth and he displayed the upper tier almost all the time. Identifying him was easy, but Paul noticed himself having the same problem he had observed when concentrating on the details of Miss Janet's appearance. At first, Matt seemed to be wearing a white lab coat. When Paul looked more closely, he saw something like a coverall of a not quite distinguishable color. Matt stood casually while Paul remained seated, but it seemed to Paul that they were equally at eye level. Maybe this had something to do with an absence of focal points in the Vale, because he had felt the same way with Miss Janet.

"Good to see you, Matt. It's been a long time. Tell me. Is this the way you really look?"

"The way you perceive me? Not much. Not even here for the most part. Definitely not beyond here. It's just something we do to help you along at the beginning. The Vale is like a Potemkin village in reverse. The whole thing really is here, but we throw up a facade to put you more at ease. How much of the Vale you see is relative to your level of progress here. At the beginning, you see very little of what is truly going on. In that respect alone, it is more like earth, where things often appeared in forms that were not fully real."

He eyed Paul for a second before continuing.

"Nope. Sorry. Not my voice either—nor yours for that matter. We don't need those any more. You'll see how it works soon."

"What about the promise of a new body?" Paul asked.

"Absolutely true, but it is a spiritual body of such glory that your current vocabulary and comprehension would fail any effort of mine to describe. It is kind of like your faith in God. While you were in the world, you couldn't fully explain it to a person who did not have it too. When you met someone there who already shared it, no explanation was necessary. Since you're not yet ready for reality, we sort of fake things around here. What you have right now is certainly not your old body, but it seems that way to you—minus the aches, pains, diseases, and outlandish appetites of course. The Vale prepares you for the body that will be fully yours later."

Matt hesitated for a second, as if trying to think of another example.

"Do you remember how Janet looked when she visited you?"

"Miss Janet? How could I forget? What beauty. In life she was at the far extreme of plain. Here she seemed to be more what she should have looked like, if her body had more correctly revealed her true self."

"You always had a preternaturally keen nose for the truth. Janet, you see, is something of a saint. The treasure she laid up in heaven always projects from her spirit to glorify God. Did you notice the incense?"

"Yes. It was entrancing."

"You'll observe that it does not cling to me, as it does to her and all true saints, even when they are away from the throne. You should know that she appeared to you here, not in her completely glorified spiritual being, but as a translation of that, which comes as close as possible to anything your spirit can now interpret."

"If you'll pardon the comparison," Paul commented archly, "you still look just like Matt Harriford."

"Most of your therapists, if you knew them on earth, will appear as I have, the way you remember them. That is for your present comfort and ease of association. You must not think that this is the shape we have as fully healed and transformed souls. Neither, at the end, will you be anything like the way you see yourself now."

"So this is the end of the trail," Paul murmured.

"Are you kidding? Don't dare get the idea that your journey is over just because you are gone from earth. This is where you finish growing into what God meant you to be from the first. You have many paths yet to follow, but they are all full of joy and the love and peace of the Lord.

"Whoops!" Matt started, turned his back to Paul, and made a few gestures that were outside Paul's line of view. "I forgot to turn that thing off."

Abruptly, the snow-covered meadow was replaced by the arcing lights and strange designs of color and shadow Paul had expected to see when he first opened his eyes. For some reason, this made Paul feel more comfortable.

Matt turned again to face Paul, resuming his previous posture.

"It was not real, you see. Just a still shot of your dramatic exit. That's the only reason it was available. You were not visible yourself, because you were already under the snow. You could still tell that Barney made it safely past the tree line. I thought you would like to know that."

"That patrol vehicle must have come back early. Maybe we were spotted. Can I find out anything more?"

"About Barney? Nope. Your earthly time line is finished. You've left the race. And you might as well forget those fairy stories about Mom and Dad being up there somewhere watching. It doesn't work like that. After a while, you'll be glad it doesn't."

"Why do you say that?"

"Listen, Paul. You are still thinking in terms of linear time—you know: past, present, and future. Forget it. You don't have those any more. You are in the Vale."

"Can you expand on that?" Paul asked.

"Okay. Like I told you, we put on a kind of show here to make you feel better while you are still learning the ropes. Before long, you are going to find out what it is like to be always in the realm of now."

"What does that mean?"

"Not much you could not have figured out yourself, if you had looked. Did you ever read Poe's detective story, *The Mystery of Marie Roget*?"

"I don't recall it."

"It was one of Poe's Dupin detective stories, like *Murders in the Rue Morgue* and *The Purloined Letter*."

"I remember Dupin."

"Well, toward the end of *Marie Roget* the narrator comments, 'With God all is *Now*.' I've asked Edgar himself about it. He says he was just trying to impress his readers with some mystical profundity. He was completely unaware that he had generated an act of prophecy by exposing an eternal truth."

"Push me, if you must," Paul said, "but this is all news to me. Exactly what are you talking about?"

"I'll try, but the best we can do is deal in broad generalities. Complete understanding will come only when you actually experience what time is like with God." Matt stopped for a moment, as if he were considering where to begin.

"Do you remember what Jesus told the Samaritan woman at the well about God?" he asked, but proceeded to answer himself. 'God is a spirit, and those who worship him must worship him in spirit and in truth.'"

"Yes."

"Now think about this. Where God is in his fullness, all beings must conform to what God is. Since God is spirit, all around him must be spirit, just as we all are when we at last come out of earth. Why do you think God used the incarnation of our Lord Jesus to come live among us? If he had come as himself in his own pure holiness our whole universe would have blown apart. It would have been like the maker of a doll house trying to move in and occupy his creation."

"I can see that," Paul agreed, hesitantly, "I guess."

"Good start. What about the name God gave himself when he first spoke to Moses from the burning bush? Remember that?" Again Matt went on to answer his own question, and Paul was content to listen. "It was not a name like those of the pagan gods the world had known. It did not suggest something he did or was the patron of, like weather, agriculture, or sex. It described something elementary about him. He called himself I AM, a name so holy that the ancient Hebrew scribes had to write it in code, the Tetragrammaton. If you take it literally, he identified himself as a being who is *infinitely simultaneous*."

"What does that mean?"

Matt sighed with patient resignation over Paul's inability to instantly grasp his meaning.

"Your reaction is typical. Just like you, most of humanity has managed to overlook that straightforward interpretation of what God said about himself. Almost all Christians would agree that God is omnipresent; he can be everywhere all the time, because he just is. We had no trouble granting that ability to God's Holy Spirit.

"Yet, most of us went right on thinking, without much thought at all, that God was trapped in time like the rest of us. Like us, he was bound always to move linearly in one direction from past to present to future. He might know things about the future that we did not, but that was just some kind of cosmic fortune-telling act. What nonsense!"

Matt clapped his hands for emphasis; then opened them outward to stress his follow-up questions.

"Why couldn't we see that for God time and space intersect in a way that gives vastly expanded meaning to the concept of omnipresence? What if *was* and *will be* have no meaning at all for God or the spiritual dimension where he is? They don't, by the way. What if God just always *is* all at one time and all of the time?

"Can you tell where this is going, Paul?"

Matt waited while Paul spent a few seconds in thought.

"Let's see if I follow you," Paul began. "If God just is, he is simultaneously in our past, present, and future. He is then, now, and whenever. For God, as you say Poe wrote, everything is always now; not in the sense of the present, but in the sense of eternity."

"Right," Matt responded. "And what does that do, for example, to the idea of predestination?"

Paul found this question very interesting. He had often been troubled by the references to predestination he found in Paul's letters to the Romans and the Ephesians. They seemed to say there were people in the world who, by failing to win some primordial lottery, were lost no matter what they did.

"This works out beautifully," he said with excitement. "If God just *is*, he is before the beginning, at the beginning, at the end of the age, at every point in between, and at all points beyond—whichever way we look. Not only that, he is there this very second and every second before and after. Predestination becomes an act of knowing, not deciding."

"You're coming along now." Matt was grinning at him. "Does that discovery tell you anything else?"

"If that's the case, God did not predestine us to our spiritual outcomes, any more than he programmed Judas Iscariot to betray Jesus. Our freedom of choice was always complete. So was Judas.' Still, God knows how things turn out, because he is always everywhere all the time and all at once."

"You're starting to get it. Prophecy works the same way. God's prophets do not get foreknowledge from God, they get an eyewitness report."

"I can see that."

"Now here's something terribly important. Think about prayer. Freedom from linear time means God's power transcends any human constraints of cause and effect. God can answer today's prayer by intervening yesterday, or last year, or anywhere in linear time from the Big Bang to the Crunch. Cause can quite easily follow effect in God's good time."

"This is getting harder to handle."

"No, it's not. You only have to open your mind."

Paul thought Matt was beginning to sound like a college professor introducing a basic course in quantum physics to a class of inept students.

"Like most Christians," Matt continued, "you are accustomed to thinking that God worked out an historic plan of salvation, step by step, over the thousands of years between Abraham and Jesus.

That is the way it looked to us, but it is not the way God operates on earth. He sees it and does it all at once over great spans of the linear continuum."

"Take it easy. It isn't just the new information I have to process. I've got to scrap a lifetime of carefully learned, mental habit."

"Come on, Paul. This is the easy part. This is stuff you could have thought up yourself. Some people have. Zeno of Elea caught a glimpse of it back in the fifth century BC, but he took it in the wrong direction. In the 1940s, C. S. Lewis summarized what a lot of theologians and philosophers had thought about it, but he knew that many people would be uncomfortable with the idea. They both told me so."

At last, Paul found something amusing in their exchange.

"My, my, Matt. First Edgar Allan Poe and now Zeno and Lewis. You always were a namedropper," he said, throwing up his hands in mock amazement.

"Not at all, my friend. Just wait until you see the kind of society we share and how we do it." Matt's expression was one of grinning delight. His impatience appeared to evaporate, and he continued in a serious, but more good-natured tone.

"If you want to break free from *was* and *will be* and move on to simultaneous infinity, you must get rid of those foggy old notions of linear time the way it used to seem in the universe of earth. That is simply not the way things are going to be for you any more."

"Okay," Paul said with exaggerated resignation. "Let me have it."

"Listen closely to what I say, because at first it may sound like the Abbott & Costello baseball routine. You have come from a place where, time-wise, you were on a sort of racecourse, actually a line of very closely spaced equidistant dots. They were so close together you could only represent them by drawing a solid line, running to infinity on either end. Each dot behind you at any given moment represented a tiny bit of *was*, yours and other people's. Every runner on the track thought he was moving from *was* to *now* toward *will be*, but the time was always *now* for all of them. Every dot identified a *was*, a *now*, or a *will be* for every runner at some time. You could remember *was* and wonder about *will be*, but you could only live in *now*, and that was always turning into *was*. *Will be* never came, because it was just the next *now*. You were all running in the same direction at exactly the same speed. Everyone's instantaneous location was *now*, and every dot out front was a *will be*. Everybody's position, while they lived on that track, was precisely relative to the position of every other life on the track, whenever it was or would be there. At the instant of every *now*, new runners popped onto the track, beginning their race abreast of everyone already there, while old runners with no *will be* left vanished from the track. No one gained on, pulled ahead of, or fell farther behind another. When runners died, they just stopped being part of the race and could no longer be counted. That was the way you saw time in a linear universe."

"I think I get it, but didn't you say God was somehow outside all that?"

"Completely. See if you can imagine God in his own time, occupying a line parallel to that linear track where humanity lives. It is also a line running to infinity on both ends, but it is not made up of a series of points in linear time—no relative components here. God occupies the whole line all at once and from infinity one way to infinity the other. Can you conceive the workings of that?"

"I'm trying," Paul answered. "For an analogy, how about a reel of motion picture film? God sees the whole movie projected at once, from end to end, but I am watching it play out one frame at a time."

"Very close. But don't forget the reel of film is of infinite length, and in God's time, it never breaks or ends. It does, however, embrace our old linear universe of earth, which has a definite end and beginning."

"I'll need time to get used to this."

"Of course you will. It is, at first, a confusing concept. Accepting it demands a very significant alteration to some very basic beliefs. That is one of the main reasons you are here. You spent your whole life, seeing things one way. Now, you have left linear time and relativity for a temporality that is neither linear nor relative. You are entering an entirely new life to experience happiness you have never imagined, the joy of completely being yourself for the very first time."

"Think I'll make it, buddy?"

"No problem. You are on your way to the great gathering of souls that God has prepared for us, and—trust me—you will not arrive one millisecond earlier or later than any of the rest."

"How can that be? You're already here."

"Believe me, Paul. I know, because we both arrive together—you, me, and all the rest. Have you heard of the harrowing of hell?"

"Isn't that the idea that Jesus, while he was dead in the tomb, went spiritually to redeem souls that died before he came?"

"Something like that, but don't you see? From here, it is all quite transparent. The saints of the Old Testament and others who had measured up to God's standard of being what they are did not have to wait centuries after their deaths to benefit from our Lord's immeasurable sacrifice. Here, that is not a thing of the future or the past. It is happening now and now is when they pass through the Vale to come before God."

Paul paused for thought.

"Sorry," he said. "I guess I have been a bit slow catching up with your terms. You say that God and everything around him are infinitely simultaneous. That means the same thing, even if you turn it around. Anything that is infinitely simultaneous has to be simultaneously infinite."

"Eternally true."

"You and I have been on earth for what seems a long time. Right now, the two of us are here talking to each other in the Vale. But it makes no difference when we lived, when we died, or how long we might be in transit. God brings all of us together at once, where and when he is. In the true, absolute, non-linear sense, we already are—always are—in God's simultaneously infinite kingdom."

"I could hardly put it better," Matt's face and voice were filled with encouragement. "Soon, and that is already the last relative term that matters to you, all else will be forgotten. You will be eternally what and where you always are."

"Since I am not quite there yet, I'd like to ask you about one of those relative old times we had on earth."

"Relatively speaking, I think I can tell what's coming." Matt was no longer smiling.

"Right," Paul said in a firm, slightly accusing tone. "Why did you lie to me?"

9

At the time of Paul's death, he had not seen Matt Harriford for nearly twenty years. During that time, Paul had continued to remember him with a degree of sadness. Matt had not set out to betray anyone. Paul was sure of that. Yet, he was equally convinced that Matt had let him down and disappointed plenty of other people.

Wherever he went and whatever he did, Matt Harriford was bound to stand out. He was dark and smoothly-rather-than-ruggedly handsome. In a way he reminded Paul of the old comic strip character, Smilin' Jack. Every movement and expression spoke of energy and interest, but the feature no one could fail to notice was his deeply resonant baritone voice. He could commandeer any discussion and authoritatively center attention on himself and what he was saying. He won a lot of arguments that way. It also made him an excellent instructor. That was how Paul got to know him.

In his late twenties, Paul was one of the younger members on the training team, but his seniors were only a few years older. When Matt came on board, he was an exception to the local order of things. He was assigned to a junior instructor position, but in his mid-thirties, was several years older than any of the senior instructors or training supervisors.

His youthful appearance notwithstanding, Matt had served in the army during World War II. He had arrived in Germany after its surrender but before the war ended in August 1945. Returned home and released from service well before the Korean conflict, he wandered around the country for a time and then spent four years getting a college degree on the GI Bill. His time with the army occupation force in Germany and further study in college had made him fluent in the German language. This easily attracted the attention of government recruiters, who persuaded him to apply for employment and eventually channeled him into Paul's organization. After initial training and a round of overseas operational assignments, he had been sent back according to routine practice to instruct at the initial training school.

Matt had an expansively generous nature that made him an instant favorite among instructors and students alike. Working at adjoining desks in one of the converted Quonset huts that provided office space, classrooms, and quarters for the training teams and their students, Paul and Matt quickly became good friends. They not only shared a working area, but also had class space, students, and curriculum-development projects in common. Occupying apartment space in the same living-quarters Quonset and finding that they possessed some of the same interests, they frequently spent leisure time together on and off the site.

The entire school compound was filled with various examples of the World War II Quonset hut. Some provided ten small bedroom-sitting-room apartments for single or unaccompanied faculty and staff members. Each apartment was equipped with a single bed, a desk with chair, a dresser, and one comfortable chair. Nearby-Quonsets provided common toilet and shower facilities, which gave the place something of a military flavor. Students were quartered in more-open Quonsets with almost no privacy, which was even more military. Other academic, administrative, management, messing, and recreational facilities were housed in appropriately converted versions of the ubiquitous Quonset. All privately owned cars had to be parked on a concrete lot outside the station perimeter.

The training area sat in a remote section of West Texas desert. More than fifty miles from the nearest discernible town, the location had been selected for at least two reasons. The surrounding terrain was readily adaptable to field training and its isolation provided a moderate degree of anonymity to the sponsoring organization.

Out of sight from the main road and surrounded by barbed wire, the site looked like a rather small, government storage facility of some kind. That was the cover story deliberately circulated within the sparsely populated vicinity. A doubtful person might have wondered what a storage facility was doing so far from transportation centers or any other government activities. Nobody seemed to care, however, since the government was known to spend great amounts of money on so many strange and foolish things. If any of the locals had been inclined to visit the site, they might have been puzzled by the rather heavily armed security patrols that operated around it. Still, they would probably have judged that to be just another outrageous example of government extravagance.

The single gravel road into and out of the site connected with a state highway, dotted with occasional truck stops, restaurants, and beer joints. These, at least, gave students and faculty access to basic necessities and the nearest thing to diversion in that part of the country.

Paul once asked Matt why people who rarely talk about God start to do so when they have had something to drink.

Matt gave Paul a wicked smile.

"Probably for the same reason that guys who never say boo to anyone while they're sober get snotty with the boss and frisky with the ladies after a bit of boozing," he said.

Matt called it barroom theology. It came up quite often when he and Paul shared a pitcher of cold beer in one of the roadhouse honky-tonks near the site, as they sometimes did after supper.

Their favorite spot was the dimly lighted Bottle Top Cafe, which was near the turnoff from the highway to the site and a reasonable walking distance from their quarters. The name probably derived from a parking lot covered with beer and soft drink bottle caps, pressed into the cracked, asphalt pavement. The Bottle Top might once have been a café—that is what the aging, lighted sign said—but the only menu items available, by the time Paul and Matt became patrons, were beer, soft drinks, potato chips, peanuts, and pork rinds. While a regulation jukebox was normally in operation, the volume was always low enough to permit normal conversation at the other end of the room. A small area near the jukebox was allocated for dancing but rarely used for that purpose, except on weekends, when more of the local ranching population might come in with wives or girlfriends.

For men who demonstrated few signs of religiosity in daily life, Paul and Matt seemed uncommonly apt to drift into the kind of discussions most of their colleagues classified as "God-talk." Their regular drinking companions soon learned to see it coming and usually moved to another table before the conversation became too tedious to bear.

Paul and Matt had studied some comparative religion in college and each came from a Christian background. It was perfectly natural for these things to be part of their discourse, but both of them realized that nothing else came up so repeatedly or escalated to such intensity. No wonder others were inclined to clear out and leave them alone when it started. Even had another person been interested in the subject, the two contenders gave little opportunity for third-party participation.

"What about *dukkha*, then?" Matt asked one night in the Bottle Top. Their two table mates had already made a quick break for the linoleum-covered bar.

"It's the Hindi word for what Buddha said life is. It is most often translated as 'misery.'"

Matt was quick to correct him.

"You know it means more than that. *Dukkha* also describes something misaligned or improperly related to other things, something out of order that creates disorder, like a bent axle that will not let the wheels track. It might describe a broken bone, but at the same time mean the bone's state of brokenness. Another example would be a scale out of balance that cannot record a correct weight.

"Buddha took that meaning to a completely new level. He said the pain, frustration, and grief that make up our lives are only symptoms of *dukkha*, that faulty condition of something poorly connected and always out of order."

"I know that," Paul replied. "He taught that we don't see reality the way it is. In fact, he says we can't. Our universe is a massive illusion. We're wrong about our world, ourselves, and our linkage to all that is. We're unhappy because our true selves, our souls, yearn to be what they are, but don't know themselves to be. Looking for happiness, we just make things worse, because we see everything the wrong way."

"Exactly," Matt said, picking up Paul's lead. "Our pursuit of material happiness turns into a blind alley, because the real universe, the reality we cannot see, is spiritual, and spiritual rules are all that count. Trying to find happiness on material terms, we sink into ever greater pain. Our unhappiness ceases, in the Buddhist view, only when we quit trying to be in control and allow ourselves to become what we really are, relative to everything else as it actually is."

Between these two men, fairly amiable discussions of religion usually produced an argument.

"That's very eloquent," Paul said, "but aren't you bordering on Christianity."

"What? How?"

"I would say," Paul grinned condescendingly, "that absent God in Buddha's outlook, his description of the fruitless human struggle of self against reality is not much different from the Christian concept of sinful pride that blinds humanity to its true relationship with God."

"How do you arrive at that comparison?"

"It's easy. Christianity says that alienation from God is the source of human unhappiness. It sees progress of the soul to its proper place in God's presence as the ultimate good. Buddha sees a universe that keeps us from knowing what is real or discerning our true relationship to it. Is that any different than St. Paul saying, 'For now we see through a glass darkly; but then face to face'?"

"Scripture quotations are cheating," Matt objected.

"Not when you throw *dukkha* at me, buddy. Just think about it. St. Paul was directly addressing the reality of God. Buddha spoke only to the concept of reality. Given that difference, they don't seem very far apart in what they are saying about the human condition and our problem with recognizing reality."

"You're saying that God is reality and *vice versa*."

"Absolutely, but not in the sense of some vast transcendental oversoul with everyone and everything as part of it. I'm just saying that everything real has its reality only by way of its relationship to God."

"Then who and what, my friend, is God?" Matt smiled smugly and tapped the table with a forefinger for emphasis.

"What a precisionist you are. You know how tricky that kind of definition can be."

"Yep. This will require at least one more pitcher," Matt said, signaling the waitress for a refill.

"Drink it yourself. I may surprise you."

"I'm listening."

"Are we agreed that humans have not been given minds to conceive or, if they could, vocabularies to describe God?"

"That goes without saying."

"We know he is not the inspired but inaccurate figure that Michelangelo painted on the Sistine ceiling. Right?"

"True."

"So what do we know about God?"

"It's your nickel. Keep talking."

"Our first big clue comes from Genesis. Remember? We—all of us—are created in the image of God."

"Come on, Paul. You just made the point that God doesn't look like us."

"I'm not saying he looks like us or we like him. That would be absurd."

"So what image are you talking about?"

"Maybe," Paul said, "we bear a resemblance to God that is much more profound. Would you agree that some element of God's nature abides in every human spirit?"

"I'll go along with that. But how do we resemble him? In what way do we share his nature, and what is that nature?"

"Gotcha! I think it is all over the Bible, but the *Reader's Digest* condensation comes in—what is it? First John?—'God is love.' Remember that?"

Matt gave him a disgusted look.

"You're just full of Scripture tonight. Aren't you oversimplifying a tad?"

"Am I? Think about it."

Conversation paused for a moment, while the waitress delivered and collected for the new pitcher and Matt filled their glasses.

"Aren't you putting a right heavy load on a three-word passage from the Bible?" Matt resumed, querulously. "Are you saying that this is the key to everything we need to know about God as he is and ourselves as we are intended to be?"

Paul waited a few seconds before answering.

"That's right," he said with fervor, "but I did not see it so clearly, until you put it that way."

"Stop blaming me for your confusion, and get on with it."

"Okay. Think about this," Paul continued. "Selfless love is not a concept anyone would make up. There is scant evidence for it. It exists in nature only as itself. You won't find any clues to its existence in physics, chemistry, or mathematics, and you can't deduce it from our economic or social sciences. The universe we can see holds no clue to love's reality. Yet, it exists as surely as beating hearts, brains, and nuclear fission. All humanity knows of it, but how? For Christians, it turns up as *agape*, New Testament Greek for the kind of love we share with God and each other, the kind of love God is."

"I know what *agape* means, Paul."

"But how do we know to look for it? How do we comprehend it when it comes? If its ideal, undiluted expression cannot be found in our world, it must have its perfect state outside the world. In that case, how can we claim to know so much about it? What makes us so certain we do?"

"You tell me."

"Bad grammar, I know, but I think it is us. It is built into us."

"Do you want to explain that?" Matt was showing signs of impatience.

"God is love. Remember? We share in that, because he made us to be a part of his truth, the truth that he is—all the reality that exists, if you think about it. That is why and how we are created in his image. All he really wants us to do is be ourselves the way he made us to be."

At this point Matt would surely have countered Paul's argument, had they not been interrupted by a loud crash from the area of the bar. In the poor lighting they could only tell that the waitress and a few others were gathered around someone who was slouched over the bar. Several more customers were headed that way to take a look.

"Let's see what's going on," Matt said, as they rose from the table.

Nearing the point of interest, Paul could see that the noise must have been produced by a near-full, glass pitcher of beer striking the concrete floor with explosive results. Coming closer, he identified the limp person at the bar as Benson Radiswell. Commonly known as Rads, he was one of the older team supervisors, who had arrived at the school from a field assignment about eight months earlier. He was nominally the supervisor for both Paul and Matt.

Paul had previously observed that Rads was a heavy and somewhat bad-tempered drinker. He was also aware that Matt and Rads had known each other during a previous field assignment. Paul and Rads had come to share mutual antipathy after a nasty incident early in their relationship. While that clash had not diminished their ability to work together, the memory of it probably explained why, until now, they habitually avoided each other off duty.

10

When Rads arrived at the site, about two months before Matt turned up, he had taken over Paul's small training team. The transition at work was no problem for Paul, because he was accustomed to handling his own projects and received minimal supervision. Working with Rads was easy enough in the beginning. When he first arrived, he struck most people as a voluble man who seemed friendly and loved to tell ribald jokes. Within a few weeks, Paul had noticed a less attractive side to his nature that was moody and waspish.

Rads did not actually insult people in the office. His bluffly arch sarcasm was always cast as witty commentary on both personal traits and job performance. Those who were not targeted at the time laughed readily at these *impromptu* jibes. The targets felt the sting of his attacks but were disarmed and unable to react, because his thrust was always disguised as good humor. Everyone learned early on that Rads did not take even a hint of criticism well; he would retaliate at length with focused, acerbic assaults against anyone who tried to match him by responding to his abuse with *repartee*.

For more than a month, Paul devoted his attention entirely to the job and tried to ignore the tension he could sometimes feel building around him. At the same time, he philosophically avoided any appearance of conflict that might make him vulnerable to Rads' caustic word play. This studied neutrality worked fine for Paul in the office, but ultimately failed to preserve his immunity from harassment outside the workplace. At a site so small and isolated, Rads was sure to confront him sooner or later.

The nearest thing to a recreational facility on the site was a dayroom set up in one end of a Quonset hut. This included a TV lounge, where a single black-and-white set provided mediocre reception from the only station with a relay tower in range of the site. Other features were a bring-one/take-one paperback library, two faded pool tables, several tables suitable for card games, and an honor-system refrigerator containing canned drinks and light snacks.

Paul usually visited the dayroom only to watch a major sports event on TV, to get something from the fridge, or to review the contents of the library. He was never inclined to join the frequent poker games there, but sometimes stopped to greet players he knew. He intentionally avoided the ongoing game one night when he had come in for a book, because he saw Rads playing.

Paul was scanning a worn copy of Robert Heinlein's *The Puppet Masters* when he heard a buoyant cry from across the room.

"Hey, Paul. Come on over. We got a chair open."

Replacing the book, Paul turned and walked toward the table where Rads was sitting in a sleeveless undershirt with three other players whom Paul only knew slightly. He could see there were drinks on the table and he noticed a one-quarter-full whiskey bottle on the floor by Rads' chair. He also observed that the sharp, professional appearance Rads usually projected on the job was drastically transformed at the moment. His face was a shade or two brighter than its normal red under his curly black hair, and it supported a glossy sheen of perspiration that seemed unhealthy in the well-air-conditioned room. Tufts of body hair exposed themselves around the neck and armholes of his undershirt.

Rads' eyes were puffy and his lips slack as he waved Paul over.

"Join us, man. We need a fifth."

Paul knew it was a mistake to taunt the man, but he could not stop himself.

"You look like you've already had one, Rads."

Rads shook his head without understanding.

"No, man. We need another player. Not enough money in the game." Rads smiled crookedly.

"Oh. That's the fifth you're talking about," Paul gestured, imitating surprise. "No, thanks. I don't gamble."

Rads still did not get the joke and Paul was a little ashamed for making fun of the man.

"Sure you do," Rads said. "I've seen you at the table."

"Not so."

Rads' face was turning ugly as he rose to his feet, absently kicking his bottle over. Luckily, the cap was on and the bottle failed to break against the concrete floor. Rads did not seem to notice it.

"What's the matter? Don't you like to play cards with your friends?"

Paul and Rads were now face to face about three feet apart. Rads was the shorter man by at least five inches. Paul knew it was foolish to give in to his irritation, but he had heard more than enough from Rads for one night. His basic dislike for the man bubbled to the surface and made him speak with unmeasured candor.

"You're right about one thing, Rads. Even if I liked playing cards, I wouldn't want to play here and now with you."

Paul saw a miniscule change in the other man's expression and realized he had pressed a button that was better left untouched. The face Rads now lifted to Paul was deceptively jovial. Paul had seen it before, when Rads was trying to engender complacency in a victim he had already selected for a round of verbal mischief.

"Hey, Paul. Don't tell me that."

While the man's appearance was familiar, it was also colored by his intoxication. Rads would not, Paul thought, be taking the trouble to mask his malevolence, as he usually did in the office.

"You don't want to talk to me that way. I'm your boss. I always thought we got along pretty well. What's the matter, Paul? Don't you like me any more?" The tone was friendly, but Paul knew Rads was just warming up.

"We're not at work," Paul answered.

"Oh, Paul. I am so very disappointed about this. What can I say to make things right between us?"

"Nothing I want to hear," Paul said, keeping his voice level with effort. Rads' repetitious, whining use of Paul's name had become an added irritant.

"Well, that just won't do, my man." Rads' voice was hardening, and his jovial expression was gone. He continued to smile, but it was a thin, mean smile that showed his contemptuous anger over Paul's rejection.

Paul checked the three players at the table, who were conspicuously minding their own business. They were apparently content to audit the performance going on above them and had no interest in becoming further involved.

"I know what, Paul."

Rads raised his eyes to look straight into Paul's.

"I'm just gonna have to kick your butt."

"Don't try."

Paul held his gaze, but peripherally, he could see Rads drawing back his right foot like a man getting ready to punt a football. His initial reaction was one of surprise. How could the man even think about doing something so stupid? It had to be the whiskey. What else could explain such foolishness?

Paul did not stop to consider if the rising foot were intended to do real harm. He was neither angry nor fearful. He simply wanted to be done with an unpleasant nuisance as quickly as possible.

Almost without thought, Paul made a quick half-step toward

Rads, while moving slightly to the right. This took Paul outside the arc of the coming kick and put him squarely in Rads' face. Then Paul locked his left arm around the now nearly horizontal, right leg and lifted it just enough to dump Rads onto his back.

Standing over him, Paul looked down to be sure that the other man had not cracked his skull on the concrete. He was relieved to see Rads looking up at him in shocked, but clearly conscious confusion. That was enough for Paul. He retrieved the novel he wanted from the library and left without looking back.

From the next day, Paul and Rads went on working together without mentioning what happened in the dayroom and no one in the office was ever able to tell any difference. Paul, as before, seemed to be exempt from Rads' verbal barbs. Whether by intention or accident, their paths outside the office crossed only incidentally, until the night over six months later, when Paul saw him stretched drunkenly across the bar at the Bottle Top Cafe.

Standing at the Bottle Top bar, Matt instantly grasped the situation and took decisive command. He motioned to one of the students he knew had driven to the place.

"Can you give me a hand to get him back to his Quonset?"

"I have to take care of Rads," he went on softly, while pointing at Paul. "Settle up his damage. Okay?"

"Of course," Paul replied, while Matt and the student shouldered Rads' limp body away from the bar toward the exit. "See you tomorrow."

Rads' damage was only the price of the beer and the broken pitcher, plus a generous tip to the waitress and the bartender in return for their forbearance and disinclination to involve the authorities.

Paul could have asked somebody for a ride back to the site, but he preferred to walk. The site was only a mile off the highway, and when the temperature was not too cold, he enjoyed being alone outdoors in the West Texas night. He had never known a night sky of such breadth and clarity, where he could stroll and meditate in a stillness shared only with the moon, the stars, and hundreds of rattlesnakes. The snakes hunted at night, but he was confident that, except when molting or mating, they would feel him coming and stay clear of him. That, at least, was what he told his students before nighttime navigation and evasion exercises in the area.

In the enveloping beauty of this vast solitary openness, his mind went back to the aborted talk with Matt. For some reason, Paul felt he was finding new meaning in old knowledge. Where else might the argument have led? That seemed important now.

Strolling beside the gravel road that led to the site, he lapsed into the kind of internal dialog he sometimes practiced when analyzing personal doubts or exploring unfamiliar situations. It was a technique of mentally interrogating himself and probably had its origin in the forms of debate to which Miss Janet had introduced him in high school.

All right, hotshot, where do you want to start?

Before the interruption, I was pointing to the biblical statement, "God is love." I suggested that love is an elemental characteristic of God's nature that he shares with humanity. That is the way we are created in his image. It is how he intends us to fit into his reality, which is all the truth there is. God wants us to participate in that reality with him and each other, but we can do that only when we choose to grow toward and into the spiritual kinship he has given us with himself.

Aren't you sort of sentimentally stuck in the New Testament? I remember God being a pretty bloodthirsty customer in earlier days.

You are looking at it all wrong. God is love, and God's law is the law of love. It, like God, is not new; it, like God, has never changed. He did not mature from an infant or juvenile God into an adult God. He was not learning on the job. There is no difference between the God of the Old Testament and the God of the New Testament.

There is only a difference in the way he was perceived and his deeds recorded by people who had yet to be enlightened by Jesus.

You're sure of that, huh?

You bet I am. In Deuteronomy, Israel was commanded to love God fully and completely, while Leviticus insisted upon loving one's neighbor as oneself. About a millennium-and-a-half later, Jesus confirmed these as the prime commandments on which everything else rests.

This is the whole story. Jesus put it all together for us. This is the selfless, holy love that binds us to God and each other. It is the critically important part of living we have to get right. Nothing else matters so much, because if we do this, everything else comes around. If we do this, we are being ourselves, the way God made us, and that embraces everything we are meant to be. Being ourselves makes all the right connections and puts us exactly where God wants us to be, in consonance with everything else that is.

Simplify. Simplify.

Okay. Think about a jigsaw puzzle.

What should I think about it?

Look at it. Many of the pieces are shaped the same and look very much alike. The more difficult the puzzle, the more this will be true. Still, each piece has a unique purpose and position within the whole. No piece can rightly fill another's place. One, and only one, placement is suitable for each piece. If a piece is exactly in its proper relationship to any of its many points of contact with the other pieces, it will be correctly related to every other point of its position and to the entire puzzle. That piece, then, is where it belongs. It is being itself, not something out of place, out of line, or out of order. It has not been forced into a false position, nor is it attempting to be what it is not and could never properly become.

I begin to see your analogy. So what?

Consider the opposite case, a puzzle piece out of its proper position. Doesn't that remind you of Buddha's definition of *dukkha*, the disconnection or misalignment between the soul and reality that creates misery and unhappiness?

What if it does?

In a limited way, the jigsaw puzzle illustrates human relationships with God and each other. It touches upon the most elementary aspect of a human soul, its identity. Because of the way God made us, the soul's identity is totally dependent upon its mutual and coincident relationships with God and other souls.

Does that matter?

Absolutely. If we are growing in our relationship with God, we are at the same time growing into a proper, loving relationship with others. This is *agape*, the kind of love we share with God and our fellow souls, because we see the same family image of God in them that they should be able to see in us. As we move closer to loving others, we also move closer to God.

Anything else?

I think so. Perhaps this explains why Christians are so strictly forbidden to hate other people. Hating and loving cannot be mixed or merged, because of the discontinuity of love that occurs when we try to do that. The two acts are so incompatible that the admission of one drives out the other. As love is the true nature of God, we share that nature with him and each other in accordance with his creative will. God loves us, and we are designed to love him and each other. Not to do one is to not do the other. We cannot turn our backs on either requirement and still be our true selves.

I'll buy that.

Paul was elated. He knew he had come to the edge of an important spiritual truth. It was hardly a discovery he could claim for himself. He had not produced a single original thought. Everything he had found was derived from an abundance of sources, even if he could not directly identify some of them. Whatever the process, he had come to an entirely new sense of what God wanted from him and all humanity. It was not at all what he had once believed. He was stunned but, oddly, not surprised.

If Rads had not passed out at the bar, he thought, the whole reasoning process would quite probably have degenerated into just another pointless exercise in barroom theology. Finishing the search in sober solitude under God's great open sky had made all the difference.

Paul was eager to share his excitement and insight with Matt. As circumstances developed, that opportunity never came, and Paul was distracted until much later from a revelation of life-changing potential.

11

Rads did not show up for work the next morning. Since Paul and Matt were the only ones in the office who knew of the roadhouse incident, they were well ahead of other faculty members in noticing his absence.

"He must feel like pickled death today," Paul whispered to Matt.

"If he's conscious at all," Matt replied quietly. "I'll go over to his hut and try to drag him out before he misses a class. If anyone asks about either of us, try to stall them until I get back."

Even disliking Rads as he did, Paul was feeling a degree of sympathy for him fifteen minutes later, when he was called to the telephone. It was Matt. Paul caught a flat tonelessness in his voice that he had never heard there.

"Tell Grogan. It looks like Rads shot himself."

"Is he dead?" The question seemed pointless, but Paul asked anyway.

"Seems that way to me. I called the dispensary and the security post. They should be here any minute." While Matt was speaking, Paul could hear the sound, rare at the site, of a siren. "I'll get back to the office as soon as I can, but I'll probably miss a couple of class periods. Tell Grogan, and get somebody to cover them for me."

"Can do," Paul said, as he heard Matt hang up.

Paul spoke to no one else in the office, but immediately went next door to the training headquarters Quonset where the site chief, Phil Grogan, had his office. This was the same man who had directed Paul's Furstenfeldbruck operation from afar. The office was an open area at one end of the Quonset, which Grogan shared with his administrative assistant and an educational advisor, so Paul was able to go directly to his desk.

Paul briefly told him what Matt had said, adding a resume of Rads' problem the night before. At the end Grogan quietly uttered an uncharacteristic expletive, immediately followed by terse instructions.

"When Harriford gets back, tell him to come directly to me. Make sure someone picks up his schedule for the rest of the day. Tell the day supervisor to get in here, and keep quiet about all of this until you hear otherwise from me."

Grogan's last order was the hardest one for Paul to obey. The sudden convergence of the dispensary ambulance and a site security vehicle on Rads' quarters could hardly escape notice in the relatively small, site community. Vehicular traffic was so rare that Paul wondered why a siren had been used at all. On his way back to the office, he saw a number of people headed in the direction from which its wail had last been heard.

A variety of tales began circulating after some students saw a covered stretcher being loaded and driven away in the ambulance. They were amplified when a group of security officers showed up to seal off the area. The stories ranged from something near the truth to a sudden outbreak of some mysterious disease. The least informed versions multiplied, when a Texas Department of Public Safety highway patrol car entered the site, followed sometime after noon by two U.S. Government Motor Pool sedans from who knew where.

Rumors grew and flew, and by mid-afternoon it was widely

accepted that the entire site compound was about to be placed under some sort of quarantine. Paul remained silent about such things, while taking over Matt's classes. Rads' classes had been reassigned by the day supervisor when he returned from seeing Grogan. The day wore on, but Matt did not return. Paul feigned ignorance when other team members became curious about the simultaneous disappearance of Rads and Matt.

Just before quitting time at five, the day supervisor, Art Dayton, told Paul that Grogan wanted to see them both. Dayton was the former instructor whose anecdotal teaching about radio reception had come back to Paul so providentially during his Furstenfeldbruck operation.

Working with Grogan at the site, Paul had come to admire his leadership qualities. The man seemed to thrive on management crises that produced panic verging on mutiny in those around him. He was fully at home, whether calming distraught people or reconciling disruptive personality clashes, and he never appeared to lose perspective or control.

Grogan's physical persona was casual, but unmistakably commanding. He was of medium height, but heavy build. Now in his late-thirties, he still had his slightly graying hair trimmed in a crew cut. His typical work uniform included an open-collared dress shirt with the sleeves rolled up to reveal muscular, oversized forearms, which he was reputed to have developed working below decks on a World War II battleship.

Following Dayton into Grogan's office, Paul came upon a man he barely recognized. Grogan was alone in the windowless room, now darkened except for one overhead light and a desk lamp. Sitting limply in his high-backed, executive, swivel desk chair—the only one like it at the site—he looked weary, if not defeated. This had obviously been his idea of a very bad day. He looked like a different person, as he listlessly waved the two men to take seats in front of his desk.

"First of all," Grogan said blankly, "if you had any doubt, Radiswell is dead. He took a twenty-two hollow point up through the mouth and into his brain. Not much chance of that being heard in the night. The pistol was found in his lap. It definitely looks like suicide, but the FBI-types who came out to investigate refuse to completely abandon the possibility of murder."

"Murder?" Paul asked in surprise.

"I don't believe it," Dayton said, more evenly.

"That's what they say. I think they are just trying to put the blocks to Harriford, but they have latched onto the fact that he was the last person to see Rads alive and also the one to discover the body. It sounds like a pretty weak assumption, but they are tying in something we did not know about."

Dayton and Paul looked anxiously at Grogan, but said nothing.

"It seems," Grogan went on, "that they have had Rads under investigation since his last assignment; they even had him in for a few interviews." He paused before adding, "I was not told."

He spoke in a low, menacing tone that suggested somebody would pay for that grievous omission. Paul could not help thinking that Rads might be better off now that he was beyond the reach of Grogan's wrath.

"Why were they after him?" Paul asked when Grogan seemed almost unwilling to continue.

"Homosexuality." Grogan obviously introduced the word reluctantly, and it produced an emotional reaction in the men who heard it. "You can bet they were squeezing him. It might explain his suicide."

Both listeners reacted with annoyed grunts.

"Who could tell?" Grogan said. "We had no indication of it. He always had a hollow leg for liquor, but we've got plenty like that. Still, the FBI seems pretty sure of their facts about Rads. It was a quite a shock," he hesitated, "but not the worst one of the day."

His two guests waited, while Grogan took a long drink from the Coke can on his desk. He seemed to be regaining some of his normally imposing personality. The desk and the chair, especially the chair, were part of that too. Grogan was hardly Grogan without them. His executive chair was a talisman of storied reputation. One could as easily imagine King Arthur without Excalibur as envision Grogan without that chair.

"As I told you," Grogan continued, "the Feds are trying to discount the suicide idea. They are looking for some way to establish—I would say they may even be willing to manufacture—that Rads was murdered last night by Harriford, who then tried to make it look like suicide by discovering the body this morning."

"Why would he do that?" Paul asked, as he felt himself passing from shock into anger. He could not seem to sit still.

"That's the easy part for them." Grogan made a calming, but directive, keep-your-seat kind of gesture. "They are accusing Harriford of being a homosexual too. Frankly, I think that is all they really care about."

"No!" Paul exploded verbally, barely staying in his chair. Grogan was now projecting the kind of presence that normally gave him control over others.

"Maybe you don't know it," Grogan continued, "but Matt and Rads were together part of the time at their last station. Since they were at the same place at the same time, the Feds already had an eye on Harriford. Now they claim to have found some things in Radiswell's apartment to incriminate him."

"As a murderer?" Dayton asked, incredulously.

"Not that, they just think he was one of Rads' homosexual partners. But don't you see? In their view that makes him a spring-loaded murder suspect. It also gives them a pressure point to exploit Matt for the names of other partners they both might have had.

"Like I said before, that seems to be what they really want. Pretending to have a murder investigation just gives them an excuse to keep Matt on a string."

"I don't believe it," Paul said, grimly. "Not any of it."

"Neither do I," Grogan told them, angrily. "Those jerks wanted to confine him to the site, pending their investigation of his alleged homosexuality. I told them to stuff it. This isn't the flaming army. Let them go ahead and arrest him, if they have evidence of murder. If they can find a judge to go along with it, put him in jail for all I care. I'm not going to be the one to cage him up, no matter what they want."

Having relieved himself of his contempt for the investigators, Grogan adopted a more serious expression and tone.

"Still, I'm worried that they'll railroad him on this homosexuality thing. I've already had to suspend his security clearance, merely on suspicion. What irony. If he were only suspected of murder I would not have had to do that.

"The way things are, he won't be able to work until this gets sorted out, and he's too good an instructor to lose over some stupid witch hunt. I don't have to tell you two what a career ender and life ruiner this kind of thing can be in our business."

Now Grogan brought his armor-piercing, black eyes to bear on Paul.

"You're about his best friend at the site, Paul. What do you think?"

"No way could it be true. But like you said, I'm his friend. That probably makes me suspect too. What can we do?"

Grogan smiled.

"Thank God, we're not the military. We'd have to restrict his movements and threaten him with court martial for sodomy. That charge doesn't usually come to trial, but in the armed forces it remains a criminal offense. Texas has a sodomy statute, but they go pretty far out of their way to avoid enforcing it. Just guess how many prominent Texans might go to the pen if they did."

Grogan brought his right palm down solidly on the desktop.

"I'm confident this will blow over if Matt can ride out the investigation," he announced firmly. "In the meantime, I can only let him do menial administrative tasks around the site and pray he doesn't choose to resign and be done with it all. I'm nearly certain the murder case will go away once the Feds lose their handle on the homosexual issue. You both know what a big *if* that is."

Now Grogan spread his hands to take in both listeners.

"The main thing at the moment is to keep his spirits up," he continued. "Let him know we support him. I also need to be informed about how he's taking it all. It's perfectly normal for him to be anxious about what's happening to him. The last thing I need around here is another act of desperation."

Now Grogan addressed them separately.

"Paul, I want you to get in touch with Matt right away. I think he'll be in his quarters. Go out somewhere for supper. Pick a place farther out; you probably don't want to run into the usual crowd tonight. Talk things over. Find out how he's feeling. Tell him about our session here, and make him understand that we are fully behind him. Be honest. Tell him I expect you to report back to me, and encourage him to come see me about anything."

Now his gaze moved to Dayton

"Art, your job is at least as tough as Paul's. Tomorrow, you have to explain to your staff that Matt is temporarily suspended while Rads' death is being investigated.

"Not one word about homosexuality!" he said, lowering his voice and exhaling each rasping word as if firing it from a gun. "I know it will leak out eventually with the FBI nosing around, but I want to spare Matt as much needless embarrassment as possible. After all, I want him back on the job—and soon."

Pushing himself back into his chair, Grogan was transformed from the tired, unhappy man they had seen when they entered. He had drawn energy and confidence from the process of talking the problem through and telling others what to do about it.

"Questions?" he asked.

They both shook their heads and looked at their laps.

"'Nuff said then. Goodnight, gentlemen." Grogan turned off his desk lamp, rose from his chair, and led them out of the office. His step, like his mood, was now brisk and positive.

12

Trudging reluctantly across the site toward the Quonset where he and Matt had apartments, Paul did some rapid self-examination on a subject he normally preferred not to think about, personally or professionally. Homosexuals were not at all welcome in the world that Paul and Matt inhabited.

Homosexuality was among those topics that were rigorously avoided by adults when Paul was growing up. He was in high school before he heard a reasonably accurate, far from thorough, definition of it. It was in a category with certain other words that, when he encountered them in magazines and literature, had no exact meaning for him. Rape, for example, was another total mystery until junior high. Even then, he did not understand exactly why or how such a thing might happen. The general belief of many parents and teachers in matters of sex seemed to be that, if youngsters did not know about it, they would not think about it. Then, surely, it would not happen.

In high school, of course, there was the boys' room. In those days parents and school authorities, alike, commonly accepted that a substantial number of post-pubescent boys were going to smoke cigarettes. That granted, the main responsibility of the school was not to prevent smoking, but to regulate it. Thus, certain outdoor areas were designated for smoking before school and during the lunch hour. Additionally, during bad weather, lunch-hour smoking was tacitly permitted to high school boys in the main boys' restroom.

There in the dense clouds that roiled above the tiles between the urinals and the toilets, the regular sexual bragging and pretense of ill-informed adolescent males augmented the generally one-time, pastoral, parent-child talk about the birds and bees. The aims and accuracy of such lewd tutoring were always questionable, but it had, by default, a significant influence on the sexual development of many young men.

In Memphis City Schools, moreover, sex education came through the back door decades ahead of its time, at least for boys. Who knew what might have been going on in the girls' home economics class? It probably was not the kind of thing that was presented in Junior ROTC armories.

To graduate in that era from one of the Memphis City Schools, physically able high school males had to spend a minimum of two years taking Army Junior ROTC. There they learned many useful things, like how to: march, salute, wear a uniform, read maps and navigate with a compass, care for and employ a marvelous array of firearms, and make effective use of a condom.

That last bit of knowledge came from a World War II navy training film, designed to scare sailors away from bad women or, failing to do that, teach them how to protect themselves against a series of revolting diseases. It convinced Paul, for a time anyway, that the most likely products of any sexual liaison were social shame, running sores, fleeting but ominous rashes, and a life that could end in agonizing insanity with tertiary syphilis.

During elementary school, what may have been Paul's first encounter with homosexuality went almost unnoticed by him.

A transient man, who had done a few chores at Paul's house in exchange for food, greeted him a bit too enthusiastically at the bus stop one morning. Lifting him off the ground and hugging him quite intensely, the man whispered what a good boy Paul was. The bus came at that moment and Paul was promptly released to board it. He was not alarmed, but he had not liked being so peremptorily handled. Besides that, the man had possessed extremely strong breath and body odors.

When Paul mentioned the incident to his mother after school, she was outraged. She sternly warned him to avoid such encounters in the future, but true to form, did not explain why. Nothing more was said to him, but he noticed an animated, whispered exchange that night between his mother and father. He did not know what, if anything, his parents might have done about the incident, but he never saw the offensive man in the neighborhood again.

By the time he was in the tenth grade, Paul had acquired, mostly from restroom chatter, a rough, distorted knowledge of the behavioral patterns that differentiated homosexual men from others. Naturally, the names he learned for such people and the things they supposedly did rose from the street and sounded repellent in themselves. Comparing all this with his earlier definition of rape, he could not imagine why anyone would want to perform acts that seemed so repulsive. Doubtful as he was, he was not about to bring up the subject with his parents. If he had known the word pederasty at that time, he would probably have thought it a synonym for male homosexuality. That was what the guys in the boys' room seemed to think. While he had heard a few rumors about lesbians, the concept utterly baffled him.

For the rest of high school, Paul thought very little about homosexuality or homosexuals, except for one spasm of self-doubt. Since he really did not know what made such men that way, or even what way that was, how could he know that he was not one of them? He was, after all, shy and awkward with girls. He dated very little, mainly because he was so shy and awkward with girls. Did that mean anything?

Then he was comforted by the incontrovertible, sometimes visibly embarrassing, evidence of his own maddeningly uncontrollable, physiological reaction to the young female form and proximity. How could anybody who felt, and so often showed, such raging pangs of desire for the closeness and touch of a nubile woman find any kind of sexual interest elsewhere? His fears were stilled. He was satisfied with his heterosexuality.

Paul had little occasion to think more about homosexuality until his sophomore year of college. The Korean War had broken out and he was persuaded by a friend to join the local Navy Reserve unit. It seemed a reasonable choice, offering paid drill sessions, a two-week training cruise each year, and most significantly, a navy active-duty alternative to being drafted into the army.

Reserve enlistment required him to fill out a detailed application, all in ink and by hand, under the close scrutiny of a grizzled, active-duty chief yeoman. He briskly placed X-marks on the form to deny ever having been: addicted to drugs or alcohol, convicted of a serious crime, disloyal to the United States, or aware of homosexual tendencies. While his knowledge of homosexuals had increased since high school, he was not precisely sure what tendencies might belong exclusively to them. He was instinctively certain, however, that his desire to be accepted into the Navy would not be advanced by asking the chief any questions about that.

Paul took advantage of his next summer break from college to schedule his initial active-duty training. This, unlike the annual two-week cruises to follow, would be a concentrated basic training course, which attempted to approximate the regular navy, 11-week, enlisted boot camp.

Paul's training was conducted in the 4th Regiment at Bainbridge Naval Training Center near Port Deposit, Maryland. There, he also learned many useful things, such as: how to do calisthenics with a nearly antique Springfield rifle, render the semaphore signal postures for "U.S. Naval Training Center, Bainbridge, Maryland," wash his clothes daily by hand, scrub and swab a wooden barracks deck to exquisite whiteness every night, stand watch over trash dumpsters, fight fires, load naval guns, avoid offending the punitive articles of the Uniform Code of Military Justice (UCMJ), and make effective use of a condom.

Yes. It was the same gruesome navy training film he had seen in high school ROTC. There must have been hundreds of copies in circulation. This time Paul could identify the thin melodrama the sexual hygiene propagandists had forged, but he was barely less intimidated by the cautionary message of the subject matter.

The class immediately following that dark expose was conducted by a navy chaplain.

"I am required to talk to you about something dirty," the chaplain began grimly. "It is a disgusting and nasty subject, but you have to be warned about it."

Good heavens Paul thought. *What could be more disgusting than the movie we just saw?*

"It is my duty," the chaplain continued, "to teach you something about homosexuality." He did not actually say much about the mechanics of homosexuality, except to quote from Article 125 of the UCMJ proscribing acts of sodomy. That was more than enough. That punitive article made it a felony to engage in specified forms of sex, whether the engaged parties were of the same or the opposite sex. By omission, it seemed to make all such acts, even between marriage partners, equally criminal. The same article punished acts of bestiality, but the chaplain never got around to that.

The chaplain's case was pretty clear. The UCMJ made active or passive homosexual behavior a felony. Offenders were subject to court martial, but would at minimum be thrown out of the Navy with a Bad Conduct or Undesirable Discharge. They would be shamed before their communities and practically unemployable for life. All sailors were required to immediately report even the suspicion of such activity. Failure to do so might make a seaman as liable to disciplinary action as the homosexual felon himself. Paul experienced a haunting recollection of Dr. George Fathringill Trumbull in the role of God from the pulpit.

This was not the last time Paul was forced to consider the real or imagined dangers to national security posed by the presence of homosexuals in government service, military or civilian. Toward the end of his college life, conscious that he was already in his draft board's sights, he began job hunting within the federal government. Like the Navy Reserve, every government agency to which he applied required him to declare his freedom from addictions, criminal convictions, treasonous intentions, and homosexual inclinations.

When one of them invited him to pursue a job that would call for a national security clearance, similar assertions had to be made on the incredibly tedious forms he submitted to initiate a background investigation of himself. This involved a rigidly formatted, precisely detailed biography of his entire life, which was blessedly not too long at that point. Even so, it required reaffirmation of the now familiar denials.

With the investigation favorably completed, he found himself employed and almost immediately transported to his organization's remote, initial-training school in West Texas. There his very first classes were dedicated to security indoctrination and counter-intelligence briefings.

Among the many things he learned from these sessions was the official government policy that homosexuals were an especially serious threat to national security and would not be tolerated in any position with access to classified information. Several reasons were given for this and a few notorious cases were cited. The overriding rationale seemed to be that homosexuals, because of their guilty secret sins, were particularly vulnerable to targeting, corruption, and blackmail by unfriendly intelligence agencies. Paul understood and accepted the logic of this, even while musing idly that in a different world, people without guilty secrets could not be blackmailed.

The security instructor pronounced the menace of homosexuals in sensitive positions so grave that mere suspicion of sexual deviancy would bring about suspension of the suspect's security clearance, pending investigation. The clearance of anyone determined to be homosexual would be permanently revoked and their employment terminated.

"Not only that," the instructor went on, "but any employee who fails to report knowledge or even reasonable suspicion of such activity by another employee may be similarly disposed of. The mere act of knowingly associating with homosexuals can justify suspension, investigation, and subsequent termination."

Am I back at Bainbridge with the chaplain, Paul wondered. He had previously congratulated himself that his new government occupation might exempt him from fulfilling any extended active-duty obligation to the Navy. Now he found that at least one navy policy would be little changed with regard to his future duties. He was still being ordered to inform against his coworkers on the mere suspicion of homosexuality.

Even in the early days of his career, Paul would encounter fellow workers who displayed effeminate mannerisms. *Effeminacy alone*, he told himself, *does not mean a man is homosexual*. Then he forgot about it. When later events seemed to belie his judgment, as they sometimes did, he could truthfully tell himself that he had not suspected a thing.

He had been surprised at times to see competent and, as far as he could tell, loyal colleagues simply stop coming to work. No official explanation was normally given, but in some cases, the interoffice word-of-mouth conveyance would confirm that the person had displayed a flaw in sexual identification.

Now Paul was going to meet his best friend, over whom a threatening net was being cast by men who did not have to prove their suspicions correct. They had only to leave him under suspicion. That would be enough to bring his reputation, career, and maybe his whole life to ruin.

He had reached the Quonset apartments. The questions could not be postponed. It was time to see what Matt had to say.

When Matt opened the door to his knock, Paul smiled at him.

"Hi, pal. Want to talk?" he asked.

Matt looked drained and uncaring. His normally smiling face was grimly drawn with lines of strain. He did not appear to have cleaned up or changed clothes since that morning.

"Not much, but I guess I ought to," Matt answered.

"Get your jacket. Let's go to Rondo's."

13

Rondo's was one of those exceptional steak houses that could be found in the more isolated areas of the West Texas desert. Right in the middle of nowhere, surrounded by almost nothing except for the beauty of its own desolation, Rondo's enjoyed a classic reputation that spanned four states. It was not at all exclusive, as long as a customer had on some form of footwear and was reasonably covered from neck to knees. It was by no means inexpensive, but the size and quality of its steaks were legendary. It even had a small landing strip with a taxiway and several parking ramps, so that better-off, distant *aficionados* with aerial mobility could drop in for one of its fabled meals. There was also a small, Old West-style, two-story hotel to accommodate customers who found themselves too full of rich food or draft Lone Star beer to safely drive or fly home.

Rondo's was about thirty miles away from the site. Given an almost vacant highway and a total absence of traffic lights, Paul was able to pull into the parking lot in just over the same number of minutes. Matt seemed lost in his own thoughts and Paul was reluctant to press him, so the trip was completed in near silence.

The main entry to all of Rondo's dining rooms led through a long, dark-wood-paneled, bar area, decorated here and there with mounted examples of a longhorn steer's massive cranial array. For the sake of comparative privacy, Paul asked the hostess at the door for one of the small, fairly reclusive, wine-colored, leather-backed booths in the bar. She led them to one in a corner of the room that was not readily visible to people entering from outside, handed them each an impressively engraved menu, and left to deliver their drink order to a waiter. Matt began looking through the menu, but Paul laid his aside.

"I suppose it would be pretty ridiculous for me to ask how you're feeling," Paul began, uneasily.

At first Matt's face cracked into a nervous smile. Then he broke into a laugh that Paul knew would have echoed through the room if Matt were not intentionally repressing it. Paul was readily acquainted with the infectious quality of Matt Harriford's laughter. As had happened many times before, he was soon caught up in it and, like Matt, barely succeeded in suppressing what would otherwise have become a reverberating roar. Approaching them to deliver their thick, frosted schooners of Lone Star, the waiter must have thought they were sharing a terribly funny joke. They calmed themselves enough to order a serving of KC tips for two and watch the waiter make his way toward the kitchen.

The spontaneous outburst of laughter must have phenomenally diminished Matt's tension. His facial expression had visibly eased and he now pushed himself back into the comfortable booth cushions. Paul could tell he was actually trying to relax.

"Whew," Matt sighed. "I owe you one for that. I don't believe I have smiled, let alone laughed, since I left you in the office this morning."

"I would lay money on it. Want to tell me how it went down with Rads, or would you rather pass on that part?"

The stress lines did not come back into Matt's face. For the moment, he only seemed softly sad.

"It was sort of ugly," he said, continuing in a quiet monotone. "I didn't really expect him to be awake when I got there. You know how I needed help, getting him back to his Quonset last night. He never came out of his drunken stupor. After I muscled him into the apartment, I just dumped him unconscious on the bed and left him there fully clothed.

"When I went back this morning, I knocked once and went on in. The door was unlocked the way I had left it." Matt hesitated, but Paul said nothing, giving him a moment to gather his thoughts.

"He wasn't in bed. He was sitting right there in front of me—same clothes and everything—just sitting there in the easy chair, wearing the same lousy clothes. The place smelled awful; I guess his sphincter let go. I couldn't see his face at first, because his head was thrown back on top of the chair. I could see the gun in his lap though. It looked like a Colt Woodsman. Neither of his hands was touching it. It was just lying there, as if he had put it down for a minute to deal with something else.

"Then I went over to look at his face. I've never seen anyone look like that. His eyes were wide open and staring. His mouth was wide open too and crusted with coagulated blood that had spilled out and dried on his cheeks and chin. I was kind of surprised to see that much blood from a head wound. Maybe his heart kept pumping for a bit. The bullet must have been a hollow point; it took part of his skull right off. I suppose some of his brains were on the ceiling, but I didn't even look. Now that I think about it, I did see them later.

"Nothing I could do to help. I just went out to the telephone and called security, the dispensary, and you. Then I stood in front of the door. I could hear the siren. After a while, I sat down on the concrete. Then they came."

Paul noticed how Matt had related the narrative of his discovery in a steady, running, almost uninflected stream of speech. The dominant tone of his delivery had been nearly as blank as his face. Paul felt it was time to break in.

"Hey, Matt. How are you doing? Are you going to feel like eating?"

"Not to sweat," Matt said in a more normal voice. "Talking about it won't make me sick, if seeing it didn't." Now his expression became less gloomy and more animated "Anyway, I'm starved. Haven't eaten all day. By the way, I assume this feed is on you."

"Too bad it's not on Grogan," Paul grinned in agreement. "He's the one who told me to do it."

At that point, the waiter returned with two large wooden bowls of chilled, crisp, romaine lettuce, carefully coated with Rondo's proprietary, creamy-white garlic dressing. This was a pungent delight, well loved by Paul and Matt, but they ate sparingly, knowing that an immense platter of blissfully marinated, genuinely charcoal-and-mesquite-broiled, Kansas City-style sirloin steak ends would soon be presented.

Munching the salad inhibited any serious discussion and the arrival of the KC tips placed it out of the question. Conversationally speaking, the next forty minutes were exclusively dedicated to small talk, carnivorous chewing sounds, and quiet gasps of satisfied, alimentary delight.

Too full to be tempted by Rondo's warm, syrupy, pecan pie, with or without a dip of hand-churned vanilla ice cream, both men settled back into their cushions to begin the digestive process, while sipping strong black coffee. It was time to talk again. Paul started it.

"What happened after the authorities arrived?"

"Which ones?"

"Our security and medical people, to begin with."

"Not much there," Matt said. "All I did was tell them how I found Rads this morning and explain how I came to leave him there between ten thirty and eleven o'clock last night. They asked me if I had touched the body or moved anything, and I assured them that I had touched nothing in the apartment this morning, except for the door of course.

"The security types took photographs, made measurements, marked off the body, and tagged the gun and some other stuff in the apartment for evidence. Then they told the medics to take away the body for examination, which they did.

"The site cops were about to haul the tagged items to their car, when a Texas DPS patrol car pulled up. The highway patrol had been notified by the site security chief, who showed up to assist them with their investigation. The patrol officers did not seem too awfully interested, because the death took place on a federal reservation. They knew the FBI had jurisdiction and would make the definitive investigation. Still, they had been notified and must make a report, so they went through the motions.

"The lead site security investigator was Doug Malone. Know him?"

"A little," Paul replied.

"He was more or less my shepherd today. I don't think I would have made it through, except for him."

Paul nodded, silently.

"After he sealed the apartment, Doug asked me to hang loose at his headquarters until the FBI got there, so I did. Four FBI agents came in between one and two o'clock. Two of them said they were from Dallas. I guess they must have flown part way out and picked up the other two in Abilene. Anyway, they blew several gaskets when they found out the scene of the death had been altered before they got there. They seemed to think we should have just left old Rads sitting there with a pistol in his lap and the flies buzzing around his head until they could find time to look things over.

"When they finally quit thundering professional indignation over the condition of the scene and the body, two of them took me and Malone back to the apartment. The other two FBI men stayed behind to go through Rads' personal effects, the things Malone had tagged and brought to the security headquarters as evidence.

"At the apartment, I could only tell them what was already in the site investigator's report, but they still had me walk through my exact moves from the morning, as well as from the night before. They insisted I go through it several times. Then they kind of ignored

Doug and me, while they crawled around and prowled through the place like Sherlock Holmes going after Professor Moriarty. On the whole, I guess they treated me pretty well until we got back to site security. Then the business turned nasty."

Matt paused and lifted his eyes to look straight into Paul's.

"What did Grogan tell you?" he asked.

"He said the FBI is trying to turn Rads' suicide into a murder case with you in the starring role."

"That is so, but did he tell you what my motive was supposed to be?"

"Sort of, but I'd rather hear it first hand. Don't worry. I'll speak up if I hear any significant differences. Grogan could only tell me about conclusions other people brought him. He does not know exactly what happened to you. He wants to know, and that is one of the reasons he sent us out to dinner."

"Okay," Matt sighed, "but I am not going into anything like a blow-by-blow playback for you. I am not at all sure I could do that. Even if I could, it would be too depressing. I had all the accusations, degradation, and badgering I could take this afternoon, and I will not spend the evening reinflicting it on myself."

"Understood," Paul murmured

"The two FBI agents that had stayed behind in the security office were the ones from Abilene. As soon as we walked into the office, one of them collared the Dallas guys and took them into a separate room. When none of them had returned after about five minutes, I asked Malone if I could leave. He started to nod, but just then, one of the Dallas men popped into the room to ask if I would mind staying a little longer. He and his colleagues had a few loose ends to tie up and maybe I could help.

"I could tell this was not the kind of invitation to which I might safely respond with regrets. Naturally, I said I would be delighted to help them in any way I could. Nothing very nice happened after that.

"Next thing I knew, the Dallas boys had me in one of the interview rooms, taking me back over and over every step and nuance of last night."

Paul noticed a rising intensity in Matt's voice, as he continued to speak in semi-quotes of his interrogation.

"Exactly what time did I leave Rads in his room? Couldn't I be more precise than a thirty-minute span between ten thirty and eleven? Hadn't I looked at my watch even once during that time? They finally got me to say that it was more probably between ten forty-five and eleven than between ten thirty and ten forty-five.

"Well, then. If I admitted that I may have been wrong about the time, perhaps I was also mistaken about where I had put him. After all, his body was found this morning in the chair. Was I absolutely sure I had dropped him onto the bed, instead of maybe into the chair?

"I told them, 'No.' I was completely certain that I had dropped him on the bed.

"How could I be so sure? Hadn't I been drinking too? Did I ever have blackouts when I drank? Might I have had one last night?

"'What are you talking about?' I wanted to know."

Matt was not now shouting, but his voice was gradually rising in timbre and volume to more clearly recreate the questioning he had undergone. His face was beginning to show some of the emotion he must have felt that afternoon. Paul was grateful that the two of them were well isolated from other diners.

"'Why are you getting so excited, Mr. Harriford? Isn't it possible you are not remembering things exactly the way they happened? Isn't it possible you have forgotten something—or made yourself forget it? Isn't it possible you put Radiswell in the chair, instead of the bed? Isn't it possible you got his pistol from where you knew he kept it, rammed it into his mouth, and blew his skull apart? Isn't it, Harriford? Isn't it?'"

Matt was turning pale with agitation, so that Paul was moved to raise his right hand in a calming gesture.

"Whoops!" Matt released his vise-like grip on the table's edge, dropped back against the cushion and began to regain his color. His voice found a more normal pitch.

"I said I wasn't going to do that, but there you have it. What I went through this afternoon is not something I can be deliberate and dispassionate about. The main problem is that I know they have barely started on me. This afternoon was only the prelude."

Matt sighed, and Paul could see him deliberately relaxing the muscular tension that had built up in his body as he spoke.

"Now," he said, "the very rational, mature, and calculating Matt Harriford will cut to the chase to tell you where he stands with the FBI."

Paul nodded encouragement, but did not speak. Interruption of any kind did not seem helpful, so he waved away the waiter, whom he saw coming to refill their coffee mugs.

"Contrary to the scene I just described, most of the exchanges this afternoon involved me trying to find out what they were talking about. They were very close-mouthed. I had to pry every sliver of information out of them, and my validity assessment of anything I got would be no higher than fifty percent.

"Their interrogation technique was great—kind of like Judo. I was the one always off balance. All the time, they kept pressing forward and pushing me back with questions coming so fast that I could hardly get an answer out." As he had promised to be, Matt was again in full control of himself.

"Let me summarize what I think I learned—you can never be sure with these guys—in some sort of chronological order. The FBI has been following Rads around for months, harassing him about being a homosexual. They say there was no doubt about that, but they held off putting the screws to him publicly. First, they wanted to milk him for the identity of any partners or sympathetic acquaintances who might also hold a security clearance. Funny they should tell me that part, since it is one of the things they're hoping to do with me."

"Weren't they giving him a perfect motive for suicide?" Paul could not stop himself from interrupting.

"I certainly think so. That's what I told them, but they claim it doesn't wash. They say they found a journal and some letters in Rads's effects which may incriminate me as one of his homosexual partners. Notice their word, 'may.' They did not show me the items or give me any kind of detailed description.

"Their logic follows the line that I at some time had a romantic relationship with Rads. I had learned, maybe from Rads, that the FBI was squeezing him. I was fearful he would rat on me. When he passed out last night, I saw a golden opportunity. Alone with him, I dumped him in the chair, found a gun I knew he had, and guided him out of this world as an apparent suicide. Then I went back today and pretended to discover the body. They say it looks like murder, and I am their one and only suspect.

"I told them I was not a homosexual, but they just smirked. God alone knows what Rads may have written, but I can tell you categorically that he never got a letter of any kind from me.

"I don't think they really believe I killed him, but until the physical evidence has been evaluated—they've taken finger prints and paraffin tests for gunpowder residue—they can act as if they do. Since I did not touch anything in that room this morning, least of all the gun, the cause of Rads' death should soon enough be settled as suicide. I suppose somebody else could have killed him, but I can't imagine who."

Paul again said nothing, but he could not help recalling his own quarrel with Rads. He had never mentioned the dayroom incident to Matt. He had told Matt only that he and Rads never warmed to each other, but sustained a working relationship through mutual tolerance. He could think of several others at the site with ample reason for hating Rads, but hardly enough to kill him.

"They'll never put together a murder charge," Matt continued, "but they want me to be a homosexual anyway. That is a weakness they think they can exploit in the same way they were trying to use

Rads. Until they have to drop it, the pretense of a murder investigation lets them hook me in whenever they like. Who knows? Perhaps, I'll cough up something they really want to know. I'm caught in the middle and I'm bound to lose. You know how it is with homosexuality where we work. Suspicion is ninety percent of the proof."

Paul leaned forward in his chair, but before he could speak, Matt went on.

"Before you feel obligated to ask, Paul, hear this. I did not kill Rads, and I am not a homosexual."

"I know that," Paul responded emphatically.

"Make sure you tell Grogan."

"I will, Matt. And he wants you to know that you have his full support."

"So he said, when he pulled my clearance this afternoon," Matt said bitterly. Then in a less angry voice he added, "I know he couldn't help it."

At that moment, Paul saw the hostess pointing out their table to two men in conservative business dress. They came over to the table and spoke directly to Matt.

"Good evening, Mr. Harriford," one of them said. "Would you please come with us?" At the same time, the other man flashed a jacket-pocketsize, leather-sheathed, laminated ID at Paul, as if to say, "Stay put." Paul could not actually read the credential from where he sat, but he was sure that it identified an agent of the FBI.

Matt clearly knew the man who had spoken.

"Where?"

"Your site security office," the agent said.

"I'd rather not," Matt responded. "Do I have a choice?"

"Not really."

"May I have a lawyer present?"

"Of course, but it may not be in your best interest."

"I'll take a chance."

Matt handed a business card across the table to Paul.

"Call this man, and tell him where to come, would you Paul? Give him security's phone number, too, in case he is delayed in getting there. Thanks."

Paul stood and watched the three of them walk out to the parking lot. It was the last time he saw Matt Harriford alive.

14

Matt paused briefly before responding to Paul's question about the lie. Then he proceeded in a serious tone.

"You may have noticed that here in the Vale everyone always tells the truth. That is the way things are from here on out. Nobody ever lies. Even if lying were possible, what motive could there be? Everyone is an open book, and nothing from our linear background makes any difference. Your question is irrelevant, but I will answer it anyway.

"First, I did not murder Radiswell."

"I know that," Paul responded. "Doug Malone was able to tell me some of what happened after the FBI pulled you in that night. He said calling that lawyer was the smartest move you could have made. Seems Doug had given you his card and recommended him, since criminal defense lawyers were not very common in that part of the country."

"That's right. I called him that afternoon when the Feds and Grogan were finished with me, and he agreed to represent me. He was a semi-retired attorney, living on a small ranch about twenty miles from the site. He sounded like a salty old boy with plenty of experience in circumnavigating the contrary side of the law. He told me to say nothing to anybody without him present. That's why I asked you to call him."

"Doug said he was hotter than truck-stop chili. He read your investigators the riot act and a few words from the Constitution for sitting on exculpatory evidence they already had on you. Before he was through, they admitted withholding physical test results proving you didn't kill Rads. They were just jerking you around, trying to uncover more homosexual connections. Pretending to have grounds for a murder charge gave them a convenient club to beat you up with.

"Doug told me they sort of wilted at the prospect of having to explain all that to a federal judge. Under the circumstances, they could only go on questioning you by your own consent. Your lawyer suggested their chances for that were slim-to-none, and Slim Harriford was through cooperating."

"That is about what happened," Matt said. "The lawyer didn't tell me and I didn't ask, but I came away with a hunch that Malone had tipped him to the evidence suppression game they were playing. Incidentally, where did you pick up a word like 'exculpatory'?"

"Have you forgotten? My dad was a lawyer."

"I should have remembered about that. I'm sure it explains your argumentative nature," Matt teased. "Anyway, they tried threatening me with a lifelong record of homosexuality, unless I played ball with them. You can imagine how far that got them. I said, 'I'm already under that cloud, thanks to you guys.' Then I told them not to worry about my employment. I would mail Grogan my resignation in the morning from somewhere at least as far away as El Paso. If they still wanted to investigate my loyalty, they could contact my lawyer, because it would take a subpoena to get another word out of me about anything. At the end, I think they were glad to see me go."

"I always knew you were innocent of Rads' death. You made two denials that night. The other one was a passionate assertion that you were not a homosexual."

"That's true."

"Hey! I thought you couldn't lie here. Right after you left, I ran into some guys that had known you earlier. Turns out this was not exactly the first time you had been under that cloud. The time before was short on evidence and did not happen to be tied to a violent death, so it passed under the radar."

"I meant," Matt continued, patiently, "it is true that I told you what you say I did. I'll admit that I valued your friendship so much I might have lied merely to preserve it a while longer, but that is not why I did it.

"I knew the truth in my case would become a terrible burden for you or anyone else at the site who believed in me. Legally, you would be required to turn me in. Morally, you might despise yourself for betraying a friend."

"I might have handled it."

"Perhaps, but why should you? Think of yourself. Simple failure to follow the rules would have made you as guilty as me of violating them. You could have faced similar, if not identical, punishment. It would have been an awful dilemma. I would not allow you to face such a choice, so I looked you straight in the eye that night at Rondo's and fed you a full crock about my sexual tendencies.

"I suspected you would finally learn the truth and you tell me you did. Yet, you found out in a way that did you no harm. I gave up a good job that I cared about very much. If I had stayed to fight the suspicion, I would still have lost the job."

"You're probably right about that," Paul said.

"I know I am. I would never have done what Rads did, but I was worried about what the constant lying and betrayal of trying to hold on might do to me and those around me. Any way you read it, a lot of people like you would have been hurt more than necessary. My lie was framed to avert that."

"I understand that now."

"Before we change the subject, let me tell you that it was not quite the lie you seem to think. I never had anything sexual to do with Rads. I could tell what his tastes were and I pitied him for being such a poor soul, but I would never have become involved with him."

"Didn't the FBI find evidence about you in his belongings?"

"They said so. For all I know, he may have written something about me. If he did, it couldn't have been anything true about a relationship. I never revealed myself to him, although he probably suspected something from the same incident you heard about after I left. He and I were at the same station then. That was a very close call. It strengthened the decision I had made long before, not to become sexually mixed up with anyone in the organization. It would have been too risky for both of us. Anyway, Rads never tried coming on to me and I was glad to have it that way.

"Think of it like this. Would you have been attracted to Rads if he were a woman?"

"I see your point. But if you were not involved with Rads, why did you quit?"

"I already told you. I had beaten the earlier accusation, but that would have all been raked back up, and the truth would have come out. Can't you see that?"

"I suppose so."

"My friend, you will find there is no pride, anger, or shame here. Besides that, I largely stopped looking at myself through those lenses before I left the world. What made that possible? Mainly, I just quit blaming others and even myself for all my less than pleasant experiences."

"Not a bad idea."

"While I'm bringing you up to date, try this little bit of data. Since you died fairly young, I outlived you by eight years."

"You what? How could you do that?"

"There you go again, thinking of time in linear terms of relativity. When we die on earth doesn't matter. You and I are already here."

"That's good to know," Paul smiled. He was beginning to comprehend, but non-linear thinking remained foreign and conceptually uncomfortable.

"Don't worry. As I told you, we preserve an illusion of *was* and *will be* here until you learn to feel differently about time and space."

"What can you tell me about the visual environment here? Are these things my own optical illusions or what?"

"You mean the funny business going on all around us: the arcing lights, spectral aberrations, and figures you can't quite make out?"

"Exactly."

"Those are actually beings moving about and other things that exist very normally in simultaneous infinity. Most of what you see from here is the multitude of souls, like yourself, on their way through the Vale. Yet, at this very moment you also are out there helping some of them the way I am working with you. Believe it or not, I am one of those you are helping. This all exists around God and because of God. That is the only reality. Buddha was right about time and space where we grew up. It was not a bit real."

Paul hesitated, trying to assimilate the picture Matt was presenting. The proposition stunned him that in God's time he himself was already in different places doing different things all at once.

Setting that aside for the moment, he turned to a question that had come to him earlier in their conversation.

"Do you know what happened to Rads?"

"He never recovered." Matt's expression was rueful. "He is in the terminal ward."

"Because of his suicide?"

"No, no. Not that. It's never that simple. He was very unhappy. What made him terminal is the same thing that made him a suicide. His death just made it all irreversible. Even God's mercy could not reach him after that."

"Are you saying unhappiness killed him?"

Matt's expression was no longer sad, but remained quite serious.

"Remember the conversation we had about *dukkha* the night

Rads died? You were getting close to something there, Paul. Rads is in the terminal ward now, because he turned himself into something he isn't and can never correctly become."

Paul found himself recalling the analogy of a jigsaw puzzle that had occurred to him on the same night, while walking alone under the starry, West Texas sky. He never had a chance to tell Matt about it.

"Isn't that a contradiction in terms?" Paul asked. "How can he be what he is not?"

"People on earth do it all the time. We even had a phrase for it. When somebody you liked did something foul to you or someone else, you might excuse the rotten behavior by saying something like, 'He's not being himself' or 'She's just not herself today.' You were closer to the truth than you knew. If he or she had been a malicious predator who did even worse things all the time, your comment would have been truer still."

"I never thought about it that way."

"Do you remember what you said that night, Paul? You argued that the human capacity for love is a reflection of God's nature in us all. That's how you explained our creation in his image. You said that all God wants us to do is be ourselves the way he made us to be."

"Must have made a big impression on you."

"It did. Oh, I would probably have argued against it then, if Rads hadn't passed out and knocked his beer on the floor. But I had plenty of opportunity later to think of it as the last genuinely important thing you said to me."

Paul, for the moment, found no response to make.

"Don't give yourself too many gold stars," Matt went on. "There were a lot of turning points in my life on earth, but that simple statement of the obvious gave me a key to the first door in a corridor full of them. It started me down a spiritual path of thought from which I never turned back."

"That's very humbling," Paul said, finding his voice.

"Why do you think I came to meet you? I owe you, buddy."

"You mean I converted you to heterosexuality?" Paul asked in pretended astonishment.

Once again, Paul heard the resounding depths of Matt Harriford's joyous laughter. Were there real echoes here? Probably not, but Paul's phantom senses told him there were. As always when Matt laughed, Paul could not stop himself from joining in.

"Rubbish!" Matt continued to roar. "However my homosexuality may have affected my life in the world, it had nothing to do with what you called being myself the way God made me to be."

Calming his laughter, Matt went on.

"Sexual preference on the earth was a tricky business, but it did not—could not—make us what we are. Neither did most of our other predilections. God made us what we are. All of us just thought for a little while that we wanted to be something else.

"Only here and now are you fully free to be your true self. Don't you see that? Back there, sexuality was part of the baggage that came with the body. In our here and now, it just isn't."

"Isn't part of the baggage?"

"Isn't. Period." Matt smiled and opened his arms in explication. "We carry no baggage here."

"Doesn't that disappoint some people?" Paul joked.

"Can't you tell? Disappointment, with one notable exception, is also something we do not have here. We are happy, because we are being what we are—all the time, not just some of it. On earth we worked so hard trying to be happy that we rarely knew happiness at all. Did you ever see the old poster that showed people in a chaotic office scene? Its caption read, 'The harder we work, the behinder we get.' That, dear Paul, is the whole story of life on earth."

"Hey, Matt. I'm still new here. Can you fill in a few more of the vacant spaces in this puzzle?"

"Sure, pal. Here comes the greatly abbreviated version of Harriford's Helping Handbook on Happiness. I could have made tons of money with this on the inspirational lecture circuit in our former life."

"I'm ready to copy."

"Have you ever known a very happy person?" Matt asked

"Certainly."

"Oh? Were they like that all the time?"

"Of course not. Nobody is happy all the time."

"Everybody is here, but that's beside the point. We're talking about the good old home planet. Tell me. What is happiness?"

"It's not so easy to define. How about contentment?"

"That is what most people would answer, those who were not thinking very hard about a good definition. What is contentment, except floating just below the level of anything interesting or exciting? A dog is content with fresh water, regular feeding, a clean kennel, an occasional bone, and a pat on the head now and then. The human equivalent of that is bread and circuses. That's contentment. Would you call it happiness?"

"I suppose not. Would completion be better?"

"Hey! I think that's as close as you could come in one word. You're too good at this game. Truth is, you came very close to defining happiness the night Rads interrupted you. You said all God wants us to do is be what we are. Don't you see, Paul? *Happy is what we are when we are being what we are.* That is why we are so utterly happy here. Here we no longer have the distractions, one big distraction, actually. Now we lack the irrational clutter that usually kept us from being what we are during our time on earth."

Paul thought again of the jigsaw puzzle with its pieces correctly placed, each one being itself in harmony with every other and with the whole puzzle at once.

"Yes. I see what you mean, but that isn't all, is it?"

"Nope, but it's a pretty fine starting place."

"Starting place?"

"I hope you understood from our discussion of God's real time that we can readily be—in fact always are—in more than one place at a time. Still, there is a certain order to things and my time in the Vale with you is done for now."

"Right in the middle?

"Yep. You have a new therapist coming up.

"Who?"

"That would be telling. Meanwhile, close your eyes. Think about it if you like. When you open them, the boss will be here—not the real Boss, mind you. That will be a very different meeting.

"See ya later, bud."

Matt turned to one side and vanished the same way Miss Janet had.

15

Paul closed his eyes, as if on Matt's command. He was confident that a therapist would show up eventually, whether he closed them or not. It just seemed like a good idea to isolate himself from sensory input for a while and think over some of the things Matt had told him. He had been given, he thought, a lot of acreage to plow.

First, Matt had taken him on a plunging dive through simultaneous infinity. Paul had often speculated that God's temporal outlook must be different from that of earthbound humanity. He had supposed that God could see and do things in time that were beyond the range of human perception, even if the precise reason and methodology for that had never occurred to him. Yet, he had not conceived that God might be simultaneously everywhere in time all the time. *Why not?* he wondered, considering all the questions it answered. Perhaps, he had just not thought much about the relationship between God and time.

Lacking that concept, his Christian belief in the afterlife had not embraced the notion that he would one day share God's panoramic experience of time and space where God is. Now he was learning that

God wanted him to see and understand big-T truth as God himself sees it, not as God's equal of course—at least that human delusion was now behind him—but as God's beloved and obedient child.

When Paul had probed the wound of Matt's lie, he found only his own resentment, scabbed over with self-righteousness. What kept him from seeing the truth before? Surely, if he had thought the thing through in life, he would have discovered Matt's selfless motive. Now he could be grateful that here in the Vale he was freed from such self-centered pettiness. Even when he had asked his friend about that old, imagined wrong, he was no longer motivated by any sense of injury or injustice. It was purely a matter of curiosity.

Matt had said something else to support Paul's own earthly reasoning about the identity of God and the way humanity shares in it. He had agreed with the importance of being yourself the way God made you to be. Everything that mattered, in this life or the last, related to how well you did that. Ultimately, it seemed to decide whether you woke up and made your way through the Vale or went off to the terminal ward. Somehow, the health of the soul was tied to the attainment of true happiness, but the exact connection was something Paul could not yet put together.

Paul knew he had faced parts of this question before. His memory of that time was not simple or entirely pleasant to review. Yet, it spoke of forces that had penetrated his painstakingly erected defenses less than ten years before he would perish in the snow. That incision of his soul had proceeded from a series of unexpected events with life-altering impact. It had changed his view of himself, God, and everything he had thought he knew about living. He was sure then and now that God had reached out just in time to pull him back from the edge of certain self-destruction—finally and forever.

Paul first met Petra March at the Teahouse of the August Moon.

Justly or not, the Teahouse sustained an international reputation gained from its title role in John Patrick's 1953 Broadway play and the Marlon Brando/Glenn Ford movie version that followed. Considerably expanded from its immediately post-World War II structure, it sat isolated upon a blackish outcropping in the Okinawan capital and port city of Naha. Whatever its true origin, it held a unique significance for natives, tourists, and many Americans living on the main island of the Ryukyu chain.

Until their reversion to Japan in the second Nixon administration, more than a decade after the end of American occupation in Japan, the Ryukyu Islands were governed by a military High Commissioner, who resided in Camp Butler, one of the many armed forces installations that dotted the southern half of Okinawa. Under the command of the general officers who occupied this position, an unusual practice developed regarding the off-base social life of a rather large military population. Contrary to the tradition of putting undesirable establishments "off limits" to military personnel, a system was created to place specified bars, nightclubs, and restaurants "on limits." This was done by displaying a white, pasteboard sign with a large, black, letter A in all such businesses that were approved for military patronage. Military members who attempted to frequent a facility without an A sign were likely to be hauled away by the Ryukyus Armed Services Police, called by its dreadful acronym the RASP.

Okinawan business owners who wanted military clientele had to apply for and undergo a sanitation inspection before receiving an A sign. Ironically, this system resulted in *de facto* approval for military use of some of the sleaziest spots on the island. At the same time the native population was empowered to exclude American GIs from its most favored gathering places merely by keeping them A-sign free.

Rumor had it that the Teahouse of the August Moon once had an A sign, but somehow that had changed. By the time Paul arrived in Okinawa, when it was a major processing and transition point for troops moving in and out of Vietnam, the island's premier entertainment establishment was conspicuously without one. This protected the Teahouse from wanton intrusion by transient GIs, excepting members of the High Commissioner's entourage who, it was said, often entertained distinguished visitors at that renowned oriental cabaret.

American civilians did not fall under A-sign restraint and were treated more like tourists. They were generally welcomed at the Teahouse, which was so popular with locals and Japanese tourists that advance arrangements were always necessary. Paul was there one night to help his colleague, Jason March, celebrate the arrival of Jason's wife, Petra, to the island.

The Teahouse open area was a large, sparsely decorated room with a small stage at one end. Groups of diners sat unshod on the floor around low, rectangular, lacquered tables. Kimono-clad young women carefully served them at leisurely intervals with a progression of classic Japanese offerings from sea and shore, perfectly arrayed on exquisite porcelain of exactly the right size, shape, and decoration. The Teahouse offered no *a la carte* option, so for almost two hours each patron was brought a long series of courses. While this was going on, other young women, made up and dressed as *geisha* entertainers, gently sang soothing, nasal Japanese songs from the stage, accompanying themselves with traditional stringed instruments. The room was filled with quiet conversation and laughter, but table arrangements were such that each group of people felt contained in its own space of association.

Petra was seated between Paul and Jason, with Paul to her left. She was a petite, olive-skinned woman, who looked to be a comfortable thirty, wearing a simple, black-sheath dress, scooped at the top to reveal her well-tanned shoulders. She had straight, black hair, cut fairly close to expose her slender neck. A high, straight forehead gave way to clear, hazel eyes that were at once intelligent and playful. Her small nose tilted slightly up, and the lower half of her face was distinguished by two, deep dimples and a puckish mouth that smiled easily and pursed slightly when she was paying close attention. She seemed a naturally cheerful and charming person. Paul immediately found himself interested and felt more than a little envious of his fortunate friend Jason.

The four other guests at the table were Richard Vering and Nolan Dunbar, both associates of Jason and Paul at Stricott-Global Consultants, and two attractive American women they had asked to join them for dinner. Jason and Petra were the only married people at the table. Vering was the same man Paul had known as Ted, the airborne radio operator on the rescue aircraft that launched out of Furstenfeldbruck during the Hungarian Revolution.

Phil Grogan, their local boss at SGC, had also been invited, but had declined. Grogan was not much the type to socialize with other employees anyway. Beyond that, according to what Jason had told Paul, Grogan strongly disapproved of Petra coming out from the States at all. Jason understood Grogan's reservations, but was rather disappointed that Grogan did not even want to meet her.

Stricott-Global Consultants was a proprietary cover for some of the organization's clandestine activities in and around Southeast Asia during the Vietnam War. The company had offices on military bases in Okinawa, the Phillipines, Vietnam, and Thailand, which actually fulfilled contracts to procure, install, and maintain specialized avionic systems for military aircraft. Its main purpose, hidden within a Secure Design component of the company, was to plan, facilitate, and execute sensitive covert operations in and near the war zone. Grogan was the area director for Secure Design.

"Has Jason told you how much of our time is spent off island?" Paul asked Petra, who at the time was having her first encounter with seaweed, prepared as a delicacy for human consumption. Her husband was momentarily occupied in a spirited exchange with Dick Vering's companion about scuba diving in local waters. Jason was an avid diver with an instructor's certificate. He loved to talk about the waters around Okinawa, which according to him provided some of the most intriguing dive opportunities in the northern hemisphere.

"Sure he did," Petra replied. "He tried hard to talk me out of coming, but I said I'd rather have some time with him here than no time at all by staying home."

Paul knew that organizational policy discouraged the idea of family members joining employees at overseas stations, unless the spouse was also an employee. That, no doubt, explained why so many members of the organization tended to remain single, like Paul, or to wed other members. The official position made good, cold-hearted sense, because most non-affiliated spouses were unwittingly trapped in their mate's cover. This was a situation that could easily bring about problems, especially when operational activities went wrong. Even when things went perfectly well, unnecessary people in the theater were a constant threat to security, cover, and anonymity.

When the worst happened, a wife back home could be told almost anything about what had become of her husband in a foreign land. A lot of curiosity could be nullified by revealing large, hitherto unknown, employee accident and life insurance policies. The unexpected appearance of a lifelong survivor annuity eased the pain and amplified the credulity of a grieving mate who was exposed only to the authorized version of her tragic loss. Bringing families into the field was an engraved invitation to disaster. Grogan's viewpoint and opposition to Petra joining Jason was grimly reasonable and certifiably practical.

"From what Jason tells me," Paul observed, "you will have plenty to keep you busy whether he's here or not."

"You bet. My coming out would not have added up if I hadn't been able to get a job here. I was teaching school long before I knew Jason. I love it and would have gone on teaching, married or not. Jason and I had been going together for over a year and had set the date for our wedding. Then he learned of the opportunity to take a job here on contract with Stricott. He wanted to apply for it, but at first he didn't think I should come."

Excellent, Paul thought. She was still buying into the cover. A lot of unenlightened spouses stopped believing in Santa Claus after a while.

"At least, that didn't stop your marriage," he said.

"Actually," she laughed, showing the full depth of her dimples, "it very nearly did."

"I see."

"I doubt that you do. We argued about it for days. He said this was the kind of work he did, and I would get used to the waiting after a while. That probably sounds quite reasonable to you."

When Paul did not react, she challenged him.

"Well, doesn't it?"

"I would not dare give it a thought," he replied without a smile. "The technicalities of a marriage contract are way beyond my experience and expertise."

"I told him 'like hell' I would get used to it," she laughed gently. "I was not going to get married so Jason could waltz off and leave me alone for months or years. That kind of thing might become a part of our life later, but I wasn't about to say 'I do' just for the sake of a truncated honeymoon and instant desertion."

"I suspect you can be very persuasive. Was that all it took to convince Jason?"

"It got his attention, didn't it?" she said amicably, but without a trace of humor. "It became our problem, instead of just being mine. Then it was something we could talk about. Once he decided that getting married was his priority, it was simply a matter of finding a way to make it work."

"And you did."

"That was when I started looking around and found out how easy it was to get a job teaching military dependent children in the defense overseas education system. If I had known what kind of opportunities it offered, I might have tried it years ago. Except for Jason though, I think I would have opted for a position in Europe instead of the Far East." She was smiling again, this time somewhat conspiratorially.

"I am impressed by your talent for negotiation."

"So was I," said Jason, who had apparently returned his attention to Petra and tuned in on the conversation.

"You better believe it," she smirked, "but it was really more of a compromise than it seems. I was still committed to complete the school year, which had barely started when we married. Jason was out here almost nine months before I could join him."

"You see," Jason commented, smiling affectionately and putting an arm around his bride. "She really is capable of compromise."

Paul knew then that the three of them would be very good friends. He was even more impressed a little later at Petra's unabashed amusement when two of the serving girls came by to demonstrate for the ladies the arcane Japanese art of turning a mere table napkin into the most amazing replica of a *phallus*.

16

In the months that followed their evening at the Teahouse of the August Moon, Paul was an occasional guest in the March home, but more often than that he joined Jason and Petra in dinner excursions around the island. Gradually, Paul developed a warm attachment to the couple that exceeded the depth of his pre-existing friendship with Jason. Such pleasant diversions were necessarily interrupted by Paul's intermittent, operational activities elsewhere.

Paul and Jason had sometimes gone operational together during the past year, but they were by no means a fixed team. That was probably why Paul, at first, failed to notice what kind of mission schedule Jason was keeping. Even when Jason mentioned one night at dinner that he was beginning to feel underemployed and unappreciated, Paul did not reckon he was being very serious. He found out otherwise quite abruptly one morning, when he was checking back into work after two weeks off the island.

The Okinawa office of Stricott-Global Consultants occupied a one-story, white, concrete-block building that backed to an aircraft parking ramp near base operations on Kadena Air Base. It was surrounded by a chain-link fence, the gate to which was usually open, since the building was never left unoccupied.

The main entrance gave access to several gray-tiled open spaces, mostly filled with workbenches, bins, cubicles, and tools that were dedicated to electronic equipment fabrication, storage, repair, and testing. The area was brightly lit and smelled of cleaning solvent. The building was fully air-conditioned, but the nearly subliminal hum of special exhaust fans and other electronic gear could also be heard. Beyond that, the sounds of work were limited to occasional bursts from a high speed drill or some other power tool being used by one of the technicians scattered among a variety of work stations.

The entire shop was casually referred to as the wire house and the people who worked there were called wire benders. Most of their activities were a direct result of SGC's contractual obligation for avionics support to the U.S. Air Force, but the wire house was also a resource for its collocated Secure Design element. The Secure Design space was less than half the size of the shop floor and was not readily apparent to wire-house visitors.

Making his way through the shop, Paul waved to several men in shirtsleeves gathered around a designing easel in animated conversation. One was busily marking up a newsprint page on the easel. Another returned Paul's wave, but none of them seemed to give him much attention as he walked out of sight into a small nook in the rear.

Facing what looked like a wall, Paul deftly punched eight numbers into the digital-code box to his right. At an audible click from the lock on the other side, he pushed the vault door open and went in. He could hear the door close automatically behind him.

Passing from the wire house into the Secure Design vault brought a stark reversal to the senses. The vault floor was carpeted and both sound and light were very subdued, except for a well-lit, glass-enclosed compartment that ran across the other end of the room. A line of teletype communications feeds and transmission keyboards were visible through the glass, but their operation was inaudible in the main room. The communications area might be filled with the clatter of incoming messages, but people outside would be aware only of a flashing green light attesting to the arrival of information. A dozen, gray, government-style desks were scattered around the main area. Those that were occupied were lighted by desk lamps, the faint glow of which was augmented by illuminated, Plexiglas-covered data boards and maps lining the walls. The only area set apart was a small office at the far-right end of the room. That belonged to Phil Grogan and provided him with separate access to the communications node. His walls, like those of that area were glass, so that his office received more direct light than the rest of the room. Oddly, one could see into it more easily than out of it.

Proceeding to his own work space, Paul could tell that Grogan was seated at his desk, conferring with someone standing in front of him. Paul turned on his desk lamp and consulted one of the lighted wall boards across the room. It already showed the status of his recent operation as complete. He pulled his typewriter stand out of its desk well, and was inserting a debriefing form into the machine when he heard Grogan speak from his office door.

"Paul, I'm glad you're here. Could you join us for a minute?"

Grogan's voice was always commanding, even when his words were casual. Paul would have immediately recognized it without knowing its source. Furstenfeldbruck and the West Texas training site were only the first places Paul had worked for Grogan. He had been in and out of Paul's professional life ever since. He was an incredibly demanding boss, but he possessed the same kind of integrity that he called for from others.

Certainly, there were times when Paul disagreed with Grogan. In such cases he was never afraid to tell Grogan what he thought, but they rarely argued. When they did, it was without animosity, and Paul knew that Grogan would have the last word. Paul remained intensely loyal to him and could think of no man for whom he would rather work.

Grogan could sometimes be arrogant and unreasonable, but

he was thoroughly lacking in most forms of conceit. Although he would verbally incinerate any subordinate presumptuous enough to call him by his first name, he hated being called Mr. Grogan by anyone with whom he had formed a professional bond. As soon as a colleague had proved his loyalty to Grogan's objectives, he was told that Grogan's last name would be a sufficient form of address. With all subordinates, however, he reserved to himself the prerogative of using first names.

"I'll be right there," Paul said, rising from his desk and moving toward the office.

Grogan stepped back inside and resumed his fabled executive chair as Paul entered.

Paul was well acquainted with the myth that attached to Grogan and that chair. No one was certain that the chair had ever been government property. If it were, the nominal attachments of office inventory and property control had vanished long before Paul first saw it. Grogan owned that chair and it followed him wherever he went. Organizational superstition had it that his career would be over if the chair were lost. Paul did not believe that, but whenever he had worked with Grogan in different parts of the world, the chair was there.

Closing the door behind him, Paul recognized the person he had seen with Grogan in the office as Jason March. Jason was still standing, even though two chairs were set up in front of the desk.

Jason was a short, dark, wiry man with curly brown hair and the look of Mediterranean lineage. He appeared now to be leaning slightly forward, ready for combat, and the lines of his face were drawn into a mask of stern determination.

This, Paul thought, *looks like confrontation.*

"Have a seat, gentlemen." Grogan was smiling.

As Paul sat down, he was surprised to hear Jason speak up, petulantly.

"I'd rather go on standing, thanks."

Paul was even more astonished to see the smile remain on Grogan's face in the presence of such insolence.

Grogan leaned back in his chair, crossed his arms, and looked up very steadily at Jason.

"My friend," he said, "I'm going to tell you a story." Grogan's suddenly avuncular tone made Paul wish he were somewhere else. This was not how Grogan operated.

Grogan paused a second and then, still smiling, went on.

"When I was a much younger man, during the last Great War the Navy sent me briefly for duty at an ammunition storage depot in Indiana. Not having been in that state before, I was puzzled by a very peculiar law that was rigidly enforced wherever my buddies and I went out to drink. In Indiana, in those days anyway, nobody was allowed to even hold a drink while standing up. You could sit on a bar stool and drink, but the minute your feet touched the floor, your glass had better not be in your hand. You could move from the bar to a table or from one table to another, but only the waiter could carry your drink."

Grogan maintained his friendly demeanor, but continued his story with a total absence of gestures.

"Why, I wondered, would such a rule exist? No one could seem to tell me, but I think I figured it out. A lot of pretty rough characters like quarry stonecutters and railroad men—well, even drunken sailors—would crowd into those bars on the weekend. Any kind of fight would most likely turn into an end-to-end barroom brawl, maybe even spill over into the street. It would be an ugly, violent, costly scene and was definitely something property owners, lawmen, and most citizens would want to forestall."

Now Grogan leaned slightly forward, inclining his head toward Jason, unfolding his arms and placing his hands flatly on the desk in front of him.

"Do you know what I concluded about that law, Jason?"

"No," Jason responded, a bit sheepishly. His face had softened and his stance was no longer antagonistic.

"I bet you'll agree when I tell you," Grogan went on, ingratiatingly. "Think about it. Think how nearly impossible it is to hit somebody while you are sitting down."

While Grogan waited a few seconds, Jason said nothing, but Paul could see that he was feeling very uncomfortable.

"Now," Grogan spread his hands and lifted them toward Jason, "are you getting ready to hit me?"

"Of course not."

"Then?" Grogan shrugged his shoulders with his palms still up and the fingers spread, while shifting his gaze to the remaining, empty chair.

Jason promptly took the seat with apparent eagerness and gratitude. Grogan was again fully in charge.

"Jason, how about bringing Paul up to speed on our discussion so far?" Grogan leaned back in his chair, now cupping his hands together under his chin. This posture gave him almost the appearance of being in prayer. Actually, he was looking directly ahead, averting his eyes from either of the men in front of him. That effectively forced Paul and Jason to look at each other while Jason spoke.

"This is going to sound pretty weak now, even to me. When I came in here, I was full of indignant umbrage at being ignored for months. It was easy to get carried away and dump all over Grogan. That was about all that had happened before he called you in."

"What do you mean, 'ignored?'" Paul asked.

"Haven't you noticed anything? When was the last time I went operational?"

"You tell me."

"That shouldn't be hard. It was the last time you and I did one together, just before Petra got here."

"That is a long time. Maybe Grogan was just giving you a little togetherness time before going full up again."

"I don't think so. I think he's trying to get even with me for letting her come here against his wishes and coercive attempts to prevent it."

"Why would he do that? We're not exactly overstaffed."

Later, when Paul recalled this discussion of Grogan and his motives, he was puzzled to realize that it had taken place with no input from Grogan, nor even the recognition of Grogan's presence by the other two. Grogan showed no physical sign that he was even listening, but the argument was evidently developing exactly as he had intended. He was learning everything he wanted to know and could re-enter the exchange on his own terms at a moment of his choosing.

"I don't know," Jason replied, "but it's a fact that he's kept me off the mission board for over three months."

"Some people would welcome that kind of break."

"Not me. I need to be making a contribution and taking my share of the operations. It's driving me nuts to be nothing more than a communications officer and glorified scorekeeper for the rest of you. Even Petra is starting to catch on that there's something eating at me. I'm afraid she may begin to think it's her fault in some way."

"I doubt she would."

"Why wouldn't she? What's she supposed to think, when she really doesn't have a clue to what's going on?"

"Who knows why people do anything?" Grogan said, stunning Paul and Jason into momentary silence by reminding them he was there.

"Jason," Grogan went on calmly and smiling again, "you have it partly right. I have been keeping you off the mission board. You misjudge my motive, however. If I could have kept you from bringing your wife over by grounding you, I would have done it, but that was never one of my options."

Grogan now abandoned his observer posture and moved forward, laying his muscular forearms on the desk as he continued to speak.

"I am a management realist. There would be no point in punishing you after the fact, unless that would serve to deter others from doing the same thing. Fortunately, I am not at the moment cursed with another employee who imagines himself to have that sort of incentive. You're the only rebel I've had to contend with lately. To your credit, I suspect some others here are delighted with an organizational policy they can blame for lengthy separations that create geographical bachelorhood."

Grogan hesitated, briefly caressing a smooth, crystal paperweight, while the other two waited for him to go on.

"Of course I don't want people thinking they can disregard my wishes with impunity, but I don't think many would see your case that way. I'm quite sure such a delusion would be overshadowed by resentment at having to double up their own operations just so I could get your goat."

"Then why?" Jason asked.

"That's a little more complicated." Grogan's face took on a grim appearance. Paul remembered seeing that look only once before. It was the day Rads was found dead, and Matt was accused of murdering him.

Grogan cocked his head a bit toward Jason and posed a question.

"Have you ever had the job of telling a spouse or other family member that their loved one is dead, while glossing over the truth or lying full out, because they are not allowed to know what really happened?"

Before Jason could respond, Grogan made a brushing-away gesture with his right hand.

"Of course you haven't. My question was rhetorical. The trouble is that I was put in that position several times when I was at the headquarters. If I sometimes don't seem to have much of a heart, I would suggest that some of mine was eaten away by that experience. I don't think I can do that again and believe me, it would be a lot tougher to do here.

"Anyway, that is why I so strongly urged you to follow the informal, unenforceable policy against doing what you did. It is also why

I have kept you down all this time. I knew you would eventually confront me, and I would have to give in. That is what I'm doing now."

If Jason meant to react to this announcement, Grogan did not permit him time to do so.

"You're back on the board, but I have to be as sure as possible that you come back safely—every flaming time. That is always a priority for every operator I have, but your situation makes it a personal imperative to me."

Without warning, Grogan shifted his attention.

"Oh, Paul. In case I didn't mention it, I'm turning you around fast to go back out with Jason in about two weeks. He's probably a bit rusty, so you have the lead. I want you to bear down hard on him while you're planning the operation. Don't do him any favors. Make sure he's one hundred and fifty percent ready. If you find he isn't I'll scrub the operation or, if there's time, replace him." Grogan punctuated his last sentence with a hard, meaningful look in Jason's direction.

Now Grogan took a loose leaf, three-ring binder from the bookcase behind him and placed it on the desk between the two men.

"Here's the objective and a hazard projection from the drop to the target. Start now and find a way to make it work. Your window on this one is narrow. That just means you've got to work harder and faster. I know I don't need to say it, but as always, you have no margin for error."

Paul saw that Grogan's rare moment of futility and resignation had passed. Decisive action always agreed with him.

"Questions?"

Of course, there were none.

17

The world calls it a rainforest for good reason. Moisture is everywhere on the jungle floor. Even wearing boots with sole treads built like a tractor tire, the going is very slow, especially when moving on an up-hill incline. Conversely, going down hill over the same kind of terrain becomes a slippery slide, where one bad move can make for a broken leg. Navigating a down slope demands very deliberate care that slows progress at least as much as struggling along the trail up. It seemed to Paul that ninety percent of any hike through a tropical rainforest was always up or down.

At least, Paul thought, *the job is done and we are on our way out.*

A title sheet beneath the transparent cover of the notebook Grogan had given Paul and Jason was labeled *Park Tray* and stamped with a "secret" classification. It bore no codewords or caveats to indicate sensitive compartmentation, but any full account of the project to which it related probably would have. One of the things Paul most liked about his line of work was that he rarely needed to know the

Big Picture, nor did he want to. His job was merely to execute limited, but indispensable, contributions that most other government components did not feel up to taking on. This project looked like a good example of that.

On the whole, Paul and Jason were being called to play a fairly small, but difficult and dangerous role in something called *Park Tray*. First, they were to carry a specific item, probably some kind of sensor, into the Laotian jungles. Then they would install and activate it at a precise location on the western end of the Mu Gia Pass. Mu Gia was one of two mountain passes coming out of North Vietnam that fed into the Ho Chi Minh Trail, which ran south through Laos and Cambodia, connecting to the east with South Vietnam.

The Ho Chi Minh Trail, so called by the American military after the communist leader of North Vietnam, was the North's logistical end run around the Demilitarized Zone that separated it from South Vietnam. It was the North's critical lifeline for moving troops, vehicles, weapons, and other supplies for Viet Cong insurgents and its own army elements in the South, Laos, and Cambodia. Heavily traveled, the Trail was both constantly targeted by American air power and massively defended and supported by the North Vietnamese. It was certainly no safe place for a couple of American civilians to go wandering through the jungle.

Electronic sensors of many kinds were commonplace in wartime Southeast Asia. Strongly promoted by Defense Secretary Robert S. McNamara as reconnaissance tools, they were part of what some military personnel irreverently called McNamara's Marvelous Modern-day Electro-Magnetic Battlefield. Over time, thousands of the things were dropped from aircraft over the Ho Chi Minh Trail in an effort to remotely discern the level and type of munitions moving along it, as well as to assess the practical effectiveness of aerial bombardment attempts to block it.

This Park Tray doodah, Paul thought, while preparing for the operation, *must be extremely delicate and important to warrant sending it in by* canopy and left both men dangling thirty feet or more from the ground. No sky light penetrated to where Paul and Jason hung in complete darkness, unable to judge at first how high they were or what might lie below. They had jumped from the aircraft almost together, simultaneously opened their parachutes at low altitude, and heard each other's parachute canopy becoming entangled in the trees. Each knew the other to be nearby

Very tall forests do not bear much foliage beneath their treetops. This enabled the men to locate each other in silence by using shielded strobe lights that could not be seen from the ground. Then each one took only minutes to secure a lanyard between his harness and parachute risers, free himself from his parachute canopy, and lower himself a foot at a time to the jungle floor.

Traveling at night was always preferable in this kind of work, but the absence of natural light below the trees and the risk of showing any artificial lights made it necessary to wait for the day. Listening to the hunting sounds of jungle rats and other creatures of the forest night, they wrapped themselves in mosquito netting and rested until dawn near the spot where they had dropped.

Moving out at first light, they were unconcerned about their abandoned parachute canopies giving away their arrival. Besides being camouflaged for the location, those billowing silks were trapped in the highest foliage. Unless specifically looking for something overhead, most people walking through jungle keep their eyes forward and on the ground to avoid whatever perils might otherwise beset them. Paul and Jason had already buried their chute harnesses and the visored helmets that protected their heads and faces coming down through the trees.

Landing where they had, it was not hard to find the Ho Chi Minh Trail. All they needed to do was continue moving east and they were bound to come to it. The trick was to intersect it as close as possible to the planting ground.

The *Park Tray* device, when fully deployed, would look exactly like a small banana tree. Banana trees are one of the more prolific forms of flora in a Southeast Asian rainforest. One, planted among many, could go unnoticed indefinitely. Inserting and activating it would be easy. The hard part was getting in and coming out without being noticed. That meant moving slowly and exercising excruciating patience in every step they took.

By the end of the first day, they felt they were getting close. They had not actually seen anyone, but the merest rumors of sound were in the air and foreign smells had begun to contend with those of the untrammeled forest.

They had still seen no one by noon the next day, but they knew themselves to be entering an area of human presence. The jungle reeked of it. The nearer they came to the target, the more densely populated their surroundings were bound to become. The peril of discovery increased with every step they took closer to the Ho Chi Minh Trail. Ideally, they wanted to avoid coming within visual range of anybody, but they knew they could never be that lucky.

They were not, but with patience, skill, stealth, and silence they were able to circumnavigate or otherwise avoid contact with the working parties, security patrols, and even an anti-aircraft-artillery (triple-A) battery they had to pass undetected. On the afternoon of the third day, they were at last in view, when the profuse vegetation permitted, of the mountains embracing Mu Gia Pass and the winding road below that rolled on south ahead of them.

Calling the Ho Chi Minh Trail a road was something of an overstatement. It was more like a pattern of barely contiguous path-like segments, running mostly through jungle, so that Paul and Jason could not keep it permanently in view from any distance, even while moving nearly parallel to it.

At their first sighting of the Trail, Paul scanned the road with hooded binoculars. After a few minutes he motioned Jason to follow him to the left, making their way north. Periodically, when there was a sufficient break in the trees, Paul would stop, use the binoculars, and move on. Finally, he found what he was looking for. It was a white-painted stone marker with a number on it, planted beside the road. Grinning, he turned to Jason, held up his palm with fingers and thumb outstretched, and pointed in the direction they were headed. Jason understood at once and gave a hand signal for, "Okay."

Things were going far better than Paul had hoped. Their navigation had brought them almost onto the target. The projected banana plantation was only five kilometers ahead. Moreover, they would be able to complete the last leg of their trek into it at night, because that was when traffic picked up on the Trail. To keep going in the correct direction, they had only to continue north, paralleling the activity to their right.

By dawn, the planting was done. Paul and Jason were moving back west toward their pickup point, but proceeding with great care. The heavily fortified Ho Chi Minh Trail was still nearby. That meant patrols and observation posts they must avoid. Detection of their presence now could ruin the whole operation.

Paul was mentally philosophizing about the upness and downness of moving through tropical rainforests, when the morning stillness was shattered by drumming bursts from high-caliber automatic weaponry. Paul wondered if it was from a Russian-made, fifty-seven millimeter, triple-A emplacement like the one they had passed on their way in. Whatever the weapon, they were hearing anti-aircraft fire of some sort and Paul doubted that the North Vietnamese Army (NVA) had sufficient ammunition to spare for test firing its guns. Some kind of aircraft, probably American, was being shot at.

The firing had stopped when Paul and Jason heard a loud explosion some distance away. Either the target had laid a bomb on the shooters, or the guns had brought down their target. Doubt was removed moments later, when a man's body fell through the forest canopy and was suddenly brought up short, suspended above them.

The covering foliage here was neither as high, nor as dense as in the place where Paul and Jason had landed. Within seconds they heard a rending sound from above and the body descended again. This time the man stopped violently between four and five feet from the ground. His parachute harness may have been equipped with a lowering device, but if it was, he chose not to waste time using it. Instead, he crossed his arms, bringing his gloved hands to the canopy-release covers at his shoulders. Then he flipped open the covers, squeezed the releases between thumb and forefinger, and tumbled to the ground in his now empty, backpack parachute harness.

The downed aviator, whose flight-suit shoulder insignia identified him as a U.S. Air Force first lieutenant, rose slowly, but appeared uninjured. Possibly preoccupied with shedding his helmet and harness, the man did not seem to notice Paul and Jason until they moved forward to help him. His immediate response was to draw a revolver from the holster sewn into his survival vest and point it at them.

"Hold on, lieutenant!" Jason barked. "We're on your side." At the same time, Paul was thinking how strange and threatening they must look to him in their camouflage coveralls and blackened faces.

Jason's comments in English kept them from being shot right away, but the downed aviator continued to point his .38, a long-barreled version of the snub-nosed ones in their own survival vests, in their direction. He was a young, middleweight, blue-eyed, Nordic type with close cropped blonde hair and a good tan.

"Who are you, anyway?" He looked very confused.

"Just two Americans taking a long walk in the jungle," Paul said quietly. "Want to come along?"

"No," he replied, plaintively. "I have to use my radio."

Still a bit dazed, the man was trying to get his survival radio out of his vest without first putting away, or laying down, the pistol. This looked like a juggling act with lethal potential. Jason had been closing in slowly and was now within a few feet of the blued-steel barrel. With his attention divided, the man's gun hand wavered, and he no longer had real control of the weapon. Jason stepped suddenly to the left, coming abreast of the flier. Now out of the line of fire, he faced sharply to the right, reached straight in front of him, and simply took the gun away without violence or resistance.

Paul stepped in from the opposite side and placed a hand gently on the man's left shoulder.

"Listen, lieutenant," he said. "This is not a good place to be. Your chute beacon is going out to everyone in range who's monitoring the Guard Frequency. That includes the NVA gunners who just shot you down. If you start talking right now on your emergency radio, it will only waste your battery power and make it easier for the bad guys to find you *and* us. Come with us now and we'll do what we can to help you."

"You can trust us, lieutenant," Jason said, offering the butt-end of the pistol. "Believe me; you will be safer with us than standing here while the NVA troops come out looking for you. Here. Take the gun back, but please put it away."

The clouds behind their young companion's eyes seemed to lift as he holstered the weapon. Confusion and indecision were gone from his face.

"What's you're plan?" he asked, quietly but firmly.

"Somebody is bound to have seen you coming down," Paul answered. "Are you alone?"

"Yeah. I was in an A1E." The A1E was an updated WWII-era, single-engine, fighter-bomber training aircraft the Air Force had pressed into service in Southeast Asia. It flew lower and much slower than its modern-day jet counterparts and was well adapted to ground support, interdiction, and harassment operations. Regrettably, it was also a much more vulnerable target for AAA ground fire. Such aircraft were commonly called Sandy, after their theater radio callsign.

Paul could not see the man's name tag beneath his survival vest, but found no purpose in wasting time on introductions.

"Okay, Sandy. Now is the time to hide, not run. Let's find something quick." With this, Paul and Jason led the way at as rapid a pace as the terrain would permit, while the lieutenant followed.

They had gone no more than ten yards when Jason touched Paul on the shoulder.

"We forgot to turn off the chute beacon," he said.

"Leave it. There isn't time," Paul replied, but he was too late. Jason was already loping back to where the lieutenant's spent parachute backpack lay with its emergency beacon automatically broadcasting a siren signal on 243 megahertz. That was the international, VHF distress frequency, monitored by every military aircraft in the war zone, as well as by North Vietnamese Army regulars who went out hunting for downed American airmen.

Confident that Jason would follow them, Paul led the lieutenant uphill in the continuing search for a good hiding place. Within a few hundred yards of where they had started, the two came suddenly into a fair-sized clearing, which rose gently ahead of them toward a large, low-lying mass of second-growth vines that covered at least a thirty-yard circle on the clearing floor. This seemingly impenetrable bramble ran on to abut the jungle beyond, which partly overhung and cast great shadows upon it.

"I think this is it, Sandy."

Moving toward the massive mesh of closely woven vegetation, Paul saw that it was entirely overspread by an opaque roof of thickly tangled vines about two feet above the ground. Up close, he managed to find an animal-hole entrance to the dark and snaky-looking cavern that ran far in beneath the cover.

"Get in here, Sandy," Paul told the lieutenant. "Crawl way back, keep still, and don't let the snakes intimidate you. Just keep thinking about Br'er Rabbit being thrown into the briar patch."

With the lieutenant moving on his belly under the second-growth hideout, Paul looked back to the place where they had entered the clearing. That was when his ears, no longer encumbered with the sounds of movement and heavy breathing, picked up distant fragments of excited, human speech. The hunters, he thought, are into the chase. Still, he stood, watching the other side of the clearing.

The voices grew more intense until Paul could barely identify the language as Vietnamese. Then Jason broke into the clearing about a hundred feet away. Seeing Paul, he stopped, taking in the vision of the hiding place he could easily identify. For a few agonizing seconds the two men looked at each other. Paul knew what was going on in Jason's mind, because he was calculating the same grimly unyielding equation.

If Jason tried running toward Paul and the safety of the second-growth shelter, he would never make it. His pursuers would be into the clearing too quickly. Even if he and Paul could make it under cover first, there would only be one place he could have gone. The men behind him would not be foolish enough to try entering the suspect warren after an armed quarry. They would probably just set the partly dried-out vegetation on fire or maybe use it for target practice until they got lucky.

Jason's choice, when he made it, would not be something idealistic or heroic, but merely an action based upon an honest measurement of the cold facts. Whatever he did, he could not save himself. The alternative to a futile dash for safety offered, at least, an opportunity to salvage the operation and spare two of the three lives now at stake.

The assessment was made at lightning speed and both men came to the same conclusion at the same time.

Paul watched helplessly as Jason waved him away, turned to his left, and ran back into the trees, deliberately making as much noise as he could. As Paul crawled into his second-growth refuge the sounds of pursuit receded. He had stopped to listen halfway back into the thicket, when he heard the sudden popping of what he realized was probably Jason letting off a few rounds from his snub-nosed thirty-eight.

Was Jason actually trying to start a drastically uneven gun battle with his hunters? Probably not. When the shots were not immediately returned, Paul suspected that Jason had fired them with intent to draw the pursuit after himself and farther away from the other two men. Paul's suspicion was confirmed a few minutes later, by several lengthy bursts of AK-47 automatic-rifle fire that went unanswered.

Again Paul was crawling beneath the second growth to find the lieutenant, his heart filled with a kind of bitterness and blinding pain he could not remember ever feeling. His mind raced wildly through a list of outraged indictments and complaints.

Why, God? Tell me. Why did this have to happen? We did everything right. The job was finished. We were on our way home without anyone spotting us. Then this lousy flyboy drops into our lives. Why did Jason have to go back on that fool's errand to turn off the radio beacon? Why did we have to be here, anyway? Why us, Lord? Why now? It isn't fair. Where is your justice? Where is your love? Why did you have to kill Jason? What happens to Petra?

Ironically and pitifully, the last question in this catechistic litany was, *What will Grogan say?*

Despite his anger with God, Jason, and himself, Paul did not take it out on the lieutenant. He knew it was not really the pilot's fault. Even if he were actually to blame, trying to bawl him out then and there would have been suicidally unprofessional.

When Paul found the lieutenant well back in their shadowed refuge, he touched a finger to his own lips to demand silence. They were not nearly safe yet. The man's response showed neither fear, nor any of his former hesitation. He seemed to accept that, under the circumstances, Paul's orders were to be followed.

Eventually, Paul detected the sounds of men coming through the clearing from the general direction in which Jason had left it. Vietnamese was being spoken, but in quieter, more labored tones than before. These men were working, not hunting. Risking a slow, quiet crawl to the edge of the undergrowth, he could see a half-dozen small figures through the mesh of dried, brown vines. Most of the men were carrying rifles and all of them were moving away from him. Now his attention was drawn to the last two men in the group. They appeared to be unarmed and were carrying something between them. As they got farther away, he could see that each of the two was holding one leg of a human body, dragging the torso and head along the ground behind. He could not see clearly enough to identify any clothing or features of the corpse they had in tow, but he was quite sure it was Jason.

Paul's eyes stung and his stomach seemed suddenly cold and empty. He had not stressed himself physically. Maybe that was why the small of his back around the kidneys ached the way it always did when he deliberately suppressed a sudden burst of adrenaline-driven action. He felt weak and impotent. He hated the men who had killed his friend. He longed for revenge against them, but he knew how irrational that was. He wanted each of them to suffer and be forced to look into the moment of his own death. Yet, he was powerless to do anything other than remain in hiding. Any movement now would be insanity. Just like Jason, he was simply doing what had to be done. He had no choice.

Paul and the lieutenant remained silent and still in their vegetable dungeon for three more hours. When Paul was reasonably certain that all human traffic in the area had ceased, they came out and stood up.

"What happened to your friend? Do you think he may have gotten away?" the lieutenant asked him quietly.

Paul looked at him, not wanting to talk at all. Finally, he spoke tonelessly.

"He didn't make it back in time to take cover, so he led the people who were looking for you away from us. Didn't you hear the gunfire?"

"Do you think they killed him?"

"I saw them dragging his body back."

The lieutenant said nothing at first. Then he spoke very softly.

"I know it doesn't help, but I'm sorry."

Paul bowed his head and briefly looked at the ground before responding.

"Look, Sandy," he said, raising his eyes to the other man's face, "they shot down one airplane. They saw one parachute canopy. They've got one body. As far as they're concerned, you and I were never here. Don't even think about using your radio, unless you want them to come back and start looking all over again."

Even as a dead body, Paul thought bitterly, *Jason goes on saving our lives.*

"But how do I get out of here without using the radio?" the lieutenant asked.

In spite of his grief, Paul smiled.

"Sweat thee not, young airman. It's a bit of a walk, but I know where the next bus stop is."

18

Grogan did not say, "I told you so."

He did say that Paul would have to handle the casualty report and all related actions, including the notification of Jason's wife.

"Do you want somebody to go with you, a female operator perhaps?" he asked, obviously excluding himself from that kind of duty.

"No. It was my operation. I'll finish it myself," Paul replied, hating the whole idea and wanting to escape.

"Make sure you read the appropriate regulations beforehand. It is a delicate business that has to be handled gently. We cannot have anything redounding to expose the organization or damage our assets."

"I understand," Paul said. He knew at the most basic, personal level that he did not at all agree with what he was being called to do. At the same time, he felt it was one of those desperate situations that offered him no alternative.

Hadn't Jason been faced with the same kind of choice? Knowing he would never see Petra again, had not Jason seen it as no real option when he ran back into the jungle? Was there some kind of difference between what Jason had done and what Paul was about to do. Most people would call Jason a hero. It would have comforted Paul to leave it at that, if only he believed that Jason had any other rational alternative.

As it is, Paul thought, *Jason did only what had to be done.* Now Paul found himself, in a different place under radically different circumstances, wedged into the same intractable position.

Paul recalled debriefing the lieutenant after their recovery about the need to alter his memory of what happened to him on the ground in Laos. From now on, Paul told him, the truth was that he had met no one, had turned off his chute beacon on landing, and had evaded capture by hiding out under some second-growth cover all by himself. Later, he had made his way out of the shoot-down area and established radio contact with a U.S. reconnaissance aircraft that called in a rescue effort to pull him out.

Obviously, the loss of an A1E aircraft and the sudden disappearance of its pilot had to be accounted for. Records in all the right places would be amended, all military members with any knowledge of the truth would be sworn to secrecy on threat of a prison sentence, and the young aviator would be medically evacuated without talking to a soul. After a few weeks at a special debriefing center in the States, he would be reassigned to some place like Greenland, carrying an assiduously updated set of unremarkable military records. He would have been fully conditioned and incentivized to tell only the authorized version of his jungle adventure for the rest of his life. If he changed his mind about that later, most people would think he was, at most, exaggerating a war story. By then, any conscientious search of the official record would confirm that he was a pitiful liar.

Paul did not mind doing this to an Air Force officer, who was sworn to serve the government and used to taking orders. Cooperation was little enough for him to give in return for having his life saved. Were it not for his lucky encounter with Paul and Jason, he would almost certainly have been hunted down and captured or killed by the NVA.

Deceiving and coercing Petra March would be something else entirely. The only oath she had taken was to become Jason's wife. Now, Paul feared, she was about to be poorly served for her fidelity. Worse still, Paul had been given the job of doing it to her.

Nearly a week had passed since Jason died, but Petra had been told nothing. Grogan must have been waiting for Paul's return.

Now Paul spent two full days consulting all applicable directives, reviewing Jason's personnel records, collecting forms, coordinating approvals, suborning forgeries, and putting together a Deceased Employee Compensation package. One thing his search of regulations had told him was that he was allowed a certain amount of discretion in the process. Most of the necessary deception could be accomplished by omission. Deception or not, Paul had one absolutely essential task. He must persuade Petra to remain silent about what little he would tell her of the way Jason actually died and the true nature of his employment.

During the afternoon of the third day he left a telephone message at the school where Petra taught, asking her to call him. Less than an hour later, the outside telephone rang on his desk in the Secure Design office.

Paul shared one of two outside lines in the office; the other line was exclusively Grogan's.

"Petra?" he answered, sensing who it was. Only Secure Design personnel normally called in on this line.

"Yes," she trilled, happily. "Is Jason back, too?"

"No," Paul said, trying to keep his voice from dropping in consonance with his emotions. "No, but I have something to talk to you about. Will you be home after school? May I come over?"

"Sure," she replied, but the chirpiness was gone. "Will he be back soon?"

"I can tell you about that when I see you. Will four o'clock be all right."

She hesitated a second too long. He knew she had been about to ask if anything was wrong, but had decided against it. She probably suspected he would not answer that question over the phone, but feared to be told so anyway.

"Yes, of course," she answered, "but don't wait. Come on over. I'm leaving right now." The dreadful seed was already planted. She hung up without waiting for him to respond.

Petra's teaching job with the government made her eligible for family housing on Kadena Air Base, but she and Jason had decided to rent off-base housing in the small seaside town of Yomitan, which was a good twenty-minute ride from the SGC facility and her school. Driving down from the main road into the near-sea-level community, which was mostly inhabited by native Okinawans, Paul spotted Petra's small, blue Daihatsu sedan next to Jason's Honda coupe. Their cars were parked under a tree in front of their white, one-story, concrete-block, tile-roofed house. It looked much the same as the houses around it. Paul parked his aging Datsun convertible behind the two cars and walked slowly toward the front door, carrying a briefcase.

This part of Yomitan was well shaded. All the doors and windows, except for a window air conditioner in the bedroom, were normally left open. Before Paul could reach the screen door, Petra was there opening it and gesturing him to come in. He could see she had been home long enough to change from her normal teacher's attire into khaki shorts with a tucked-in, loose, white blouse. She was barefoot, which was normal, since she and Jason preferred traditional *tatami* matting on the floors. Her short black hair and diminutive figure gave her an almost nymphal appearance, but her face was not at all gay. Her normally full lips were drawn into a tight seam, and her eyes were wide and frightened.

Paul paused at the door to remove his shoes and set down his briefcase.

"Don't make me wait." Her voice was quivering and slightly shrill.

She had turned to face him, standing about three feet away with hands on hips. "Is Jason in some kind of trouble? Has he been hurt?"

"I'll tell you right away, but please sit down first."

Paul could see that this approach was not working.

"Sit down?" Now she was angry, and the vocal quiver was gone. "Am I a child? I will not sit down. Not until you tell me what's happened to my husband."

Paul had known this would not be easy. He had not even begun and things were already headed out of control.

"Okay, Petra," he began, modulating his voice very carefully. "This is hard for me too, but I've got to say it. Your husband and my friend, Jason, is dead."

Neither of them moved for a few seconds, as if they were figures caught in the glare of some suddenly exposed, grotesque tableau. Then she took a few steps back and lowered herself slowly onto some floor cushions. She was not looking at him any more. Her face was cast down toward her right, while her left hand came up and absently moved its fingers through her hair.

Paul felt uncomfortable standing over her. The afternoon sun no longer gave light to the windows of the front room. It seemed dark and cold, even with the temperature around eighty degrees, so he turned on an overhead light and several lamps before he came back to sit, no longer in front of her, but at her left side.

Paul felt he needed to physically touch her. They both needed that, but he was afraid of surprising or angering her. Finally, she stopped stroking her hair and brought her left hand slowly into her lap. Paul reached across and placed his fingers gently under her forearm. She did not lift her head at first, but raised her hand to clasp his softly. At last, she turned her tear-filled but steady eyes to look at him.

"What happened?"

"Wait a minute," he said, scanning the room and spotting a box of tissues.

Why, he scolded himself, *didn't I think of this when I was up before?*

When he brought the box, she let it sit untouched on the floor in front of her. Since she remained sitting, he again sat down beside her.

"Don't pamper me," she said without anger. "Just tell me what happened to Jason."

"He was killed serving his country."

"What do you mean?" she asked, incredulously. "He wasn't in service. He was an electronics engineering consultant, like you."

"I must confess to you; that is not quite all he was."

"What then?"

"He was employed by a very sensitive government organization you have never heard about. For obvious reasons, you will not hear about it from me."

"Was he a spy?"

"Let's not get into definitions."

"Whatever he was, you're saying he lied to me about what he did for a living—who he really was."

"Only about a part of his work that he had to keep from the whole world. He was still the man you married in every way. Even about his job he told you part of the truth. He just left out some details you were not meant to know."

"Only the details that were likely to get him killed," she said, tartly.

Paul did not react, so after a moment, she spoke in a level voice.

"You're bringing his body back, aren't you?"

"The truth is we don't have his body. I saw him dead myself, but I never had possession of the body. There was no way to bring it back."

"Back from where?" she demanded.

"I could lie to you about that, but I won't. It is one of the things I just can't tell you."

"How long do you think you'll keep your secrets after I go to the press? Wait until they start turning over rocks." Her jaw had tightened and her anger was rising again.

"We hope you will not do that. It wouldn't help you any, but it might do significant damage to the national security."

She had begun clenching and unclenching her fists.

"National security? You must be insane. Do you think I care about that?"

Paul did not reply. He knew that engaging her in debate would gain him nothing.

"I'm not the only one who'll miss him, you know." Her voice was becoming ragged and weak. "There were other people in his life: parents, siblings, nieces, nephews, and close friends."

"I'm counting on your help with that. Considering the distances involved, I expect everyone else will accept whatever you say for a fact."

"What I say? I don't know what to say, because you won't tell me anything." Her anger was not subsiding.

"I have in my briefcase official reports, a death certificate, letters, and news items fully establishing that Jason March died testing avionic equipment in a military aircraft that crashed in Thailand, killing all on board. The bodies were burned beyond recognition but identified by the flight manifest and personal effects that survived the fire. I also have a certificate of cremation for Jason's remains with your signed consent. If you wish, I will provide an authentic urn containing inauthentic ashes. Or you may prefer to say that the ashes were scattered at sea; I can provide certification for that too."

"How very thoughtful," she sobbed bitterly. "You won't even let me bury him."

"You may want to attend a memorial service in the Kadena Main Base Chapel on Saturday afternoon. The people there will be primarily Jason's colleagues. Memorabilia like copies of the eulogy will support the official version of what happened to Jason. They will be entirely truthful, except by omission. It will be a completely legitimate service with genuine mourners. I hope you will be there."

"How can I?" She covered her face with her hands.

"Because he is dead and you loved him. Do you think his spirit will be any more or less there because his remains are not?"

Angry again, Petra stood up and glared down at him.

"This is nothing but a massive fraud!" she shrieked.

Staying on the floor, he looked up at her.

"Not so much as you think at this moment. Jason died honorably, doing dangerous work he cared about. At the end, he deliberately sacrificed himself to save others. He was your husband, and you loved him. Do you love him less now?"

Scalding tears were streaming down her cheeks, her whole face was on fire with rage, and she was screaming.

"He betrayed me! Now you're lying to me! You expect me to suck it in and keep my mouth shut just to cover your butts. Why should I do that? Tell me why!"

Paul thought of the, as yet unmentioned, instruments of compensation in his briefcase: the quarter-of-a-million-dollar life insurance policy of which she was beneficiary, the generous lifetime annuity, and Jason's final pay and benefits check for more than $100,000. Would an appeal to her patriotism help? No. All these together would not keep her from blowing the lid off the organization and making a mess of everything. She needed a much better reason. His only hope was to exploit her grief.

"Because..." Paul said with an unintended catch in his throat. Rising to his knees to look directly into her eyes, he took both her hands in his. "Because Jason would want you to."

She crumpled back onto the floor cushions as if Paul had hit her in the stomach.

He waited several minutes on his knees, while Petra drew tissue after tissue from the box in front of her. She was trying to wipe away her tears, but they kept on coming.

Finally, she looked up at him. Her voice was now weak and defenseless.

"You'll have to help me with this."

"You're right," he said, feeling tears well up in his own eyes, "I have to."

The last time Paul saw Petra on the island was at Jason's memorial service in the Kadena Main Base Chapel. He had offered to escort her, but she insisted on coming with another friend of Jason's, someone who also taught at her school. She had rather deliberately avoided any contact with him after his formal duties were complete.

Paul arrived late to find the service in progress. The chapel was large, but the group was fairly small, mostly people from Secure Design and a few from the wire house. Even sitting on the aisle at the back of the gathering, he could see Petra and another woman in the right front pew with Grogan.

Paul wondered if Grogan had been in touch with Petra before today. Probably not. More likely, he had introduced himself at the door of the chapel and tacitly claimed the obligation of escorting her. Did she know what an uncommon gesture of respect this was, both for Jason and for her? Paul doubted it.

Petra had on the same black dress she had worn to their first meeting at the Tea House of the August Moon. Today she had added a small, black, pillbox hat with a short veil that hid none of her face. From his angle Paul watched her in quarter profile as she looked up at an Air Force chaplain, who was standing away from the pulpit to present a brief homily. He took his text from Jesus' parable of the Pharisee and the tax collector at prayer in the Temple.

The chaplain noted the contrast Jesus had drawn between the meticulous observer of religious law, proudly thankful for not being like the man next to him, and the penitent sinner, humbly confessing his fault and begging for mercy. His theme was that we deceive ourselves about ourselves and others until we understand our equality before God, who alone knows the truth about us and loves us anyway. His point in this venue would have seemed for most people to be that Jason was now with the Lord, who has compassion for all who come to him for help and pardon.

Paul, to the contrary, could only think about the false righteousness of the Pharisee who was content with his life because he was deceiving himself so well. Given the events of the past few weeks, Paul much more easily related to the Pharisee than to the tax collector. He did not like that, but he could not bring himself to see it any other way.

Later, one of the operators from Secure Design delivered a brief eulogy. It was a carefully constructed tribute to Jason as friend and colleague, but made no mention of the values to which he dedicated his life or the work he was doing when he died.

Paul had been asked by the two men who set up the service if he wanted to speak, but he had declined. Thinking how he would feel now, looking down at Petra and talking about her husband in such a superficial way, he was glad to have made that decision. It would have torn his heart in two.

As he watched her face, he realized how lovely and strong she looked.

If only things had been different, he found himself musing. He promptly and relentlessly repressed that thought.

At the end of the service everyone stood, while Grogan led Petra and her companion out by the middle aisle. Paul was standing alone in the last occupied pew on the left. Petra was on Grogan's right arm.

As she approached Paul, Petra made and held eye contact for several seconds. Her facial expression never changed, but her heart at that moment withheld no secret from him. Her gaze told him wordlessly of her undying contempt. She understood how he had manipulated her while she was weak. She would keep the peace for Jason's sake, but she would always hate Paul for it. He grieved over that almost as much as he mourned for Jason, but he knew she was right. He had earned every ounce of her scorn.

19

Paul was getting drunk again, looking blearily across the Mekong River from his usual table on the veranda of the Beer Bar. The word Beer was all that was painted on the sign out front, so that was what the bar was called. This did not matter much to Paul, since he was drinking Irish whiskey from his own sewn-denim bottle bag with a drawstring at the top.

Actually, he was mixing the Irish with bottled water over ice cubes that might well be loaded with incipient hepatitis. Knowledgeable people said using the ice was just as dangerous as drinking the thoroughly untrustworthy water here.

No matter, he thought. *Nothing in the ice should be virulent enough to survive immersion in a double measure of John Jameson & Son.* He told himself this every night.

In fact, he knew the risk but was unconcerned about it. He failed to appreciate what a conspicuously dramatic departure this represented for a man like him. What had become of the Paul who was so relentlessly dedicated to synthesizing facts, calculating probabilities, and creating plans immaculately designed to eliminate the least opportunity for error? That Paul could still be found at work, but had stopped functioning off the job.

What of the other Paul, whose previous involvement with alcohol had been limited to a few social beers or an occasional glass of wine with dinner? The off-duty Paul now spent his time drinking whiskey at the Beer Bar and elsewhere, unless he was directly involved in an operation. That situation was becoming worse as significant operations declined. He had not been actively operational in over a month.

The incidence of operations was progressively slowing down because of President Nixon's phased Vietnamization of the war and the concomitant disengagement of U.S. Forces all over Southeast Asia. There was hardly enough clandestine work left to go around. Paul fully expected to see Stricott-Global fold its tent and disappear from the theater in rather short order.

A year before, Paul would have been happy to see the hot war ending. That would have let him return to the familiar Cold War threats his earlier career had been all about. Now he was indifferent to everything, so long as he was drinking. Sometimes he wondered why, but not when he was sober. Then he knew why, but when he drank, he forgot about it again. Falling asleep in an alcoholic stupor usually kept him from dreaming. Even sober, his painful hangovers sometimes offered temporary refuge from memory.

He hated his memories. There was Jason, standing at the edge of the clearing, making up his mind to sacrifice himself for the mission, Paul, and a total stranger. That was not bad, was it? Jason was being heroic. Nobody had to feel sorry for heroes, did they?

But Jason was not the only image Paul remembered. There was Paul himself, looking straight into Jason's eyes and knowing exactly what Jason was thinking. Paul knew precisely what had to be done, but Jason was the one who had to do it. Every time Paul faced that memory, he felt himself back in the same place, working his way through the same problem, arriving at the same, inescapable conclusion, and willing Jason to do what had to be done. It was the only scheme that could work, so his dear friend Jason had to execute it just the way Paul would, had it been his to do.

As he had done so many times before, Paul tried to work through this guilt by reasoning with himself.

"Greater love hath no man than this," Jesus said, "that a man lay down his life for his friends."

Why are you quoting Scripture, Paul?

Because it describes what Jason did for me and another man he did not even know.

But that was not nearly the same thing that Christ did.

You've got that right! No resurrection for Jason. All he got was a long, bumpy drag through the jungle to be dumped God knows where.

Don't say that about "no resurrection." You're getting pretty close to blasphemy. You know better than that.

Maybe, but what difference does it make? I failed Jason. If I had found another solution to the problem, Jason would have seen it too, and he would still be alive.

How could you know the unknowable? Are you God?

No, but why didn't God help us both? He could have, you know.

Did you ask him to?

Yes. No. I don't remember. I didn't have time for that. I was too busy trying to solve the problem. I would if I could do it over.

Solve the problem, or ask God for help?

I don't know. However you look at it, I lost control of the situation. That is why Jason died.

Don't be so arrogant.

Arrogant? I'll give you arrogance. Look what I did to Petra afterward. I cynically tricked a tormented, grief-ridden widow, a woman I could have loved myself, into accepting the unacceptable. It was the same old thing, Paul's Law of No Choice. Whenever Paul sees no alternative to doing something lousy, it's okay for him to do it. If somebody dies, too bad. If they're emotionally scarred, it just had to be. Do you buy that?

Nope, but it's certainly making a basket case out of you. You don't really think all this drinking helps, do you?

Shut up, motor-mouth.

When Vietnam began winding down, Paul's operations from Okinawa had started to decline. This left him entirely too much time to spend with himself: too much time remembering what he would rather forget, too much time thinking about what he remembered, and too much time learning how to self-medicate the pain of thinking by drinking. He was getting sick of himself, so he leaped at the first opportunity to transfer into what he thought might be a more active operational environment. That was how he found himself in the twilight of the war as acting chief of SGC Secure Design at a small Thai air base farther up the Mekong from Nakhon Phanom, where Jason and he had launched their Laotian action.

When it was too late, Paul realized what a poor choice he had made. One month after he arrived, the assigned chief took leave to attend to family problems at home. Paul became acting chief, and somehow the real one never came back. Now Paul had less work to do than ever before, more things to provoke his unwelcome memories, and a whole lot more time for drinking.

Paul normally made it a point to avoid his SGC associates when he was off duty. It would not be good for organizational discipline or his professional reputation if they knew how much and how often he drank. Instead, he had built up a companionably social affiliation with a rather wild group of Air Force NCOs, whose habits in town were sometimes even less meritorious than his own.

This particular night the sun had just gone down behind him, when he was roused by a shout from inside the Beer Bar.

"Take a look at them fireworks, Pete!"

Paul reacted to this, because these days in this place his name was Pete.

Paul recognized the gravelly voice of Chase, one of his Air Force drinking pals, but his attention was immediately drawn to distant skies across the river in Laos. At first the action was too far away to hear, but two airborne gunships were ganging up on a target. Tracer rounds lit up arcing air-to-ground firing trajectories from two different angles to make the eastern sky look like a staged pyrotechnic display. They were apparently using rapid-fire mini-guns, which would have only produced minimally audible humming sounds even at much closer range. Then at least one of the shooters found what both must have been hoping for—some kind of munitions cache or convoy. This produced a series of bright flashes, followed eventually by significant reverberations from across the river. Billowing clouds of flame mounted into the sky like the setting sun lighting up a rapidly moving bank of thunderhead clouds. The gunships had finished their work quickly, but an anticlimax of secondary ignitions and explosions went on for several minutes before subsiding into a mere glow from residual fires.

"What happened to Vietnamization?" asked Chase, taking a seat at Paul's table.

"That isn't Vietnam," Paul replied.

"Who do you think they were targeting, Pathet Lao or NVA?"

"Your guess is better than mine, Chase."

Chase was strictly a nickname for the balding, heavyset technical sergeant in his mid-thirties, who was making himself comfortable at Paul's table with a large *Singh Ha* beer bottle in his ample fist. He was wearing a Hawaiian-style sport shirt over tan slacks; American military uniforms were normally not seen off base. His Air Force buddies called him Chase because of his approach to engaging prostitutes in clubs that offered such opportunities. When his companions were preparing to catch the last bus back to base, Chase would begin a frantic selection process to get himself off the street before military curfew set in. Always successful, he was famous for giving ribald accounts of his adventures in various brothels of the town.

Chase took a long pull at his beer and adopted a rather limp posture in his chair.

"Tell you what, Pete. I'm about ready to take the pledge."

"What pledge? You gonna quit drinking?"

"Not that, man. I'm swearing off women."

"You, Chase?" Paul laughed. "I don't believe it."

"I wouldn't either before last night."

"Tell me of this great epiphany."

"I have never had any woman leave me in the dust like this," Chase moaned.

"If that's the end of the story, I wouldn't mind hearing it from the beginning."

"Man, you just don't know."

"Did it start the way all your other stories do, just before curfew?"

"I'd say so, yeah. But it sure ended different. I have been whipped to parade rest."

"Okay, okay. Give me the story."

Chase took another big drink of beer and composed himself for the tale by setting down the bottle and leaning toward Paul with his elbows on the table.

"I was at Happy Harry's. You've been there, haven't you?"

"Once or twice." Paul remembered it as one of several bars, catering mainly to American military personnel, which also offered opportunities for the intimate companionship of young women. Happy Harry, as far as Paul had been able to tell, was actually an older Thai woman who seemed to be equally in charge of the premises, the bar, and the girls.

"Well, like you said, it was getting late, and I was starting to look around. You know how I go about getting off the street."

"I've noticed."

"The main trouble with looking for a girl late, the way I do, is that most of the good-lookers are gone by then. As old as I am, I don't mind that very much. I'm usually ready to accept comfort over beauty, if you know what I mean." Here, Chase took a quick sip from his bottle.

"Anyway, this time the only one left was number nineteen. You know how they all wear their own little badge with a number on it."

"Yes."

"I'd never seen this number nineteen girl before. She wasn't too old, but she was kind of skinny and her face was pockmarked. Still she had a nice smile and a soft voice, and the mama at the bar said she might be more fun than I thought. Whatever. She was the last one there, so I went up with her." Chase paused, not for a drink, but for effect.

"Go on," Paul said. "You've got my attention."

"You're not going to believe this, Pete."

Paul noticed that Chase's voice and manner were not quite as boisterous as they normally were when he described one of his escapades.

"Try me."

"You know what this kind of transaction is like all over the world, don't you? Normally, women like this just can't wait to finish business and get to sleep. At my age that's okay. I need my rest too."

Paul nodded without speaking, and Chase continued.

"But this one was different."

"Was she?"

"Oh, yeah. She didn't want to sleep at all," Chase said with an unaccustomed note of desperation in his voice. "She turned out to be a genuine, dedicated nymphomaniac."

"You're kidding," Paul said, arching his eyebrows.

"I only wish I were," Chance responded. "I know what's going through your mind, Pete. Maybe you think that is as good as any man's erotic dream can get. I would have said the same thing before last night. Let me tell you, it's the most humiliating thing that ever happened to me. She wouldn't let me go until I was in the dirt—body, mind, and soul. I was so sore, beat up, and worn out, I would have run out of there at first light, if I could have run at all. Fact is I could barely walk. I'm still exhausted."

Chase fell back from the table into his chair, as if to demonstrate his fatigue. He had obviously enjoyed telling the story, but Paul could see signs to suggest a degree of truth in what he had said.

"Chase, that's quite a yarn. Have another beer. You'll probably want to head home early tonight."

"Now you're talking."

For a time they chatted about the coming monsoon season and the Thai custom of drenching passers-by with water to hurry up the rains. After sharing a single serving of inflammably piquant, prawn soup in separate bowls, they revisited the firefight across the river, while Chase drank two more large beers and Paul continued to diminish his whiskey supply.

Then, quite unexpectedly, Chase brought his fist down hard on the table.

"That's it! She's not going to get away with it."

"Who? What?"

"No woman's going to do that to me. I'm going back there now and show her what kind of man I am. She thinks she got the best of me, but I'm not through. I'll show her."

Paul could see that Chase was not angry, only embarrassed and drunkenly determined to prove himself to himself.

"Are you sure you want to go back there?" The idea seemed more than a bit foolish to Paul.

"You bet I do. Come on. I want you to see her.

Paul thought this a bad idea gone worse.

"I don't know about that. I have a pretty early morning coming up."

"Oh, come on, Pete. Don't wimp out on me now. You've got nothing better to do. Bring your bottle and let's go over to Harry's."

By then, Paul had put so much Irish into himself that he could no longer tell a bad idea from a good one. It was not the last poor choice he made that evening.

Outside the Beer Bar, they called over two *sam lor* drivers. A sam lor is the Thai version of a tricycle-mounted, rickshaw-like carriage. Sam lor drivers are wiry, tough little men, normally good-humored but dangerous to offend.

"Say, Chase," Paul offered with drunken bravado. "Why don't we pay the drivers for a race to Harry's?" Having committed to the excursion he was beginning to be influenced by Chase's daring attitude.

"Why not?" Chase seemed happy with that.

The drivers were agreeable and Paul was about to get into his carriage, when Chase had another thought.

"I've got a better idea. See if we can get them to let us drive. I've always wanted to pedal one of these things."

What a dumb thing to do, Paul thought, but being drunk, he said, "Let's go for it."

This was a much tougher sell, but twenty-five dollars each in advance persuaded the sam lor drivers to seat themselves in the carriages while Paul and Chase mounted behind their respective handlebars.

"Know how to get there, Pete?"

"I think I can find it."

Starting off was awkward for both of them, because the seat and handlebars were adjusted for much smaller men. They rode almost a block before they achieved a natural feeling about the way their feet connected with the pedals. Since they were going to be racing, they could forget about the seats.

Gradually, they built up speed along the smooth, level, well-lit road that ran south along the river. As they began to apply themselves, the cool, night air rushed by their heads, and the seated drivers behind them began to shout encouragement in Thai.

The machines were toughly constructed and lovingly maintained, so both men were soon flying down the road at considerable speed. With no other traffic in sight, they were riding abreast. That was their vehicle configuration until Paul, stimulated by the physical exertion, decided to change things.

"Hey, partner, have you forgotten? This is a race!" he shouted to Chase on his right.

With that, Paul applied himself more vigorously to the pedals and began pulling ahead. Chase was also putting on speed but could not overcome the three to four yard advantage Paul had gained early on.

Sailing down the river road, Paul was getting far more exercise than he was used to in recent days. Instead of tiring him, that and a competitive desire to win filled him with euphoric energy that seemed to lift the alcoholic mists which had so completely enveloped him. For the first time since Jason's death, he experienced a sense of limitless exuberance. He somehow thought he was seeing the world around him with greater clarity, and it appeared to be less dingy and tawdry than before. He was suddenly and intensely conscious of being alive, and that, at least for the moment, no longer seemed like such a bad thing. The better he felt, the harder he pedaled.

Paul could not look behind him, but the driver's excited chatter in the back suggested he was well ahead. He thought that was wonderful, but he did not want to give an inch. The faster he went, the less he cared about anything else. He kept trying to push the sam lor's pedals harder and faster. He was no longer riding to beat Chase. He just wanted to go faster. That was what got him into trouble.

Paul became so absorbed in his quest for speed that he almost missed the turn he was supposed to make in order to climb a short block to his destination. Having overshot it by several feet, he was forced to turn right so sharply, with insufficient braking, that he very nearly turned the sam lor over. He was suddenly flying up the uneven surface of a dirt road that ended just ahead, where he could see a red, neon sign that said Harry's. He felt himself losing control of the vehicle. His speed was too great for the wheels to maintain traction over the stones and ruts of this road.

Probably fearing for his own safety, the driver bailed out of the carriage screaming some things in Thai that Paul could not understand. Regardless of why the driver jumped or what he meant to say, his sudden departure produced a drastic weight shift in the sam lor, and the back wheels, stressed beyond their inertial limits, broke away to the left.

At that point, the only thought in Paul's mind was that this would likely cost him at least another twenty-five dollars. That was just before the sam lor went down like a wounded horse dropping onto its front legs. Paul was propelled over the handlebars and into the dirt directly under the Harry's sign.

Paul came down hard, but he could remember more severe landings in a parachute. He knew how to fall, even when he had no control over the angle of descent and was befuddled with drink. Mentally examining his body while stretched face down on the ground, he decided that nothing important was broken.

As he carefully started picking himself up, he heard Chase arriving behind him at a much safer speed. Still on his knees, Paul could feel gentle hands reaching to help him. At the same time he heard a soft, feminine voice speaking with urgency.

"You okay? You okay?"

Looking up into the neon light, he saw a slender young Thai woman with a pockmarked face smiling down at him.

Paul sat back down in the dirt, laughing uncontrollably.

"Hello, number nineteen," he finally drawled.

Paul was not surprised the next morning to find himself skinned, bruised, and sore. He did not notice his other injury for nearly a week.

20

The flight surgeon was an Air Force colonel. Paul was certainly not in the Air Force, but his association with Stricott-Global Consultants made him eligible for pay-as-you-go treatment from military healthcare facilities like this small USAF dispensary in its remote corner of northeast Thailand. The doctor had just performed a careful examination of Paul's complaint, which related to a very noticeable protrusion slightly above the groin.

"Your suspicion was correct," the doctor told him. "You have an advanced inguinal hernia, but it is still a case for elective surgery. It can easily wait until you get back to the States."

"So I can still do my job?" Paul asked.

"I don't know your job and I suspect you won't tell me much about it." The colonel paused.

Paul was aware that SGC's cover ran a little thin, at least with some of the senior officers on base. When Paul said nothing, the colonel smiled knowingly.

"Might it ever involve something like jumping out of airplanes and running around in the jungle?" he asked

"That could happen," Paul responded with a deliberately blank expression.

"Then the answer is no. Can you imagine what your scrotum might look like after a parachute opening shock? By the time you landed, and certainly afterward, you would be a helpless invalid. You would not be able to evade, survive, or do anything but lie on the ground and beg somebody to shoot you."

"In that case," Paul said, still with a straight face, "the surgery is no longer elective. I need it now." With his management responsibilities, Paul had few opportunities to go operational, but he did not want to miss one by being unfit. As slow as things were in Secure Design at the moment, he could delegate his duties for a week or two.

"If you like," the doctor told him, "I can put you on the med-evac C-9 out of here tomorrow to the Phillipines. You'll be there for a week or so and limited to non-flying duties for about a month after that."

"Okay," Paul replied.

The following day was Tuesday. By early afternoon that day Paul had been processed into the large Clark Air Base hospital in the Phillipines. At that time, it was a major treatment facility for Vietnam wounded and other military patients coming out of Southeast Asia. Paul had arrived carrying his false passport, a matching Department of Defense identification card that said he was a DOD civilian contractor, and a carefully sanitized set of medical records, which included the flight surgeon's referral notes and medical orders for his hernia repair.

Delivered to a bright, two-patient room on one of the hospital's upper floors, he was directed to a high bed nearest the door to the corridor and given a set of green hospital tie-ups, a light robe, and a pair of cloth slides to walk around in. He could see that the bed to his right near the window was assigned but for the moment not occupied.

Moments after changing into hospital garb, Paul saw his unconscious roommate rolled in by an orderly and transferred to the other bed, which was immediately curtained off. He reckoned without asking that the man was recently out of surgery.

Over an hour passed. Paul was sitting up in bed reading, when a tanned, reasonably young, but balding man came into the room. He was wearing an Air Force major's uniform under a white lab coat with a folded stethoscope sticking out of the breast pocket, so Paul presumed him to be a doctor. He addressed Paul in a brisk manner.

"I'll be with you in just a minute," he said, ducking behind the other bed's curtain.

He emerged after several minutes, scanned the chart hanging at the end of Paul's bed, and looked up quizzically at Paul.

"I'm Dr. Barth, Mr. Goetz," he began. Peter Goetz was Paul's current *nom de guerre*. "I am to be your surgeon," he smiled, "but unless you are in no great hurry to get back to work, I have some bad news. Your flight surgeon sent you here one day too late and a week too early."

"What are you telling me, doctor?"

"By the inalterable directive of our scheduling gnomes, we do hernias only on Tuesday, which is why your companion," he pointed to the curtained part of the room, "is still sleeping so soundly. He just had his repair. The problem is that you will have to sit here, watching him recuperate and enjoying our marvelous cuisine until next Tuesday morning. One week later, you will be able to wing your way back to the shores of the Mekong."

"That may work for military members," Paul protested, "but I'm paying for this, and an extra week means a lot of money out of pocket for the doubtful joy of wandering your halls."

"I fully understand," the doctor said, mildly, "but here is your problem. We can probably work with you to shave a few days off your post-operative inpatient status. You could spend that time in the Bachelor Officers Quarters waiting for your transportation to become available."

"Would that get me home any sooner?" Paul asked.

"No, and since you are already registered here as an inpatient, we cannot negotiate the front end of your stay. You can certainly choose to sign yourself out, but if you do, our gods of regulation, accountability, and red tape will no longer permit you to come back for your procedure."

"Could you refer me to a civilian hospital?" Paul asked.

"You could find a physician and hospital yourself, but…" the doctor paused, meaningfully, "I would recommend against that. Tales are told about some wealthy locals attempting extreme and illegal measures to get family members into this hospital. There must be some reason for that, don't you think?"

"I get your message, Doc. Are there any options?"

"None that I know of. I'll speak to the ward nurse about a special pass policy, but those things are also governed by pretty strict regulations, and she is not a very accommodating person. Considering where you've been, maybe a week of quiet rest will be therapeutic for you."

Paul did not respond and Dr. Barth exited quietly. Paul resumed his reading. He had brought several books with him, but he could tell they would not be enough.

After a few hours Paul heard some activity behind the curtain to his right. Then a man emerged from it, moving gingerly and bent at the waist to an angle of about forty-five degrees. Paul learned, first by observation and later from experience, that this was the characteristic pose of those who had recently undergone hernia surgery. They had been sewn up quite tightly and any effort to stand erect or even nearly so was an exquisite agony.

The man was blond with a ruddy complexion and looked at Paul through blue eyes filled with discomfort. His current posture and condition made it impossible to judge his age or height.

"Hi, I'm Pete Goetz," Paul said.

"Don," the other man grunted. He carefully edged his way along the wall and into the toilet.

When Don had returned to bed in the same fashion, Paul

offered to pull back the privacy curtain for him. Don thanked him and promptly closed his eyes. That was the last time they spoke until the following morning.

The breakfast trays had barely been taken away when Dr. Barth came by on rounds. He acknowledged Paul, but went directly to Don's bed.

"How are you feeling this morning?" he asked.

"Better than yesterday afternoon, but I haven't been out of the room yet."

"Let's have a look," Barth said, pulling the curtain around them.

Paul heard a few low-pitched comments that apparently drew guarded laughter from Don.

"You're put together tighter than ever before," the doctor was saying, when the curtain reopened. "Now I want to see you moving up and down the hall. No marathons, but get out there. Right now. Walking is the best medicine, and it will speed things up if you adopt a more military posture as you go."

Don winced at the suggestion of standing at something like attention.

"Don't worry, father," Barth added. "Nothing you're likely to do is going to damage the sutures. You're not going to pull anything loose."

"Still sure you want the procedure, Mr. Goetz?" the doctor asked, turning to Paul.

"It looks like my only way out of here," Paul smiled.

"Don," Paul asked, when the doctor had gone, "the nurses and orderlies here call you captain, but Doctor Barth just called you father. What line of work are you in?"

Don, now sitting with his legs over the side of his bed and facing Paul, grinned amiably.

"I am by calling an Episcopal priest," he said. "At the moment I am an active-duty Air Force chaplain at Da Nang."

Paul cringed inwardly at his painful memory of the Air Force chaplain at Jason's memorial service.

"I don't get it," he said. "My flight surgeon said I could put off this surgery, if my work did not involve flying."

"So did mine," Don replied.

Paul did not ask for clarification, so Don went on to amplify his response.

"I'm qualified to go along with the Jolly Greens when our PJs go out on search-and-rescue operations. I didn't want to give that up."

Paul knew the military jargon *de jour* and was a little embarrassed for implying that the chaplain's surgery might have been postponed. Jolly Green Giant was the nickname for large HH-3E search-and-rescue helicopters that carried highly skilled Parajumpers (PJs) into enemy infested jungle areas to pull out downed airmen. These were the same kind of people that would have been out looking for Paul's A1E pilot in Laos, had he been allowed to use his survival radio. Unlike Paul's well-planned missions, every sortie Don made ran incalculable risks.

"I guess I have a limited understanding of what chaplains do," Paul said.

"Not all of us are blessed with the same opportunities, but surely you have heard of Army chaplains ministering to troops in combat."

"Looks like I failed to make the connection. So what should I call you, Don, captain or father?"

"Don will do, Pete. Now, I think, it is time to start my hallway workout."

"Want company?"

"If you think you can keep up," Don cracked, creeping from the bed to the wall.

They had barely left the room when the less than compassionate ward nurse, a grizzled, hard-faced major, came up to Don, who was gradually navigating the wall in a suture-restrained crouch.

"Want to get well fast, captain?" she asked.

"Certainly," he replied.

"Good. Then stand up *straight!*" she barked, sharply thrusting his shoulders back to the wall.

The look on Don's face promised a scream, rather than the response he made from between clenched teeth.

"Thank you, major. I feel better already.

Paul realized for the first time that Don was over six feet tall.

Walking the hall became the primary occupation for both men in coming days and introduced them to much of the ward population. Their corridor was long, wide, and brightly lit. The men who shared it and inhabited the rooms beyond were very diverse. A few patients, like themselves, were merely dealing with the kind of medical events one might find in any hospital. Others were combat injured, recovering from serious and often disfiguring wounds that would keep them in surgery and therapy for years to come. Some of these were just recovering from one critical surgical procedure to the next.

Other combat victims were being watched and sustained in hope they would stabilize enough for treatment or transportation back to the States. Some did and some did not, but the doors to their rooms were normally kept closed.

Wherever doors were open, Paul and Don usually found someone who welcomed a chat and the company of other people. This was particularly true of those who were immobilized for treatment and for whom small services, like scratching an itch, fetching something, or helping with a bedpan, might be performed.

The most heart-wrenching case for Paul was an Air Force sergeant who had been caught in a Viet Cong sapper attack on the fuel dump at Cam Ranh Bay. Thanks to the quick reaction of somebody with a CO_2 fire extinguisher, he barely survived the blazing aircraft fuel that engulfed him when a satchel charge went off nearby. Now he was never free from pain and discomfort. Swathed in gauze dressings, his body was constantly bathed in pungent-smelling, therapeutic liquids that sustained his fight to recuperate enough before going forward with surgery and other treatment. Yet, he boasted in a cracked voice of how much attention he was getting from the pretty, young nurses. "It sure beats where I was," he said, sardonically.

In their journeys through the ward, Don identified himself as clergy only where his vocation was clearly called for to comfort or benefit a patient. When that happened, Paul watched, listened, and honored what he recognized as Don's ministry.

At the appropriate moment, Paul would join hands with Don and the patient in prayer. That seemed all very natural and right to do, but it set Paul thinking about how long it had been since he had prayed with someone else. Moreover, it forced him to examine a fact he had deliberately hidden from himself. Since the loss of Jason March and the events that followed, Paul had steeply descended into a life without prayer.

However little Paul might appear to have practiced his faith in adult life, he had never, until that tragic episode in the Laotian rainforest, stopped praying for himself. Even when he prayed for others, it was really for himself—for something he wanted for them. He had always presumed that God cared about what happened to him, even when he was not doing much to show his concern for God.

Now, his hall rounds with Don were making Paul understand that even his former attitude about prayer was a contradiction. Going to God for himself or others without actually giving himself over to God's will and control was a spiritual sham. It may have been better than no prayer at all, but he had still been fooling himself. He was playing cards and betting with toothpicks, but expecting God to pay off in real money. The incredible part was that, regardless of Paul's arrogance, sometimes God had.

Something returned to him from the night Rads died. He remembered concluding that as one became closer to others, one came closer to God and *vice versa*. That, he had thought, was how the soul found its proper place in the reality of God and all that flowed from him. That was how the soul turned toward God to see itself and others in relation to all that is true. Sharing even slightly in Don's ministry to the ward patients was calling Paul back to that insightful moment. Was it only his reasoning mind that had brought him to that conclusion, or had God been leading him to find it?

Paul had been confused and disappointed by quite a few things, since he first stood poised before that stark, spiritual revelation; surely, that was what this was. They included: Matt's lie and the treachery of others he had trusted, the deaths of comrades like Jason, his callous treatment of Petra in the name of some greater good, an ever-increasing reliance on his own Law of No Choice to justify himself, and his recent, high-speed dive into a life of remorse, guilt, self-pity, and drunken denial.

Now, he began to see how he had gradually withdrawn from the near victory of that night in West Texas. That was when he had thought for a moment he saw clearly what God wanted from him. Afterward, he had lost sight of his need to be looking at God and others. He had turned inward to look at himself, instead.

Paul had not stopped believing in Christ. He had not stopped thinking about God. He had just contrived to center those beliefs and thoughts upon himself. That way, he did not have to think about the reality of God and other people. They existed only as he imagined them to be. They were available or not as he chose.

First, he had built a wall to keep God and everyone else out, while still calling upon God for protection and help and expecting other people to behave themselves. Then he had stopped even asking for help and no longer cared what others did. The same wall he had used to shut God and the rest out, he now saw made him a prisoner within.

No more, he thought. He had to be rid of that wall.

Now, he must learn to pray all over again. The theme of the chaplain's sermon at Jason's memorial service came back to him, Jesus' parable of the Pharisee and the tax collector. This time, Paul would begin praying like the tax collector, with the only prayer he had any right to make; *God, be merciful to me, a sinner.*

While Paul and Don talked a great deal about the needs and problems of the men they found on the ward, they never actually had a conversation about religion. That topic did not come up when just the two of them were together. Don liked to talk about his wife and daughter back home, the people he worked with at Da Nang, and his hopes for someday being called to a parish in his native Maryland. Paul identified himself as a Baptist and spoke of neutral events in his life with a carefully cultivated technique that avoided any potential conflict with his cover.

On the other hand, they prayed with and ministered to others every day for almost a week. Paul felt for the first time that he had begun to see the Christian life, not from a back-row pew, but standing side-by-side with a simple man who was earnestly and effectively living it. The Holy Spirit that Paul had thought gone after his childhood conversion was not just back in his life; Paul was beginning to understand that God had never been absent.

Paul had not needed to be evangelized. He had always believed in God and was well informed about Jesus' teaching. It was all there throughout his life, even in barroom theology. What he had avoided seeing, because he had been looking the wrong way, was all this amazing love in operation. Dr. Barth might repair a hernia, but Father Don had encouraged the renewal of a soul without even knowing it.

Paul was prepped for surgery on Monday, which included body shaving, castor oil in orange juice, and seemingly endless enemas. On Tuesday morning, his empty stomach was complaining of its denial, while he waited to be drugged and taken to surgery.

Don finished packing his AWOL bag and stopped by Paul's bed to shake hands on the way out.

"You know, Pete, I couldn't say this last Tuesday, but I have really enjoyed this stay and you had a lot to do with that."

"You'll never know, father, just how much it has meant to me."

Don hesitated, probably reacting to Paul's unaccustomed use of his clerical honorific.

"Somehow, I think you just told me. God bless you, Pete."

"And you, father."

When Don had gone, Paul reached into the top drawer of his bedside cabinet and pulled out the Gideon Society Bible he had seen there the day he checked in. Sitting up in bed, he opened it to the Pauline letters he loved so much. His eye fell randomly on a verse in First Corinthians.

> But as it is written, Eye hath not seen, nor ear heard, neither have entered into the heart of man, the things which God hath prepared for them that love him.
>
> I Corinthians 2:9 (KJV)

Paul paused and gave thanks before reading on.

21

Recalling his experience with Father Don as a pivotal point of his spiritual life, Paul was stimulated to continue the investigation Matt Harriford had begun into the role of happiness in the life of the soul. Maybe the next Vale therapist would take it further. Paul opened his eyes hopefully.

"Grogan?" he croaked.

"Who were you expecting, St. Peter?"

It was Phil Grogan all right. Grogan of the graying crew cut and jutting jaw, wearing a wrinkled, white dress shirt with the sleeves rolled below the elbow and the collar open and tieless. Robust and forcefully overpowering as usual, he was sitting, as always, behind a desk in that same high-backed, executive, swivel chair that he had hauled all over the world with him.

Paul had last seen Grogan in that chair in Grogan's headquarters office when he was being briefed for what turned out to be his final operation. By that time Grogan had risen in the organization to become chief of operations. That was the top spot that almost everyone who had worked with him had been convinced he would one day hold.

"I can't believe it, Grogan. I know you were a powerful guy, but how did you ever manage to bring that chair to the Vale?"

"Nah, I didn't. Symbols aren't important here. In fact, there are none. Everything here is real, not symbolic. The chair is just a stage prop, like the desk and some of the other things you see. They make you feel more at ease in the beginning. You've already been told about that. They'll gradually be withdrawn."

"I suppose I'm being foolish, but they seem to help."

"Sure they do. It was the same for me when I came through the Vale, but you're half right about the chair. I was allowed to have it here—sort of a security blanket—until I was ready to turn loose. I was a regular jerk when I first came over."

Paul decided not to say anything about it, but it was fairly evident that Grogan had outlived him, the same as Matt. He knew for certain that Grogan had been alive to send him out on that last operation. Paul no longer found such concepts outrageous or discomforting. He was beginning to accept, or at least adjust to, some of the conditions of simultaneous infinity and their effects in his new life.

"About this time," Grogan went on, "the patient normally asks why we're doing all this."

"Well," Paul replied, "I can understand why I have to be prepared for something as radically different as simultaneous infinity. All the information I am receiving is certainly interesting. In fact, I am looking forward to going ahead with what Matt Harriford started to tell me about happiness."

Grogan nodded, supportively, but without smiling.

"We'll get to that," he said, dismissively.

Paul guessed that theatrical suppression of his own heavenly fulfillment was probably part of Grogan's therapeutic persona. Paul had to admit that a grinning, cherubic Grogan would have been hard for him to take seriously. This Grogan clearly wanted Paul to ask a question, so he would.

"Okay. I am a little puzzled by the need for theological exploration at this stage of my development."

"That's what most people say. Has it been your observation that all your previous theological opinions were accurate?"

"Not entirely, but why does that matter now that I'm here?"

"Let me give you a clue, Paul. Souls pass through here from just about every known religious persuasion, denomination, sect, and cult, not to mention several hundred you have not heard of. They wake up here, because they have met God's standard of being themselves the way he made and intended them to be. God established those standards at the same time and in the same way he created those souls. They were all built to be happy. God made them that way on purpose."

"Then why weren't they all happy?"

"They are now, but of course you're talking about their lives on earth. You ought to know the answer to that by now. They were not windup toys. Even God could not—would not—force them to be happy. For that to happen, they had to be, or at least try to be, what they are. They had to want to fit into the universe God's way."

As Paul thought again of the jigsaw puzzle, he was distracted by something dissonant in Grogan's earlier remarks.

"Wait a minute, Grogan. What about those other religions? Are you telling me that people who were not Christians still wake up here?"

"It happens."

"They were not dependent on Jesus Christ for their salvation?"

"Oh yes they were, Paul—one hundred percent dependent. None of us would be here without that."

"I am confused. Doesn't this fly in the face of a whole lot of Scripture and Christian tradition?"

"Doesn't it though," Grogan replied a bit wearily. "It is one of the toughest things for a lot of souls who come through here to understand at first. It is harder, I think, for some Christians than for many others. The truth is that most religions embrace some degree of exclusivity. Just look at the ancient Hebrews. It shouldn't surprise you that Scripture produced by them and later Christian writers are laced with examples of that kind of exclusion. That does not nullify Scripture. It only means you have to pay close attention to when, why, and by whom that Scripture was written."

"And tradition?"

"The same thing holds for tradition, but more so. Where do you think tradition comes from? It derives and accumulates over centuries from all kinds of sources. It is thoroughly man-made and is more a matter of social habit than anything else. It becomes hallowed and accepted by virtue of age more than accuracy. It does not come with 'use by' or 'discard after' dates, but some of it should."

Grogan seemed to be caught up in thought for a few seconds. When he spoke again, his tone was slightly more tutorial.

"Tell me, Paul. Why did Jesus come into the world?"

"To save the world, of course."

"Correct. At least, that is why he said he was there. Now, how much of the world do you think he meant to save?"

"All of it."

"All people everywhere? Everybody throughout all time?"

"Yes."

"So you're telling me that all people everywhere have been reconciled to God through Christ. Right?"

"Right."

"Well then, the deal is done, isn't it?"

"What are you saying?"

"Look, Paul. God wants to be reconciled to us. We are the ones who balked at that. The fact is humanity made reconciliation impossible. We will talk more about that later. Anyway, that is why God took human form as Jesus Christ. He came to make the impossible possible. God did it all. We could not win, so God won for us. All we have to do is accept his gift and our freedom."

"But what about evangelism? Aren't Christians commanded to spread the Gospel of Christ throughout the world?"

"Absolutely. How else could the truth become known to those who desperately need it? That is the irrevocable mission of Christ's Church on earth. Has the very human church sometimes gone astray? Sure, but it has still done more good than any force in human history, save Christ himself."

Here Grogan leaned forward and gestured with both hands.

"Think, though, of all the souls who have not heard of Jesus or who, even having heard, remain constrained to follow the faith of *their* fathers. Think of those among them who sincerely and energetically try to live in accordance with the laws of God, as they perceive him and his laws. Are they all bound for the terminal ward?"

"I would like to think not, Grogan. But what you are saying sounds awfully close to cultural relativism, where anything goes as long as it's indigenous and sincerely believed."

"No way! Every soul that wakens here does so by choice. On earth they chose to love God and their neighbors within the context of their experience. They awoke here to go on doing that. Mightn't that make them eligible for the mercy that flows from Jesus' sacrifice for us all?"

"What do you say?" Paul asked.

"The cultural context of their choice is a technicality. Did God create our souls to perish over a technicality? There are no technicalities here. We have only God's immutable law of love. Every soul was created in accordance with that law and no soul that lives up to God's standard of trying to be itself goes to the terminal ward. God made that standard. He alone knows how it applies and to whom. His law always prevails.

"Why do you think Jesus was so firm and clear in his command to 'judge not'? We are simply not equipped, even here, to weigh the worth of a soul. You think adapting to simultaneous infinity is tough? It is child's play compared to that. Only God can do it. When it comes to God's judgment of a soul, the proof is in the waking."

"Okay," Paul responded, "but didn't you say that everybody's salvation depended on Jesus?"

"That should be obvious. All those who wake up here do so by the grace of Jesus Christ alone. Some may have been following him in truth without knowing him by name, but without the name of Jesus and what he did for us all, there could be no redemption for anyone. That's what it took to save the world.

"Any more questions about that?"

"No, but it was a pretty big chunk for me to swallow. I expect I'll be chewing on it for a while."

"Good. Then let's proceed." Grogan did not wait for a response.

"You said you wanted to follow up on what Matt was telling you about happiness. Let's take a crack at that.

"Paul, there are some things most of us did not get right in life, even with a lot of trying. Where would you say most people on earth, all of us to be truthful, go wrong in looking for happiness?"

What was it Matt had said about happiness? *Happy is what we are, when we are being what we are.*

"First," Paul began, "let's say that being what we are means loving God and all the other souls He has made."

"That will do for a start."

"Add to that something Matt Harriford told me, that being what we are is what makes us happy."

"You're on the right track. Keep going."

"Happiness, I suppose, is the one universal goal of all people. If you break it down, happiness is the hoped-for end of everything we do, but most of us don't really know what it is or how to get it. Some of us think its contentment."

"Is it?"

"No. Matt convinced me that contentment alone will not define happiness."

"Go on then."

"Matt seemed to think I was on to something when I suggested that happiness might be described as completion. Of course, I meant the completion of ourselves. On earth we generally expected to find happiness by having enough money, possessions, recognition, power, or some other thing the world uses to measure success. These are the images of happiness we pursued on our own, all by ourselves. If the other things we've said about love, happiness, and being ourselves are true..." Paul stopped, when he realized that finishing what he had started to say made no sense.

Grogan just watched him.

"It can't work that way, can it, Grogan." It was a statement, not a question.

"You're right," Grogan said, almost without inflection. "Now try putting all that into a single, declarative sentence."

"We cannot make ourselves happy by ourselves. We can't even take care of ourselves by ourselves. It's impossible."

"Congratulations, Paul. You have just identified the source of most human grief since the dawn of the race. Loving God and other people is not just what we are made for. It is what we are. Like a hammer is made to drive nails, we are made to love God in a state of absolute dependence. Doing anything else is like the hammer calling itself a band saw and then trying to be one. It is absurd and eternally dangerous. You might as well turn the family car over to a five-year-old in freeway, rush-hour traffic."

"I'll accept that," Paul said.

"If you were reading the story of the *Fall* in Genesis right now, how would you interpret the meaning of original human sin and our alienation from God?"

"I would suspect that the problem was more basic than simple disobedience, although that would certainly be enough. I have thought about this before, by the way. I even mentioned it to Miss Janet, when she was here. I would say the actual sin was when our progenitors decided to take responsibility for their happiness out of God's hands and into their own. They wanted to take care of themselves all by themselves."

"Is that the original sin?"

"Yes, and I think much more. Wouldn't it account for original sin and all the sin that followed? Just look at humanity. Weren't we all obsessed with controlling our own lives, other people, and everything in reach? It may be easier to recognize in America, because we so thoroughly enshrined self-reliance there. Still, isn't every soul on earth convinced to some degree that a good life and the chance for happiness depend on getting greater control?"

"Couldn't we just put that behind us and live differently?" Grogan asked.

"I don't think so. Not as long as we're there. We may come to see that both the method and the motive are wrong, but in life, none of us is ever fully rid of that deceptive notion. It taints us all, not so much as a curse for the sin of our ancestors, but because it lies within each of us to do it too—and we all do. Isn't that what was wrong with the first beings we call human? Hasn't the same thing been wrong with every one of us ever since?"

Paul found himself being carried along a path of thought he had long ago begun, but never taken to its logical outcome. He had started to see some of it that night in West Texas, walking back to the training site from the Bottle Top Cafe, but then Rads had killed himself, Matt had been accused, and Paul had let the truth slip away from him in all the confusion. Now, at last, he could see it clearly.

"Doing what God created us to do—being what he made us to be—makes us happy. Nothing else can, because as you suggest, nothing else equates to being what we are, properly oriented to God and everything he has made. Trying to be any other way puts us at odds with God and everything else.

"We become unhappy, because we are pursuing our own happiness in our own way, desperately ignorant that we are moving in exactly the wrong direction. Trying to be ourselves by ourselves, we do not just go nowhere. We go away from God. Our misery and pain, our unhappiness is the totally natural outcome of our choice: action and reaction, cause and effect, sin and punishment."

"You are quite right, Paul, but you have also struck on another one of those things that these sessions are good for. You may remember what I said about souls coming in here with all sorts of odd ideas and opinions from their earthly experience. We try to help them smooth out the bumps. You would not believe how many people come here thinking that God has punished them for their sins while they were on earth."

"Well, Grogan, didn't he? There are plenty of passages from both ends of the Bible to support the argument that he did."

"I know, I know. I am sure biblical truth will come up in another session." Grogan gestured diagonally upward with both hands, as if waving away an insect trying to land on his desk.

"Right now, let's stick with punishment. I have one simple question for you. Do you really believe that the God of love you have spent so much of your life learning to know is such an implacable tormentor of sinners?"

Paul was surprised by the question.

"Isn't it right to fear God?" Paul asked.

"Yes, but in a natural way. Fear God, because you stand in awe of his indescribable holiness, majesty, and power; don't live in constant terror that he will arbitrarily smite you every time you slip. Just think about how many times you slipped in life. Do you think God ever sent you punishment equal to your sins?"

Paul hesitated before answering.

"No, and I sometimes wondered about that. Are you telling me there is no suffering for sin?"

"Don't be ridiculous. Of course there is. Sin is bound to bring suffering, but not because God wills it. It's as natural as any other cause-and-effect relationship in our old universe. Justice is built into everything God makes."

"Now you're refuting your own argument."

"Not really. Remember that we are built for love—selfless *agape* love, God's kind of love—by the love that God is. Turning away from God and turning away from that love is the same thing. Either amounts to turning away from being ourselves and you just told me how serious an error that is."

"Is that the totality of sin?"

"You almost said so yourself just a moment ago. Think of a sin, if you can, that does not involve a failure to love either God or other people. This is something that, even as Christians, we all chose to do all the time. Our suffering for that was totally predictable. That is the way our universe worked. God is responsible for making things that way, but you mustn't think that he punished us in any other sense."

"Hold on, Grogan. If sin naturally caused suffering, what good was repentance? How did we obtain mercy?"

"Simple. Can't you figure it out yourself? You sin, you repent, you pray, and God in his mercy forgives your sins. In that process he comes between you and the natural consequences of your behavior. You benefit from a true miracle, one as supernaturally stunning as the parting of the Red Sea—a mighty act of God that contravenes laws of his own creation. Such is the unspeakable grace of God."

"That's all there is to it?"

"Practically speaking, it's really quite a lot. Have you read Dostoevsky's *Crime and Punishment*?"

"I saw a television version once," Paul replied.

"Too bad. Nineteenth-century, Russian literature does not usually adapt well to the twentieth-century screen, big or little. Maybe you remember that young Raskolnikov commits a brutal ax-murder. Then he goes around tormenting himself with guilt and fearful apprehension. In the end, he is exiled to Siberia, but not before he finds forgiveness and reconciliation by turning to God. He has become himself. His punishment was always in his own hands, not God's. God only cared about his redemption."

"He redeemed himself by being the self he was meant to be?"

"Actually, God redeemed him because of that. God does not give up on any of us. Some of us, on the other hand, become so absorbed with our own independence, so obsessed with controlling our own lives, that we irrevocably abandon him and our only hope for happiness."

"We want to do it our way," Paul said.

"Correct. We start by merely insisting we have our own way about everything. Then we begin to resent people, groups, customs, institutions, and even God for intruding in our lives and encroaching on our control. The closer they come—the more they demand of us—the more we despise them, so we say and do nasty things to keep them away. Eventually, everything we care about is bound up in having our own way, and the walls we have raised succeed in shutting out God himself."

"That sounds uncomfortably familiar," Paul interjected. "I was wrapped up like that for a while after Jason's death."

"Was that truly where it started?"

"No, but that's what brought things to a head. I thought for a while that what happened to Jason and what you had me do to Petra were the causes of my problem. Actually, the problem was me."

"What do you mean by that?"

"As a young man I had sold myself on the idea that if I tried hard enough, I could control what happened to me and my work. There was no such thing as chance in my philosophy—just poor planning. When things went wrong, it was never coincidence or an accident. Somebody was to blame. Since the *Park Tray* thing was my operation and I survived, the guilt was mine."

"Even on earth I didn't blame you for that, Paul."

"I know now, but you remember how meticulously I organized and planned things. Good planning was the right thing to do—no question about that. The trouble was that I deceived myself into believing I could do it all. By the force of my own will and intellect, I could keep bad things from happening. The only surprise is that I got away with it for so long. It took a very long time before something finally came along that was bad enough to shake me out of my complacency.

"Then Jason was killed doing what I knew he had to do to save me and the operation. How could I explain that? There was no such thing as chance, so it had to be my fault. I couldn't handle that kind of guilt, so I blamed God. I forgot about the prayers he had answered before and blamed him for not hearing ones I had not even uttered.

"When I got back to Okinawa, you ordered me to take care of Petra. I despised myself for doing it, but it fit in with my old thinking about order and control, so I did it. I didn't blame you for it, because it seemed the only thing to do that made sense. I had exiled God from my heart, so I could no longer blame him. I formed the conclusion that some things, however rotten, were justified by the absence of any alternative. I called it Paul's Law of No Choice. That left me without God and hating myself. It was the worst period of my life."

"I knew you were having trouble then," Grogan said gently. "I was glad to see you pull out of it."

"I didn't pull out of it on my own. What you saw was an act. After a time God supplied the means to awaken me from my self-imposed nightmare. I was done for otherwise. How could I have so completely abandoned God and myself?"

"I understand perfectly," Grogan responded. "Many souls, most actually, explore that dark passage to some depth. Too many persist, ignoring God's efforts to call them back, until it is too late. Perversely, they triumph over God by permanently rejecting him. Their ultimate declaration of independence from God becomes spiritual suicide. Contrary to his will for them, they at last become something God did not make them to be. They cannot be themselves any more, because their true self is dead. Their eyes no longer open, because they look only within. They do not respond to any effort to waken them, because they care about nothing outside their self-made prison of fear, anger, spite, envy, hate, and ugliness. Nothing is left but the terminal ward."

"That is grim, Grogan."

"I'll say it is. It is the only grief that penetrates here. Even God weeps for the children he has lost. He grieves most of all."

"Matt said something like that about Rads. He told me that suicide was not what sent him to the terminal ward. He said it was what brought Rads to suicide that did that. It was more than the FBI harassment, wasn't it?"

"A lot more. And his homosexuality was no more relevant to what he became than a bad marriage, chronic indigestion, or lots of money might have been. Everyone got thrown around back there on earth by all sorts of influences. Good, bad, or neutral, those were only incidental to what the soul became. That depended on the choices made, the roads traveled, and, most of all, the faith that grew from the heart."

"Mostly faith?"

"Certainly. Rads lost his hope for happiness when he gave up his faith: faith in God, other people, and everything he knew about. At the end, he only had faith in himself. Then that failed. He had no place left to go. The tragedy is that he will go on being just like that forever. Nothing will ever be different for him. That is his everlasting torment, but God did not send it to him or him to it."

"Don't some people have no faith to lose?"

"But they do have it, Paul. Don't you remember what Jesus said about children? 'Of such is the kingdom of heaven.' We are all born with faith. It is an elemental, part of the basic package. Unfortunately, we do not all keep it or allow it to grow. Sometimes, like Rads, we lose faith in faith itself.

"Faith in God just means recognizing that nothing else can make us happy. Happiness is simply the state of being what we are. God's grace and reconciliation are always available to each of us, but not until we accept our inability to find security and happiness anywhere else. Our great leap of faith is away from self toward God. From there on, he helps us find and become the real selves we had almost forgotten we were."

"And that," Paul inserted, "is how we find happiness."

"You've got it. Happiness is not many things, but one. *Happiness is the authentic experience of self.* Here, you are coming to know, in a more perfect and permanent way, what you once felt only in intermittent episodes. Soon you will find yourself to the fullest measure in the holy presence of God."

"But on earth that kind of happiness seemed nearly impossible to attain," Paul replied. "Even then, it passed so quickly."

"You're only half right. As a Christian, you experienced it quite often: for example, in prayer or at those inexplicable moments of inspiration, when you knew you were being touched by God. You could not make it happen though. Neither could you know when it would. Such moments of ecstasy were brought to you by the Holy Spirit, when you were able to receive them. What was impossible for you to do on earth was to sustain that experience."

"Why?"

"That should be plain enough. At some point in our time on earth, almost every Christian thought that coming to grace through faith ought to bring the happiness of total self-recognition for life. Ha! Not in that life, right?"

"I suppose not."

"You can be sure of it. The universe we were in gave us scant opportunity to glimpse the full truth of God's reality. We had treacherously short attention spans and were easily distracted. We had a lifelong struggle to keep focused on Jesus, and we failed every day. Think how much harder it would have been without those fleeting glimpses of glory, the flashes of happiness, when we were only trying to become what God made us to be."

"God knows," Paul almost whispered.

"Indeed, he does. If you remember, He made a rather large point of experiencing that first hand," Grogan said with an expression that surprised Paul by being nearly beatific.

"Any more questions, Paul?"

Paul remembered how Grogan always closed a discussion with a call for questions that were rarely asked. Paul had plenty of questions left about the Vale, but he chose to ask only about something this session had brought to mind.

"Just one. You said a while back that God does not create souls to perish over a technicality. He is a loving God who mourns every soul lost to the terminal ward. Yet, he sees everything that takes place throughout eternity all at once."

"That's right."

"Why then does he create souls he knows will fail?"

"A very good question, but it is based on a misconception. Perhaps, I should have said something about that." Grogan seemed to be frowning at his oversight.

"Think of this. God is omniscient, but he is not a fortune teller. This is not a contradiction. Yes, God occupies all time all at once, but remember that he creates our old linear universe to exist outside his spiritual, simultaneously infinite reality. Everything here is always *now*, but our old universe has a beginning and an end. God creates it all at once from one end of its linear continuum to the other."

Grogan paused, as if he expected Paul to understand. When Paul gave no sign of comprehension, he continued.

"Don't you see? All souls are created free. Once they exist, God knows what choices they make, all the way from Adam and Eve to the last man and woman who draw breath. Before creation there is simply nothing to know."

Paul caught his breath.

"That makes awfully good sense. Why didn't I see it before?"

Grogan merely smiled and shrugged. Then he reached out, turned off his desk lamp, and disappeared, along with the desk and the chair.

22

Paul was not bothered by Grogan's abrupt termination of the session. It was such a typically groganesque way of doing things. Judging from Paul's observations so far, souls in the Vale, and presumably beyond, retained their identities. They were not totally swallowed up in the un-ness of a Buddhist nirvana or absorbed into the communal oneness of a transcendental oversoul. They merely left behind everything that was not really them when they came away from earth.

He remembered how Grogan had called happiness the authentic experience of self, because here or on earth, it was the essence and outcome of being one's true self. The genuine self-interest of the soul lay in an earnest striving to rediscover and become its natural, God-created self. That rewarded the soul in its innate yearning to be itself with the true happiness for which it was made.

This was fully opposed to the tempting disaster of self-centeredness, which threatened the soul's very life. Paul was reminded again of how far he had gone into his own swamp of despair and how long he had dwelled there, abasing and abusing himself over Jason

March's death and his own unjust treatment of Petra. Instead of looking outside himself to God and the people around him, he had retreated behind barriers of self-loathing and bitterness that kept God and everyone else at a distance.

Until God and the rest of humanity had found him anew, wandering through that Philippine hospital ward with Father Don, Paul had been deliberately headed down the same disastrous road that Rads had taken. He might not have been on Rads' path to suicide, but he was, without question, traveling in the same self-centered direction that finally led Rads to spend eternity alone with himself.

Unimpeded by reason and grace, an egocentric life led to the terminal ward, where the twisted soul chose to spend eternity imprisoned by and with its own self-made self. Reversing the fairy tale of the Frog Prince, a being of great beauty turned itself into one of supreme ugliness. It would not permit itself to be saved by God's healing embrace. It preferred the perversion it had made of itself to the grandeur God had given it to start with.

How tragic.

He felt a chill and wondered why. Until now, no negative sensation had touched him in the Vale. Then he remembered what Miss Janet and Grogan had said. Grief for the lost was the one pain that entered here, and even God felt that.

Rushing past the memory of his lowest point in life, Paul began to think about some of the things that had followed his Philippine experience. That had been his great turning point. Through prayer, Scripture, and inspiration, God had gradually taught him to worship anew. During the years after the Vietnam War, working in Europe and the Middle East, his attention was more and more drawn away from himself toward God and other people.

He by no means became a saint. He frequently failed himself, others, and God, but now he realized what was happening. The guilt from which he formerly fled was now an alarm and a signpost to his constant need for reconciliation. Repentance, atonement, and pleas to God for greater faith and the strength to follow it were daily events.

His job still called for precise planning and foresight, but he gradually came to understand that everything was not in his own hands. He lived in a world of chance in which God was his only dependable resort. He still had to make choices, sometimes in situations with grave potential. He still had to calculate probabilities, but knew he could no longer count on the results. By himself, he would always be at the mercy of forces that knew no mercy. With God, he could face those forces, do his best, and have the heart to keep on going. His life was no less dangerous, but much happier.

Later, while he was assigned to his organization's headquarters near Washington, D.C., Paul unexpectedly came face to face with some of the things Grogan was saying in the Vale about happiness.

Paul's organization was very small as government agencies go. For one thing, its services were limited. Providing for them required only a modest support structure to maintain a relatively compact operations component. Another reason for its diminutive size was the need for absolute anonymity.

Even in the post-WWII days, when Paul came on board, almost no direct recruiting was done. Prospective employees were generally screened from lists of applicants to other agencies and quietly siphoned off during the hiring process. Nobody was taken on without a microscopic background check, extensive psychological testing, probing personal interviews, and a commitment to lifelong, draconian, secrecy contracts. Polygraph testing was eventually incorporated into the recurring process of employee screening. Employees terminated for failing to meet retention standards were monitored closely thereafter to be sure they did not forget the sanctity of their security oaths.

Originally spread across several military installations in and around D.C., the organization had finally found residence in a specially built, obscurely located office park in the rolling hills of southern Maryland. From the outside looking in, the park was exclusively occupied by a group of small, high-tech firms primarily dedicated to contract work for the federal government. To a casual observer, this might explain the presence of some rather extreme security applications that could not be concealed. This was the headquarters where Paul was assigned from the late 1970s until his death.

For operators like Paul, staff duty at the headquarters meant performing occasional field operations, supporting operators overseas, and perpetually updating contingency plans. On the side, staff members were encouraged to take on additional duties, filling gaps for which personnel positions were not officially funded. Once he felt comfortable in his primary functions, Paul began looking for something extra he might like to do. His search for avocation brought him one afternoon to visit Dr. Wendell Bythington, who was the one credentialed, full-time historian in the organization.

Bythington's domain was a very oversized office, lined with books, government-gray filing cabinets, and four-drawer safes. The space was also dotted with reading stands that upheld ponderous reference volumes. The room was a model of organization, except for a half dozen tables, all of which were covered with high-stacked, mixed columns of varied types of correspondence: file folders, letters, electrical messages, photographs, diagrams, and seemingly random scraps of paper with barely legible handwriting on them.

When Paul entered, Dr. Bythington was standing at one of the tables, surrounded by gray, cardboard, file-storage boxes. Bythington looked like a retired NFL lineman who had aged beyond his forties, gone to pot, and grown a scraggly gray beard like the one with which Don Quixote is commonly portrayed. He dressed without much attention, but was rarely seen without a jacket and tie. Detecting Paul's approach, he looked up and smiled.

"Can I help you, Paul?" Bythington was a heavy smoker, whose teeth were revealed by his wide-open smile to be nearly as brown as the well-tanned face above them. Paul had wondered idly if his complexion might also be related to tobacco staining from the well-caked pipes that stood in a rack on his desk.

The two men knew each other well. Paul often came in to consult the historian about target profiles when he was putting an operation together or updating the plans library. With his universal access and long tenure, the old man probably knew more about the organization than anyone on staff, past or present.

"I'm looking for a way to fill my extra hours, Doc. Got any suggestions?"

Bythington's smile broadened.

"I have a couple of history projects you might be able to help with, but what we really need right now is an archivist. Just look at this mess," he said, spreading his arms to encompass the paper-laden tables. "And this is not even a fraction of the job that needs doing. We have thousands of file boxes in the archives vault next door."

"An archivist?" Paul said. "Isn't that some crazy guy with a beard that goes around throwing bombs?"

"No. That's an atheist," Bythington countered the joke. "I'm telling you straight, Paul. We badly need one."

"An activist?"

"No, an anarchist."

"Oh, I see. An alchemist."

Bythington abruptly produced a perfect imitation, voice and gestures, of Jack Benny.

"Now cut that out," he said. Then he added in his own voice, "You know I mean an archivist, and I suspect you have some idea, however primitive, of what one does."

Now the older man propped himself against the corner of his desk, crossed his arms, and directed his operatic tenor persuasions to Paul with great seriousness.

"Unlike most government agencies, we do not retire our official documents to the National Archives—someday maybe, but not in my lifetime or even in yours."

"It's easy to see why," Paul responded. "We're not like the CIA or any other outfit. We have no public persona. Any overt evidence of our employees and funding is scattered among a bunch of real and fictional government functions with no relationship to covert activities. Officially, we don't exist. What we do is hidden from all but a privileged few at the very top of the food chain. Even our tasking is filtered through leaders of the recognized Intelligence Community. Then they merge our efforts with their own before reporting back to whatever policy maker asked the question or called for action in the first place."

"You must understand," Bythington countered. "It's because of our exemption from regular oversight that we need to work harder in-house to preserve the record of our successes and failures. You know how after-action reports and active-project files help mission planners avoid repeating costly mistakes. You use them all the time. With the help of a few additional-duty historians, I have a pretty good handle on our history, but at the moment we have no archivist. Nobody is tending the store to preserve the actual records, without which our histories cannot be documented by future researchers."

"Isn't that kind of a glorified file clerk's job?"

"Not a bit!" the old historian thundered. "You'd be handling the real stuff of history. What do you think historical research is about, if not going back to original sources to find out more than the primary historiographer thought to write up? Looking back from twenty years ahead, people will have questions that I cannot imagine now. A contemporary historian writes what he thinks happened within the narrow frame of reference to which he is dedicated at the time.

"An archivist, on the other hand, preserves the true documentary record for later researchers whose panoramic view of the past will include a lot of our future. Without the record itself—the documents that speak of what was thought, said, and done—tomorrow's inquirer just has to take my word for everything and cannot pursue new questions. An archivist is the true champion of the record. He permits the development and evaluation of history to be an ongoing conversation between the present and the future."

"You make it all sound downright noble," Paul grinned.

"It is, my boy. Check with Grogan and see when he can spare you for a month. The National Archives gives a good course for new government archivists and I want you to go."

Paul was eventually persuaded to accept a part-time archivist position. That was how he became acquainted with the archival world and the National Archives institution.

He spent almost a month using his own name, but projecting the identity of a mid-level manager from a little-known government department, to attend the course for beginning archivists. He was introduced to archival principles like *respect des fonds* and *provenance*, which bring order and accessibility to the documents and artifacts of the past. Modern archival science, he learned, had been born of the French Revolution, which explained the origin and perpetuation of all those French names.

The training taught him methods and procedures for identifying, collecting, organizing, cataloging, and preserving the most fragile elements of the national record. Besides visiting other records-preservation projects around Washington, his class also toured various areas in the sprawling National Archives headquarters on Pennsylvania Avenue. It was all fascinating stuff, but he found himself most affected by his first personal experience of the National Archives rotunda.

The rotunda gives access to an exhibit hall, but Paul was mainly captivated by the gray, marble grandeur of the rotunda itself and the near holiness of its three most important displays: the Constitution, the Declaration of Independence, and the Bill of Rights. The rotunda is not a church, but it is very church-like in ways that one may not always feel in the greatest cathedrals of the world. It is coolly beautiful, and its vast, high spaces make soaring, transcendent statements. The primary document displays are barely readable, encapsulated as they are in a greenish, preservational haze to prevent further deterioration. For Paul, even that gave a hint of surreal reverence to the surroundings. He was evidently not alone in those feelings, because the chamber tended to be hushed, however many tourists were present.

Why, he wondered, had he never come here before? Then he realized he had probably been kept away by the typical snobbery of a D.C.-area resident, who too readily sneers at most things tourists do. Whatever the reason for his past neglect, he became a rotunda devotee, stopping by almost every time he came to the headquarters on business. He often went there, when he was in D.C, just to pause, be still, and meditate. He was especially likely to visit when he was wrestling with a difficult or elusive problem, something hidden that called for surroundings where he could directly confront and cross-examine himself.

One early-October, weekday morning, after getting some technical advice in one of the main offices on the Pennsylvania Avenue side of the massive complex, Paul got permission to transit the first floor connection through the exhibit hall to the rotunda. He only wanted to stand a while and think, so he moved around the outside wall to station himself at a point next to the main entrance from Constitution Avenue. To his left he noticed a fairly large group of what looked like middle-school students entering and progressing slowly, along with their teachers, in an orderly line toward the main document display.

Emptying his mind of distractions, Paul had dismissed the presence of others around him when he felt a light pressure on his left arm. Turning his head, he found himself looking down at Petra March, wearing a green, knee-length, cloth coat with a white, silk scarf and a black, fur hat. Aside from her warm, fall clothing, she looked much as he remembered her from almost eight years past. Her normal smile was missing; he had not seen that since before the day he told her about Jason's death. Her expression now, he thought, only reflected curiosity.

"What are you doing here?" she asked, directly but not harshly.

Without thinking, he responded with a half-truth.

"I'm an archivist. What about you?"

She gestured toward the line of youngsters.

"I'm escorting a school field trip." She looked up at him with slightly lifted eyebrows. "Aren't you with Stricott-Global any more?"

If she wanted the full truth, he thought, she would have to frame her questions more carefully.

"Not now." He hesitated, wondering what else to say. "How are you doing?"

She dropped her right hand from his arm, but held his gaze.

"As well as could be expected," she said flatly.

His face must have betrayed him, because she suddenly reacted with a slight smile.

"I'm sorry. That must have sounded terribly melodramatic," she said.

"You never need to ask my pardon for anything, Petra. I'm grateful you're even speaking to me."

"Now look who's being melodramatic," she responded, melodically, showing him a full grin. Then her mouth pursed slightly, and her tone, when she spoke again, was more serious.

"I have not put Jason behind me, but I have worked on getting rid of the bitterness. That was unworthy of him. It was unfair to his memory. I could not go on hating you without being mad at him. I didn't want to do that, so after a while, I gave you a pass."

A wave of gratitude and release washed over Paul. He had not thought ever to hear forgiveness from Petra, but here it was, sudden and unbidden. He wanted to speak, but his throat and tongue would not obey his mind.

Petra appeared to grasp his difficulty.

"It's good to see you, Paul," she told him briskly. "Now I must get back to monitoring the students." She fumbled in her handbag for a moment.

"If you would like to talk sometime, give me a call," she said, pressing a card into his hand and moving quickly away.

Paul pondered over the card until the end of the week. It simply identified Petra March, which suggested she had not remarried, as a middle-school teacher in Columbia, Maryland. He knew he wanted to see Petra again, and that forced him to ask himself why. As long as he had thought her forgiveness impossible, there was no point in looking for her or trying to talk to her. Now that was a closed issue. In a matter of seconds she had torn up that excuse for him. She had left the decision totally up to him. *Let the past stay where it is*, he thought, *or risk bringing it back and face the future.*

Be honest with yourself. What kind of future are you thinking about?
Nothing romantic.
Oh no? You wouldn't kid me, would you?
I suppose something like that might come out of it, but it isn't what I'm looking for.
What do you think this is, a Gene Autry movie? Are you going to kiss your horse and ride away from the girl?
Okay, I get it. She's smart, charming, and very pretty. I could fall in love with her. I can't ignore that possibility.
But you have a history.
Not exactly one I want to remember.
That's for sure, and neither does she.
But she forgave me.
Not quite. She forgave the archivist who doesn't do undercover work any more. You were hardly forthcoming about your true career situation.
I don't think her forgiveness was that conditional. It sounded like a position she came to honestly over time.

Maybe so, but how do you think she'd feel about your dishonesty in the present time?

Good point, but it makes no difference as long as nothing romantic starts to grow.

Are you really dumb enough to believe that?

Perhaps not. For now though, I would like to go on basking in some of that unearned forgiveness.

If you say so. Just don't say I didn't warn you.

Petra's card contained both school and home telephone numbers. Late Friday afternoon, Paul called the home number. When a child's voice answered, he asked for Petra.

"Just a minute," the child said and left the phone. In a moment the voice was back,

"She can't come now. She's bathing the dog."

"Okay. Just tell her Paul called. I'll phone back in about thirty minutes."

Paul spent the next half-hour rather puzzled. Jason and Petra had no children. Might she have been newly pregnant when Jason died? Such a child, he reasoned, could be no older than seven, and the voice on the phone had seemed somewhat more mature.

When he called back, Petra answered the phone laughing.

"Paul?"

"Yes."

"Well, you have now penetrated my own secret life, including a dirty dog and the young man of the house, Bobby. Does it surprise you?"

"I think not, but I'll admit that a child's voice was not what I expected to hear."

"I don't suppose so," she replied, pleasantly. "My sister, Katya, moved in with me two years ago when she was getting a divorce. Somehow, she, her children, the dog, two cats, and a colony of gerbils just stayed. It worked out well though. I take care of the mortgage payments while she buys the groceries and pays the utility bills."

"Not bad. Who does the cleaning?"

"We both work, so we have someone come in twice a week. We split the cost of that."

"I would say Katya's husband lost a real asset."

"I've said that too," she laughed. After a pause, she asked, "Why did you call?"

"You said I should phone if I wanted to talk. Well, I do. It's been a long time and I'd like to catch up on what has been happening to you."

"You just caught up with most of it." She hesitated a few seconds. "I promised to take Bobby and Patty to the Renaissance Festival tomorrow afternoon. Want to come along?"

"I've never been to a Renaissance Festival. What should I wear?"

"Unless you want to come in period costume, jeans will be fine. Be sure to wear comfortable shoes or boots, because there will be a lot of walking."

"Should I pick you up?"

"How well do you know Columbia?"

"Barely."

"Can you find Town Center?"

"Is that where the lake is? I had dinner once at Clyde's by the lake."

"That's a wonderful spot. I'll meet you in front of Clyde's at one o'clock, and we can take my car to the festival."

Paul spent the evening asking himself if this was such a good idea. All he got were smart-aleck answers.

23

Columbia, Maryland, was James Rouse's dream of a small city, built from the ground up to suit the needs of people, rather than the demands of commerce. It was barely ten years old and decades still from completion. Set midway in what real estate people called the Baltimore-Washington corridor, it was made up of rapidly growing, but still uncrowded, communities of enthusiastic citizens who truly enjoyed where they lived and were invited to take advantage of the vast, wooded spaces the renowned developer had intentionally left open to leisure and entertainment purposes. Rouse, famous and wealthy as he was, proved his conviction about Columbia by living there himself.

The shores of Lake Kittamaqundi at what was called Town Center were a beautiful example of the Columbia spirit. The tiny lake itself was alive with ducks and trumpeter swans, and the embankment around it gave space for an annual city fair, music concerts, and even free movies on some summer evenings. An early, if not original, key to the lake front was the implantation of a branch of Clyde's, a long-established restaurant that Paul knew well in D.C.'s Georgetown district.

Petra met Paul on Saturday afternoon in front of Clyde's long, windowed facade facing the lake. She was wearing fashionably faded, bell-bottom jeans with a loose-sleeved, brown-and-green print blouse and had two lively, preteen children in tow. Together, they walked back uphill to the lot where her car, like his, was parked. She drove a short route that brought them into a sprawling, unpaved parking area behind Symphony Woods. Paul remembered parking there several times when attending concerts at the Merriweather Post Pavilion open-air amphitheater.

Leaving the car, they followed faux Old-English signs along a wide wooded path that led gently upward to the festival grounds. The children led the way, forcing Paul and Petra to move at something faster than a stroll.

"Columbia is a very different kind of place," Paul commented.

"I think so. This is where I settled when I came back from Okinawa, and I have never regretted it. You should have seen the place when it was really young. It's far from finished now, and I expect some of the eventual additions will be disappointing, but there are limits to how much open space can be taken away. It may not be perfect, but it beats any town I've lived in, including the one where I was born."

"It seems to combine elements of comfort and vibrance at the same time."

"That's right. The social climate is familiar and new all at once. This is only the second year we've had the Renaissance Festival here. I think the Renaissance-fair idea started on the West Coast, but it seems to be spreading all over the country. A lot of the actors and artisans move around from one festival to another. We loved it last year."

A large banner above the festival entrance read: "Prepare Thyself for Merriment." That was unquestionably what they found inside. The grounds included a large L-shaped meadow, adjacent to a wooded lane filled with working blacksmiths, fortune tellers, witches, musicians, dancers, and countless stalls and tents that offered period clothing, jewelry, and *objects d'art*, quite a lot of which carried rather high-end prices. Fervent haggling was heard everywhere, and the artisans and merchants kept up their good-humored banter in character with the period.

The festival theme embraced a visit by reigning Queen Elizabeth I to an English country fair, complete with a royal procession through the grounds, accompanied by quaint musical instruments and fanfared by herald trumpeters. Afterward, members of the queen's party conducted various entertainments around her royal pavilion or moved through the grounds to mix with the commoners.

Quite a few visitors had come in costume. Some had dressed elaborately as nobility or men-at-arms. Others were plainly clad as monks in brown, rope-cinctured habits that sometimes bore a resemblance to lately dyed bathrobes. Many women had simply chosen to wear a long skirt with a peasant blouse and a bright-colored kerchief or sash. The temperature was cool, but the sky was clear and the sun rewarded those more lightly clad. Visitors who had dressed for the occasion blended easily with the festival performers and seemed to enjoy an air of license denied to those who had come in more contemporary garb. Paul noticed how the antics of these bolder patrons added to the enjoyment of more timid fellows like him.

A theater-in-the-wood provided a stage for fractured Shakespeare, comedic Italian plays, and various medieval jugglers, tumblers, and magicians. The main meadow made room for armored equestrian contests, archery fields, and other real or imagined games of the era. Besides the royal pavilion, there were stalls for procuring drinks, pastries, turkey legs, and piquantly marinated beef. The brisk October air was laden with the fragrances of wood smoke and cooking meat. Near the pavilion a pair of the Queen's bravos was slowly turning a brace of suckling pigs over a small open pit.

Going from one place to another, patrons were constantly accosted by ragged-but-witty beggars, crafty-but-bungling knaves, and wandering, buxom wenches. Brash young swordsmen moved through the crowd, exchanging ribald insults to provoke and stage comical duels.

The children were enthralled, and so, Paul had to admit, was he. Petra appeared pleased with all three of them. Distracted by the sequential events of the festival, Paul and Petra had no opportunity to talk of anything else until half-past four o'clock. That was when the children suddenly bolted across the meadow toward the sprawling human chess board in front of Queen Elizabeth's pavilion. At first alarmed, Paul took off after them without a glance at Petra. He soon slowed his pace, when he saw them running up to a woman, who, except for her blond hair and three-or-four more inches of height, could have been Petra herself. Even before Petra caught up with him, he knew this must be her sister and the children's mother.

As he approached the small group, he felt Petra come up and push him playfully from behind.

"Paul," she said, coming along side, "meet my sister, Katya."

"Sorry about the foot race," Paul told them both. "I didn't know where the kids were headed, but the minute I saw Katya I got the message. Except for height and hair, you two are dead ringers."

"The only authentic difference is that I got the tall gene," Katya noted, demonstratively stroking her long, yellow hair. "But you're right. The likeness is uncanny, considering we are not twins. I'm two, full years older."

"And I have never been allowed to forget that," Petra protested. "Every school teacher I had in the lower grades would ask if I were Katya's sister and then tell me that I must try very hard to be just as good a student as her. I told them I would certainly do better than she had, and I proved it in every respect but one."

"What was that?" Paul asked.

"I was more apt to get in trouble with the teachers, but never about grades. Maybe I had more character."

"Mainly, you had more mouth, but you were a character all right," Katya announced cattily. Her voice was far throatier than Petra's.

Together, Paul thought, *they sound a little like Joan Crawford and*

Debbie Reynolds. They were both smiling over their old, and no doubt, vigorous competition.

"Listen, you two," Katya said. "I finished my work early and thought you might like a break from escort duty. Besides," she added, putting her arms around her children, "it will give these two a chance to show me around."

"What do you think, Paul?"

"Good idea, if it's okay with Bobby and Patty."

It obviously was, so Paul and Petra left the festival and got back to the parking lot by the lake shortly after five.

"I don't know about you," Paul said, when she had turned off the engine, "but in spite of being surrounded by savory vittles all afternoon, I didn't eat much. Now I'm hungry. Want to grab a bite?"

"I'm not ready for supper, but I could use a substantial snack," she replied. "Want to try Clyde's?"

"Precisely what I had in mind. You must be clairvoyant."

"Just don't call me Claire."

"You've got it."

The area adjoining Clyde's ornate, long, lacquered-wood bar was still crowded with devotees of Saturday's televised football games. Given that, Paul and Petra struck a lucky hiatus between afternoon browsers and evening diners to obtain a table for two against a window overlooking the lake and woods.

"Would you like to split a baked brie almondine?" Petra asked, without opening the menu.

"I don't recall ever baking a brie, but I'm game to try it. Do you think a bottle of chilled Riesling would help it go down?"

"Beyond any doubt," she announced with approval.

Their agreement saved time with the waiter, who promptly produced the bottle with a basket of sliced French bread and disappeared. They touched glasses and sampled the cool, crisp, white wine.

"I like your sister."

"She's great. I've become so used to having her and the kids around; I think I shall have severe withdrawal symptoms when they leave."

"Is that likely to happen any time soon?"

"Not soon, I think, but eventually."

She broke eye contact and gazed out at the lake in the fading, autumn sunlight. Paul noticed the firm line of her mouth. She was thinking about what she wanted to say next. To give her time, he said nothing.

Instead, he devoted his attention to the rapidly darkening woods across the lake. The fall foliage had begun to turn, but the leaves were not yet falling. The close-grown trees gave an impression of deep forest beyond, even if he knew them to form only a thin curtain between this man-made lake and the heavily traveled, divided highway beyond. From what he could see at the moment, he might as well be looking across some secluded mountain tarn.

After a moment she turned back to him and spoke.

"You can't understand—no one could—how lonely I was when I first came here."

"And angry?" Paul interjected.

"Oh, yes. That for sure," she sighed. "Not just with you. I was angry with my country and myself, and God help me, I was especially angry with Jason. My entire life was a mess, but I did not care enough to do anything about it."

She hesitated.

"That last part may not be quite right. In fact, I didn't know what to do and I didn't care enough about myself to try finding out. Thinking about what was behind me was too painful, so I tried to concentrate on the future. You can guess the trouble with that. Refusing to acknowledge my miserable present, I kept sinking deeper into its self-perpetuating gloom. Of course, this was all years before Katya and the children came."

She stopped abruptly.

"Are you a Christian, Paul? I don't think I ever asked."

"Yes."

"Were you then?"

He could tell she was talking about their time on Okinawa.

"Only in the sense," he replied, "that I grew up in the Church and accepted Jesus' teachings about God and humanity. By the time you and I met, I had almost stopped asking questions about how that affected me in the real world. If I thought about God at all, he was off somewhere, and I had to manage my own life here and now. I thought, for example, that I had to keep Jason alive. Then he died, and it was my fault. It wasn't, but that was the only way I could see things in a world without God."

Paul wondered if he should have said that part about Jason, but Petra's expression remained one of interest, so he went on.

"I was a wreck for quite some time. It's a long story, but after a while something remarkable happened to help me see that God is always near. I was the one keeping him at a distance by trying to do everything myself. I do better with that now, but I still catch myself struggling to take over. At least now I recognize how I am going wrong and why. God is unbelievably patient."

Paul was a little surprised to see a smile growing on Petra's face.

"I feel almost," she said, "as if I were listening to myself."

At that point the waiter appeared with an over-four-inch rind of brie cheese, sprinkled with almond slivers and baked to a warm, runny, richness within. Serious conversation came to a halt, while they pierced the rind and smeared its contents, rind and all, onto the crusty, French-bread slices, which they devoured with zest.

"Thank you for introducing me to this," Paul said, when they had mopped the last creamy remnants from the serving plate. "It never occurred to me before that brie might be served hot."

"It's a favorite here," she replied, while he emptied the last of the bottle into their glasses.

Paul sipped his wine and waited for her to resume.

Moving her napkin from her lap to the table, she began to speak.

Her look was sober, but pleasant. The doubt and reticence he had detected before the meal were fully gone, and her voice was firm.

"You must have noticed my fairly solemn mood when I first started talking about the past. I don't visit there much any more, and I wasn't sure how I would handle it now. I was also nervous about exposing myself to you, because I was uncertain about your current feelings for that other time. What you said about yourself encouraged me to believe you'll understand the thing that has happened to me. In a way, while you spoke, I felt I was looking into a mirror."

She took a small drink of wine and continued.

"I told you how disillusioned, angry, and self-hating I was when I first moved here. I may have chosen Columbia because it was different, and I desperately wanted something to change in my life. I wanted to be at peace with myself, but I didn't find that at first. Instead of feeling lonely among lots of other lonely people, I found myself alone in a crowd where everyone seemed to be having a perfectly wonderful time. Besides that, I was a single woman in a world of couples, and I could not then bring myself to face the dating scene. Columbia is very much a people place, but I didn't want other people—especially happy ones—in my face. I found myself avoiding them as much as I could.

"Like you, I came from a Christian background. I have always considered myself a believer, but I stopped any regular church attendance after I left home. I was embarrassed enough to go back to attending Sunday services when Jason and I wanted a church wedding, but that only lasted a few months.

"The day you told me Jason was dead, I was so filled with anger and hatred that there was no room for God. That's why I didn't want to go to the memorial service when you first mentioned it. How could God help me then? Jason was dead. Nothing else mattered. The memorial service might have done me some good, if only I had been willing to think of someone other than myself.

"I don't remember blaming God for what happened to Jason. I

don't think I hated him. I just couldn't imagine him being relevant to what I was going through. As it was, I did not want God or anybody to save me from the path I was taking. Misery had become my one and only traveling companion, and I was not prepared to give it up for God or anything else."

Paul related to Petra's painful recollections, but remained silent. For the moment, she seemed to be informing herself as much as she was speaking to him.

"I know now that what I was doing after I got to Columbia was nonsensical and self-destructive, but at the time, I was becoming almost comfortable with my rejection of everyone and everything. I had learned how to ignore the world I no longer wanted to be in. I taught school without caring much about the students or making friends among the faculty. The rest of my life was circumscribed by eating, sleeping, and being alone.

"Weekends were the worst. At least, I had to be at school on weekdays. I tried going to church a few times on Sunday, but I found nothing there except the bitterness I brought with me. I came and went quickly, so no one could talk to me or invite me to do anything. At home I might turn on the TV, but I didn't sit down to watch it or even listen to it from a distance. It was just background noise to keep me company in my self-imposed isolation."

Paul could remain silent no longer.

"You don't have to tell me this, Petra," he interrupted, fearing the distress this memory was evidently bringing back to her.

"It's okay," she responded with strength. "I'm just now getting to the important part." She reached across the table and briefly pressed his hand to assure him she wanted to finish her story.

"I rarely went out, except for maintenance shopping. Columbia has a great shopping mall, but I refused to go there any more than I had to; the shoppers seemed just too cheerful to bear. Then one Saturday afternoon, I suddenly experienced a compelling urge to get out of the house. I rejected the idea at first, but it quickly became an obsession. The next thing I knew, I was locking the front door behind me. By the time I got to the car, I felt like a convict breaking out of prison. I drove aimlessly out through Ellicott City toward Catonsville and on into a countryside full of hills and horse farms.

"At one point, I thought I was taking a paved side-road, but it turned out to be a curving driveway that went up a small hill into a church parking lot. I had pulled into a parking place, planning to back up and leave, when something prompted me to turn off the engine and get out of the car. Before I knew it, I was standing on the pavement, closing the car door."

Paul saw a look of energetic excitement take over Petra's face. As if in counterpoint, her voice became steadier, and she spoke more deliberately.

"That was when I got a good look at the church, which was still a short distance away at the top of the hill. Another building to the left looked like a house, but my attention was held entirely by the church. Some additions had been made to the rear of the building, but the spired, limestone-block sanctuary was the core of the place. The stones exuded a gentle dignity and strength that only distinctive structures normally give off. Yet, its design was non-distinct. It looked very much like the snow-covered, country models that used to be common on Christmas cards. It reminded me even more of some of the old, stone churches I'd seen in films about rural England. Those places were in some cases many centuries old. This one might have stood nearly a century, but certainly no more. Still, it filled me with awe as I approached it. Do you know what that's like?"

"I can understand it. Places of worship, especially very old ones, can easily inspire such feelings. A skeptic would say it is just a matter of cultural conditioning, but that doesn't explain it. More pious observers would suggest that the influence of prayer and continual human traffic with God have actually seeped into the walls and the earth beneath to create an enduring sense of holiness within."

"The latter," she said, "is exactly what I found inside. I never meant to go in, of course, but there were only a few steps up to the red door and it was unlocked. I resisted opening it, but I was drawn in by an impulse stronger than my will. Either that or I yielded to my own unbidden desire for discovery. I honestly cannot recall which.

"Beyond a small vestibule was the nave, full of pews on either side, leading up to a carved wooden pulpit and a white marble altar trimmed with gold. The inner walls were of the same stone as the outside, but some sections seemed darker than others. Except for the vigil lamp on the altar, the only illumination came through tall, gothic, stained-glass windows on each side and a rose window behind the altar."

She hesitated for a few seconds and Paul could see that she was reliving the event, not simply recalling it.

"I was not," she went on, "reared in a liturgical tradition. Kneeling was not part of our ritual, but somehow, I wanted to genuflect before entering the nave. I did not choose to do it; I simply had to.

"Inside, I found a dark, cool, quietly soothing atmosphere. I felt, not just welcome, but welcomed—even called. I moved into one of the right-hand pews. The kneeler was already down, so I knelt and something entirely new took over my senses. For the first time in my life, I prayed without forming words or sentences in my mind. I remember my lips moving, but I cannot tell you what I said or if I said anything. Every moment of suffering I had known since Jason died flowed out of me in a way I still cannot describe. At the same time comfort, peace, and joy rushed in. I was all at once still and listening, while being blown about like dead leaves caught in a thunderstorm.

"I truly cannot say how long I knelt there. Eventually, my mind quieted, but I was still euphoric. In some incredible way, God had called me, healed me, and set me on a whole new path in spite of my stubborn resistance.

"I was still kneeling, but had lifted my head when I heard a gentle man's voice to my left say, 'Welcome to St. Athanasius.' Please don't let me interrupt your prayer, but you looked like you were finished, so I thought I might speak.' That was my introduction to St. A's and the rector, Father Don. It's a long drive, but I have been going there ever since. You should come with me sometime."

Paul smiled warmly and said, "Maybe I should."

"Tomorrow?"

"All right."

He paused a few seconds before reaching across the table to gently take her hand.

"Thank you for telling me your story, Petra. I would say we have both found our way back from a very dark and dangerous place. I won't go into the details of my own transition, except to say that you were right. We traveled many of the same roads and were granted the same merciful kindness all along the way."

Releasing her hand, he asked what sounded like a casual question.

"Incidentally, what is Father Don's last name?"

When she told him, he laughed.

"I've often heard that God works in mysterious ways," he said in measured speech. "I was not aware until now just how hilariously coincidental some of those ways can be."

24

In the Vale Paul remembered how his relationship with Petra had been solidly relegated to one of dear friends only, when she discovered he was still working for the same organization. Paul had known he would have to tell her eventually, but the subject came up sooner than he expected.

Paul sensed Petra's suspicion when he visited St. Athanasius' with her, and Father Don rushed up to greet him as Pete. After church, he cleared his conscience by volunteering the whole story and Petra generously deigned to overlook his former half-truths.

No matter, he thought, *that romance never bloomed.* He knew how greatly blessed he was in being able to reclaim his connections with Petra and Father Don. His reunion with both of them had contributed enormously to the happiness he enjoyed for the last few years of his life.

"Good, Paul. I see you are ready."

Paul was startled out of his thoughts and realized with mild surprise that he had not closed his eyes this time between sessions. He must be getting more comfortable with the view.

The nasal voice he heard was sharply penetrating and well

remembered. It did not inspire any particular emotion here, but Paul suspected it would have on earth. Lifting his head he saw the unforgettable form of Dr. George Fathringill Trumbull. He was dressed, as Paul had nearly always seen him, in a well-tailored black suit, white shirt, and dark tie; that was his preaching uniform. Had God from the pulpit come to the Vale to get him?

"Pastor, what are you doing here?"

The preacher peered at him from behind those thick, steel-rimmed glasses he always wore. His thick black hair was slicked into place and held there by some sort of hairdressing, as it had been when Paul knew him. In the same way, his stiff, prim bearing was exactly as Paul remembered it.

Pounding his Bible for emphasis or pacing in front of the pulpit during the invitation, impatient with the reluctance of sinners to come forward and be saved, he had seemed to Paul to be a man in a hellish hurry to get God's work done. Every sermon Paul could remember was built around the threat of eternal damnation and laced with an element of urgency, lest time run out before the sinner's critical decision to follow Christ was made. Then, how sad, it would be too late. The missed opportunity might turn into a sentence of death and torture forever. He had made it sound as if God were waiting outside to get even with anyone who hesitated to make the right choice right away.

"What's the matter, Paul? Didn't you think I would make it here?" Dr. Trumbull was smiling a bit slyly.

When Paul did not answer, the smile broke into a broad, toothy grin that almost concealed his cheeks.

"I wouldn't blame you a bit," the preacher said. "You'd be right to think of me that way. Looking back on it from here, I know it has to be one of God's major miracles that I did make it. I thank him constantly that I was judged by his standards and not the ones I laid out for so many people I knew on earth. How could you stand me, son?"

Hearing the man's confession, Paul reacted automatically by feeling a touch of empathy with him.

"Oh, pastor, don't blame yourself too much. You thought you were doing the right thing."

"Well, of course I did, but I wound up doing a lot of wrong that misled a lot of people and even drove some of them away from God." Paul recalled that the preacher was an intelligent and well-spoken man, except for his tendency toward verbose and runaway sentences when he became excited.

"By the way," Dr. Trumbull proceeded, "before we go on, let me explain something to you about sympathy and things like that. Here the only souls we feel sorry for are the ones in the terminal ward."

"I know about that."

"What I'm trying to tell you is that you don't need to sympathize with me when I tell you what a fool I was in life. Here we know all about the mess we made on earth and the people we hurt, but we don't have to feel sorry about them—not here.

"How could heaven be heaven if we had to go around grieving for our sins in the world? We needed to do that there, not here. This is heaven, boy—the last stop before you get there anyway. You're close enough to it that all your sorrows and everyone else's are over. They just fall away and don't ever come back.

"We're here for joy and reward, not worry and remorse. We don't need to beg forgiveness, because we've received it. It's not to my credit or yours—just God's."

Paul was stunned by this uncharacteristic outpouring of unconditional love.

"Pastor," he said, smiling back at him, "I wish I had heard you preach like this back then." Paul was barely aware that the familiar presence and accents of the old preacher had brought back the easier, gentler tones and forms of his own speech as a child.

"I do too, my boy. I could have done more for the Lord, if I had. Actually, I did. In my later ministry the Holy Spirit showed me how wrong I was to try scaring people away from hell instead of blessing and loving them toward heaven.

"Of course, I had to find another kind of church to do that in. It's frightening how many full-grown people want to be yelled at and scared about God.

"You left the Baptist Church?" Paul asked.

"No, no. I lived and died a Baptist. Baptist doctrine wasn't wrong; I was. Did you ever see that bumper sticker? 'God said it, I believe it, and that settles it!' That describes a biblical literalist, and that was me, boy. All you had to do was read the King James Bible. Everything you needed to know was right there in black and white. Everything truly was, but not the way I went at it.

"I admit it. I was a plodder in those days. It's always easier for a plodder if he has a book of regulations. He doesn't have to think. He just reads the rules.

"Praise the Lord. His Holy Spirit got hold of me about that too. He sat me down at that Good Book for many long nights. I had to study it, think about it, pray over it, and think about it some more, until I learned more about what it was really telling me.

"That's another reason I had to find a new church. There are so many people who don't want to search the Scriptures or even be asked about such things. They just want the preacher to tell them what the Bible says on Sunday morning, so they can go home, feeling like they've heard God's Word, and get on with their lives.

"Naturally, there were some literalists in my first new church. Some other members were a different sort. They came at the Bible like it was the cafeteria they went to for dinner after the Sunday service. I called them cafeterians.

"Cafeterians were always looking for passages of Scripture they thought said something good about whatever it was they wanted to do. That might not have been so bad, but then they would figure how the Bible said it was wrong to do something they didn't want to do themselves. Then they would count anybody who did those things to be the worst kind of sinner.

"They were sure that all those Scriptures they approved of came directly from the mouth of God. Any that went contrary to what they liked would be questioned, doubted, denied, and thrown out faster than last week's fish.

"What were you later on, Paul, a cafeterian or a literalist?"

"I didn't do much serious Bible study until I was almost forty, Pastor, but I'd like to believe I was somewhere between those extremes. I think most Christians are. Once I gave it close attention, I realized that not everything in the Bible is meant to be taken as factual reporting. There's plenty of that there, but to me it seemed more important to look for the truth the Bible was telling us. It gave us plenty of history and rules. I didn't ignore that, but more than anything else, it seemed to be a source for what God wanted all of us to know about him and his love for us.

"I wouldn't dispute that for a minute," the preacher said. What was your favorite part of the Bible?"

"No question about that. I've always loved the letters of the apostle Paul."

"I can't argue with you there. Outside the gospels, there's no better guide to Christian living. And yet, those letters have been abused and misinterpreted in ways that did great harm. Just look at how Paul's words were twisted to defend terrible sins like slavery and suppressing women."

"If you read all of what he says on those subjects, you couldn't possibly think he meant that," Paul observed.

"I've heard it from the apostle himself," the preacher told him. "Remember what I said about the cafeterians in some of my later ministry. Some of them were always looking for biblical justification to hold other people back. Truth is, I could have found them almost anywhere. It's a hard trap not to fall into, when you want to keep things the way they've been all along.

"I can't blame people who've been raised a certain way for thinking that's the way things ought to be. Mama did it. Daddy did it. They and your teachers and preachers told you it was right and anything else was wrong. Then everybody you knew reenforced it by example, and you lived it day by day.

"Maybe it was slavery or women keeping their place. It might be racial segregation, anti-Semitism, or excluding people who are different. Some people would like to keep disabled folks from getting in the way just by refusing to make a few changes that would let them get out of the house and move around. Others are willing to perpetuate plain old poverty just to preserve their own advantage.

There's a long list of systematic injustices going as far back or forward in the human story as you might want to look.

"Some of them can be so big and overpowering, like slavery, that nobody even notices the smaller ones until the big ones are gone. It's like trying to see candles sitting around a great big searchlight you're looking straight into. You won't even know the candles are there until you put out that big light.

"Humanity hardly did anything about slavery until the nineteenth century. Then in most places they got rid of it. Just think about how long we had it before we thought about doing that.

"In our country segregation grew right up to take its place. If that was any better than slavery, it was no less oppressive. The candles were still pretty hard to make out beside the searchlight of segregation.

"There was anti-Semitism all over Europe and, in its time, America for nearly two thousand years. Most folks didn't think it was so bad until Hitler came along to show us how mean people can be to other people they think are not quite human.

"American women got to vote in 1920, but it was forty years before everybody was so shocked to learn that many of them were not happy doing nothing but cleaning house, bearing babies, raising children, and growing old at home.

"Do you know where I'm going with this, Paul?" the preacher

asked, but did not wait for an answer. "Every time we came to a point where enough folks realized something was terribly wrong—whenever the balance began to tip toward eliminating some kind of systematic social injustice—what do you think happened?"

Again he did not wait.

"Let me tell you. People who hadn't studied their Bibles in years came up screaming that taking that injustice away would be scripturally unacceptable. They said whatever was being talked about wasn't really unjust anyway, because that was the way God made those people. They said it would be against nature to change anything, because that was the way God wanted it. Why else had we been doing things that way for so long, if it weren't the natural God-driven order of creation?"

"And that," Paul interrupted, "is how St. Paul's letters of almost two millennia before became the ready-made justification for any false proposition that aimed to maintain the *status quo*."

"Absolutely, and that is where you can separate the sheep from the goats. Before the tipping point was reached, most people didn't equate living that old way with wickedness—with failing to love those other souls the way God intended. After the tipping, you'd see good people, usually not enough of them at first, coming out to set things right. There was another bunch though, most often too many of them at first, who would whip out Scripture and shout to high heaven what heaven least wanted to hear.

"That's one of the reasons it always takes so long to change the things that need changing most. The people with the least love in them convince themselves and others that they're doing God's will by holding out.

"That's what gives the Bible and God's people who love it such a bad time in so many quarters. I can say that, because I was once one of those who did it. The Lord straightened me out about that too. His Holy Spirit spanked me until he got my heart right about the misery, sorrow, and ugliness at my own front door. Then I was given at least some opportunities to make amends before I was called here."

Paul simply sat in silence. This man he had despised for so long had just given him a compelling lesson in humility, love, and redemption. On earth, it would have brought him to tears of joy. Here it gave joy without the tears.

Had not Dr. Trumbull said there was no remorse in the Vale? If that was so, and it must be, it had not stopped him from presenting a masterful projection of emotional events from the past. Here in the Vale he could speak plainly of his own mistakes and mankind's failures, while purely rejoicing in the happy reality of God's grace for everyone. Paul lifted a silent prayer of thanksgiving for the preacher, his message, and the holy clarity they had brought to him in this place.

"Pastor, that is the finest sermon you've ever given me, and some of the best preaching I've ever heard. Thank you. It seemed to be designed especially for me."

Dr. Trumbull smiled and bowed his head for a moment. "It's mainly why I'm here," he murmured. Then, he resumed speaking in a more conversational tone.

"Of course, we don't read the Bible here. We have its primary sources and major characters among us. Still, I cannot forget how very important that holy library of history, law, wisdom, prophecy, and truth was to us on earth. We had nowhere even nearly like it to go to about God.

"Think of its contents: creation, the faith of Abraham, the law of Moses, the history of Israel, God's revelations through prophecy, the apostolic letters, the gospel of salvation, and the teachings of Jesus about God's love, mercy, and justice. They did not speak only to the ancient Hebrews and the Christians of New Testament days. They were a living, continuous medium, like prayer and inspiration. They brought God's truth to all humanity throughout all time."

"I understand, pastor, but it was so important to me then that it still is now."

"Oh, yes. I do know all about that. Can't you tell?"

Then Dr. Trumbull turned to one side and went, presumably, wherever the rest of Paul's visitors had gone when they left him.

25

This time Paul closed his eyes, shutting out all else, to be alone with his thoughts. He was reasonably sure that Dr. Trumbull had brought him the most important message, except possibly for the exploration of simultaneous infinity, he had heard since entering the Vale. It was less what the old preacher had said than what he had shown. His experience, judgment, and confessions had seemed to tie together most of what Paul was learning about the identity and nature of a human soul.

It is all about love, he thought. *Our human souls are made for it, the agape kind: the love God is, the love he has for us, and the love we are made and intended to share with him and each other. Finding our place within that community of love is how we grow into what God made us to be.*

What was it Matt said? *God made us what we are, but we all think for a while that we would rather be something else.* From what Dr. Trumbull told him, getting past that snag was only the beginning. Once we knew what we were supposed to be, we were barely prepared to start looking for the role God expected us to play.

On earth, Paul thought, that would have suggested taking a

360-degree evaluation of where he was and what lay around him. In Paul's former work a 360-degree analysis described what one did, either at the beginning of an operation, or when the course of events began running significantly counter to plan during one. If an operation were starting to fall apart, the recommended tactic was to stop for a second, a minute, or whatever time it took to assess everything that was happening and every contributing factor. Instinct might work in a singular crisis, but it was a poor tool for focusing resources to avert a multi-dimensional catastrophe, especially if the disaster was already in progress.

Why, he wondered, was he thinking like this? He was no longer on earth. Here, doing 360 degrees would merely mean opening his eyes and looking all around, but that would tell him no more than he already knew about his situation.

Now that he thought about it, Paul realized that almost everything Dr. Trumbull said to him had something to do with discerning truth and bringing it to others. What a full circle that seemed to make with what Miss Janet, Matt, and Grogan were telling him. That, of course, had been the old preacher's life, but how did it relate to Paul now? Why did Dr. Trumbull indicate that his message was specifically designed for Paul? Why should that matter to him now that he was in the Vale?

Paul was still sitting there with his eyes closed to disengage his senses. Then everything internal just turned itself off. He could not tell what had happened, because he was no longer there to know it. Anyway, that was how it seemed to him when he looked back on the event. While it was going on, he could not think about the Vale or anything other than the sudden, massive intrusion of shock and pain into his body.

Body? What body?
In the Vale Paul had forgotten the existence of any stimuli that

did not relate to his overwhelming realization of total health and serenity. Now a stunning suffusion of agony coursed through the framework of his entire being.

What's happening to me?

A violent, stretching pressure took hold of him. In seconds he felt as if he were about to be dragged inside out of himself.

What is it?

A crushing weight kept hammering into his chest. Pain radiated from the area around his sternum. The tissue-wrenching pressure from within came back over and over. Each time it seemed more demanding than before.

What?

Again.

Lord, have mercy. Am I dying all over again?

His limbs shook wildly. Lightning bolts of pain completely engulfed his awareness. They brutally invaded every ganglion of his nervous system.

Stop. Oh, please stop.

Now, he was heaving convulsively. Explosively, he vomited up the burning, sour refuse of a tortured belly. Between one heave and the next, he gasped desperately for breath without success.

Got to breathe. Why? Got to.

At last, his internal passageway cleared, and he drew in huge gulps of stinging, painfully cold air. With that, he began to be dimly aware of himself. He was not actually conscious, but he knew he was alive.

Alive?

He could not think, but he was sorry that it hurt so much to live. His head throbbed rhythmically with piercing flashes of pain. His chest was wracked by great spasms of coughing. He shivered against a sensation of dull, persistent cold that had penetrated every muscle and bone in his body.

Slowly he began to register other stimuli, but could not relate them coherently to himself. All his senses seemed to be speaking at once, chattering in directionless confusion that told him nothing useful: blinding light, sudden darkness, blurry sight without seeing, agitated voices, metal clanging, something like heavy doors being slammed, the taste of rust on his tongue, an acrid stench of kerosene, quieter voices and engine noise.

Invisible hands were yanking him around, tugging at his extremities and cutting or tearing away his clothes. He was being tumbled roughly onto his right side and held there, facing up against some cold, smelly, metal surface. He felt stabbing, hot pain in his left buttock. What followed was a warm glow that quickly spread throughout his body.

For a moment, some vague memory turned him into a child under warm blankets in a dark, cold room. Everything was as quiet and still as fresh-fallen snow. Then he knew nothing.

26

This was not a bit like waking up in the Vale. Within seconds Paul's senses had given him sufficient evidence to warrant opening his eyes. These were not the subdued, artificial senses he had known during his sojourn outside the world. They were raw, earthbound realities, all the more painful and intrusive for what seemed like their long absence.

His nose told him, as soon as he regained consciousness, that he was in a hospital. He conjectured it to be a prison ward or possibly a prison hospital. Certainly, he was clad in the drab dress of state-supported hospital inpatients everywhere. He lay in something like a hospital bed under bright, incandescent bulbs that were bare, except for the wire-mesh guards that encased them.

His captors had saved his life, but they were no less his captors. They would not treat him like a misfortunate civilian lost in the woods, miraculously snatched from the jaws of death by the alert forces of the State Ministry of Interior—no chance of that.

Paul recalled how Americans are sometimes confused when they read or hear of a foreign country's Ministry of Interior. Some are apt to associate it with the U.S. Department of Interior and think it has something to do with native people and national parks. In fact, the Interior Ministry in most countries has to do with internal security. In dictatorships or totalitarian nations, it invariably comprises the state secret police and oversees at least some border security functions.

Paul knew he had been snatched from a place that was infinitely better than this one or anywhere else on earth. That was all too confusing at the moment. He wanted to think very carefully about the things he had seen and heard before being pulled out of his snowy tomb in the meadow. Given time, he would try to figure out how he went to the Vale without really dying and why he had to come back here now. All that was very important, but it would have to wait.

For now, he must prepare to meet the consequences of his less than welcome rescue from paradise. He was clearly alive and in the world again. Given that, he was indelibly programmed by nature and training to remain so.

He awoke alone, so he quickly examined himself. His stomach was empty, and his body was full of pain. He ached in more places than he could identify. He was, no doubt, weak and shaken by the experience, but that would pass quickly—at least, as quickly as he needed it to. Being weak and confused could have its uses in a situation like his.

There was no mirror in the room, which was basically a chain link cage on all sides with his bed in the middle. Still, he could feel a significant number of stitches through a thin gauze bandage on the right side of his scalp. The area around the dressing had been shaved well above the hairline. He vaguely remembered his head throbbing after the rescue. Someone probably got him with a shovel while they were digging him out. This and a suspicious pain over his rib cage when he moved were the only significant injuries he could detect. That, he thought, was a blessing indeed, and he offered up a brief prayer of thanks.

He knew he had been bathed, because his former trail stench was replaced by a heavy, but much less offensive, antiseptic odor.

A slow drip injection tube ran from a mounted, clear-liquid, IV bag to his left arm. He could not tell what the bag was dispensing, but he suspected it was limited to purposes of hydration and nourishment. His consciousness did not detect any effects from drugs at the moment, but then, he was not trying to move around.

How long had he been here already? At least twenty-four hours, he assumed, and possibly more. An absence of aftereffects from drugs or shock suggested to him that it had been longer. He could barely remember being injected with what must have been a heavy sedative dose just after his rescue. More drugs had almost certainly been administered while his body was recovering from the freezing cold and shock of his experience. This was all guesswork, of course. The austere decor of his room did not extend to a clock, and his wristwatch had been taken from him. There were no windows in view, so no way to determine if it were night or day.

While Paul was making these observations, a male attendant abruptly came in and observed that he was awake. He removed the IV from Paul's arm and silently began packing used gauze pads and what must have been other medical waste items into a stainless steel instrument pan to the left of Paul's bed.

Paul greeted him with what seemed an appropriate question for someone waking up in a strange place and a foreign country.

"Where am I?"

The orderly looked at him, but made no reply. He just went out, taking the pan and the IV cart with him. Outside, he carefully and conspicuously relocked the wire-mesh door between Paul and the rest of the establishment.

With the orderly gone, Paul considered the events leading up to his interlude in the Vale. Barney, who was almost into the trees, had passed out of sight when the surface snow gave way and Paul was enveloped by the cavity below. Before he could assess its depth or size, his entire world was blotted out by the massive collapse of snow coming in on him from every direction. Feeling so much snow packing itself so closely and firmly around his body, he knew he would not have to wait for hypothermia to kill him. He expected to suffocate or possibly drown. He could not remember which, if either, had happened. Had he been clinically dead or merely unconscious? Who could tell?

He was at least unconscious when the troops dug him out, but he did not think he could have possibly survived in that hole for more than a few minutes. From what little he remembered, they must have revived him with some rather brutal application of cardiopulmonary resuscitation. He suspected he had sustained a cracked rib or two in the process. He decided it would not be very fair to complain about that.

How did the troops get there anyway, and how could they have known where he was? That was not very hard to work out. It must have involved one of the calculated risks Barney and Paul had taken in deciding to make a run for it across a decidedly dangerous area near a river that was bound to be closely watched.

They had gambled that the regular appearances of a patrol vehicle meant there was no fixed observation post within view of the meadow. He should have known they had guessed wrong when he saw a patrol vehicle leaving the road in Matt Harriford's magic lantern show in the Vale.

Recalling that fact, Paul could easily reconstruct the episode. Some clever fellow in the observation post that was not supposed to be there must have spotted Barney and Paul right after they entered the meadow. Under the full moon, they would have stood out against the snow like two clumps of mud on a white carpet.

Maybe we should have gone on using the parachute panels to camouflage ourselves for the run, Paul thought. That would not have worked, he realized, because a 200-pound man wearing a parka and carrying a heavy pack is pretty hard to cover up in such bright, white scenery. You can throw back the moonlight with white parachute silk, so as to blend an unmoving target with the snow, but that will not hide the shadows of two men on the run in snowshoes. The only mistake the two of them had made was being foolish enough to do what they had done.

When the observation post identified them, it might have sent out its own vehicle, if it had one available and ready to roll. More likely, it radioed the patrol vehicle already on the road, which hurried back to the meadow in time to see Paul going down, but not in time to stop Barney from making it into the woods. Since they did not have much chance of catching Barney, they swooped down and saved Paul.

Paul entertained no illusions about the humanitarian concerns of the Ministry of Interior troops who had pulled him out. He was quite certain that somebody in uniform would be in to see him soon, and that person would expect Paul to tell him something. Before that happened it would be a good thing to review his cover story, revisit his legend, and assess the probabilities.

Barney, he hoped, would have finished the operation and been out of the country, or nearly so, by now. If Grogan did not already know about Paul's problem, he soon would.

Paul's legend had been running before he and Barney began executing the operation. Any effort to trace the person identified in Paul's phony passport would find evidence of a comfortably fixed, South Carolina furniture distributor with no immediate family, who was currently on a sporting vacation somewhere in Europe with no fixed itinerary. That would hold up for a time, unless something leaked and the press got hold of it. No counterintelligence agency in the world could shred a good legend faster than the American press.

Chances were that nothing would leak for a while. Paul would probably be held *incommunicado* until some higher-level interrogators got a crack at him. The longer his low-level captors held him, the better his chances would be. They were less likely to have well-trained or experienced interrogators, and their authority to abuse him would probably be limited. Any time they spent employing their amateur talents would give Grogan more opportunity to perform some of his magic tricks. Paul knew his ability to endure, resist, or even survive would diminish considerably when he was moved to a higher headquarters. He entertained no illusions about the possibility of escape. Given his probable situation, that would be a non-starter.

Paul thought about Vanja Durov, his long ago mentor in techniques for surviving captivity and resisting interrogation. His real name was Ivan, but he always insisted on being called by the diminutive nickname, Vanja.

Vanja was a dark, black-haired man of medium height, who was built straight up and down like a fire hydrant. He was a hard-looking man of Russian descent, who was far harder than he looked. He often spoke with an ironically caustic, typically Russian sense of humor about some of life's more distressing possibilities; he had known most of them.

Vanja was the organization's authority on getting out of prison alive, because he had survived more than a year in Moscow's infamous Lubjanka. Lubjanka was the KGB's, maximum strength bullpen for top-notch Soviet interrogators, who felt they had a reputation to uphold. His imprisonment, like that of the Soviet operator who was eventually traded to get him back, was never made public. Coming out of Lubjanka alive and unbroken made Vanja a very special person to everyone who knew about it.

Vanja's most remembered contribution to Paul's education in such matters was the advice to avoid any appearance of arrogance or defiance.

"Who do you think you are," Vanja laughed, when Paul had said something about simply refusing to talk, "John Wayne or Jimmy Cagney?

"If you clam up or come back at these guys with a smart lip, they'll just bust it for you. Hey! They don't like you to start with. Don't give them any more reasons to hurt you. What good is that? You'll be taking enough punches without provoking any extra ones.

"Will a beating or two every day improve your ability to hold up? Not likely.

"If you antagonize them too much they may get carried away and overdo it. Then you're dead and they have nobody to trade—bad for them, but the end for you.

"Naturally, you can't tell them what they want to know, but you can at least look like you're trying to help. Keep talking. Act disappointed when they jump at you and call you a filthy pig of a liar. The more you stick to your cover, the less they'll believe it, but as long as you keep talking they may think there's a chance to find something in all that garbage you're spilling. If they think that, maybe they won't beat on you so much. That wins you some time: a day, a week, a month, however long you can stretch it. Whatever time you gain, gets added on to how long you keep going. Strong, silent toughguys don't last long playing *Truth or Consequences* with professional bullies. Don't try it."

Vanja had been right. Time was what Paul needed most, time to survive and pray for distant events and forces to work in his favor. He was totally powerless to help himself. What a familiar ring that had.

He had decided for the moment not to concentrate much of his attention on what happened to him in the Vale. He would think about that later. Yet, he remembered what Grogan had said about faith in God that brings the authentic experience of self. If he could hold on to that, even while his mind and body were being abused, he would be happy in the only sense that happiness mattered for now—in the comfort of his soul.

He would try not to forget that his adversaries, regardless of their purpose and methods, were souls created in the same image as his. He would pray for them to be merciful, even as he prayed for the strength and wit to obstruct their efforts to exploit him.

He would remember Vanja and become the very soul of innocence, distress, and deepest gratitude for the heroic exertions of those valorous Interior Ministry troops who had saved his life. He was only a private tourist, who had been separated from his hunting party, become lost, and inadvertently stumbled into the wrong country.

Nothing in his pack would suggest anything else. Even the white, silk panels could be explained as components for a hunting blind.

It was not much of a cover story, but he would stick to it. No one would believe a word of it, of course.

Nobody did.

Paul was not surprised or intimidated by the small, semi-automatic pistol the uniformed interrogator unholstered and menacingly shoved into his face. Despite his primal instinct to survive, he found no fear in the prospect of dying.

Go ahead, major, Paul thought. *I've done this once already.*

The major exposed himself as an amateur with handguns by bringing the pistol close enough for Paul to get hold of it. Paul knew he could disarm the man in a second. It was tempting, but what good would it do? Behind this one stood a long line of interrogators, like those who had preceded him, eagerly waiting for their turn. Besides, aggressive action was not compatible with Paul's current cover.

The thing to do right now, Paul told himself, *is to grovel and whine.*

"For heaven's sake, don't do this! What have I done wrong? I didn't mean to wind up in your country. It was all an accident—a huge mistake. I didn't know I was crossing the border. Why do you want to kill me? Please don't shoot."

Paul's voice gurgled with terror. His eyes fastened fearfully upon the man's finger, as it continued, purposefully but slowly, to squeeze the trigger of the weapon being aimed squarely between them.

"I'm no spy, I tell you. I'm just Jack Nolan from South Carolina. I sell furniture; that's all." Paul's tone was frantic, and his words kept running into each other, like a chain-reaction, rear-end collision on a metropolitan beltway. He was waving his hands and looked as if he would fall to his knees at any moment.

The officer's hand was steady, and his trigger squeeze continued until they both heard a metallic click from the pistol's hammer falling against a firing pin that failed to make contact with a live cartridge. Paul thought this would be a good time to let his legs go out from under him, so he did, sprawling limply onto the floor.

"Dear me," said the Ministry of Interior officer in perfect but accented English. "I must have forgotten to load the chamber. Oh, well. There may be another occasion. Just remember, Mr. Nolan. Your life belongs to us. We saved it, and we can take it back. You are being very foolish to withhold your cooperation from us."

"But I'm doing everything I can to help." Paul was now sitting on the floor, and his voice was softer but, if anything, whinier. "I told you how grateful I am to your troops for saving me from the snow. I've told all your people, and I just told you the same thing again, but…"

"Stand up, Nolan!" the officer barked. "You make me sick," he sneered, as Paul gingerly brought himself something less than erect, using his hospital bed for support. "Don't you understand what you have done? You are in my country illegally."

"I don't mean to be," Paul sniveled, rather convincingly he hoped. "We were hunting on the other side of the border when a blizzard came up. The snow was blinding, and I got separated from the party. Even after the snow stopped, the sky was overcast, and I couldn't get my bearings. I thought I was going west, but I must have been coming east for more than a day. As I keep telling you, I am not at all familiar with this part of Europe."

"We found a perfectly serviceable compass in your pack. How could you have been lost?"

"I looked for it after the storm and couldn't find it. I must have panicked. I was sure I had lost it in the snow."

"How very awkward for you."

"Anyway, the next thing I knew, I was swallowed up by that snow pit that caved in on me by the river. I would have been a goner if your people hadn't come in so quickly and dug me out." Now Paul's voice had modulated to less of a whimper. "How can I thank you enough?"

"How?" the officer asked. His face was now a contorted mask of disdain and irritation, as he brusquely returned the pistol to its holster.

"I'll tell you how to thank us. Quit treating us like idiots. Don't you know the moon rises in the east? The sky was quite clear when we found you. Stop lying to me. Tell me how you really got here."

"I'm no good at night navigation, and I tell you I'm not lying," Paul protested.

"No? Then why do you say you were out there alone?"

"Because I was alone," Paul said a little more steadily than before.

"Oh, really? Then who was it that our observer saw going ahead of you into the forest?"

"I saw no one else. There was absolutely no one with me."

"We saw him."

"You couldn't have. I was alone."

"Stop insulting my intelligence."

"I'm trying to help, but I don't want to lie to you. I was entirely by myself."

"I have no need to talk to fools!" the officer shouted, slapping Paul across the face and knocking him to the floor.

Paul was relieved to note that it was a firm blow, but not a tooth-loosener.

Thank you, Lord. He whimpered and massaged his jaw, suggesting the injury had been much worse. He bit the inside of his cheek and managed to spit a little blood to amplify that point.

Not counting the threat to shoot him, this was only the third time he had suffered moderate violence at the hands of his low-level questioners. Just as he had hoped, a higher headquarters seemed to be keeping these people on a short leash about physical duress. That was a benefit he knew would run out when he was moved up the chain of command.

"I will be back, Nolan, and there will be others as well," the major grumbled, going out and securing the lock on the wire-mesh door.

27

Paul's austere surroundings gave him no sure means for telling time. He could only guess that the crude but intensive interrogation in his hospital cell and several even more depressing parts of the building had gone on for more than three days. After a while, he was allowed to take a much needed shower, given some rough workingman's clothes to wear, handcuffed, and told that it was time to go.

The only personal items he still had were his boots. They had been through a lot and showed it. They too would have been taken, he supposed, had their appearance been any more attractive.

His body had sustained more adversity than his footwear, both before and during his captivity. He felt the pain and did not try to hide it. He wanted to appear weak, wounded, and confused. That strategy may have been less effective than Paul would have liked, but he reckoned it spared him a few gratuitous blows from the bush-league players he was up against at the Ministry of Interior hospital facility. At least, he still had his teeth and was visibly in about the same condition in which he had reawakened to the world.

No more of that, he told himself, grimly. *Now I'm going up to play hardball with the big kids at headquarters. They will be about as patient, empathetic, and gullible as a hungry tiger tracking a stray goat.*

He was wrong.

Instead of delivering him to durance vile in the capital city, his keepers took him to the international airport just outside it. Here he was unshackled and turned over to a functionary of the American Embassy, who presented him with a new passport just like the old phony one, which had been confiscated. Paul had to sign for this with his real name, as well as for a book of $500 in traveler's checks, a business-class ticket from Frankfurt, Germany to Baltimore/Washington International Airport, and a standard ticket to Frankfurt on the local national airline. He was also given a carry-on bag, his only luggage, which he later found to contain toiletries, a change of clothes, a cheap wrist watch, a handful of West German coins in a plastic bag, and a most welcome pair of comfortable loafers in his size. Having already breathed a silent prayer of thanksgiving, he asked an added blessing upon the headquarters-staff operator who had thought of the shoes.

The man from the embassy had the charm and demeanor of a desk clerk in a no-star hotel. He spoke no more than fifty words, including directions to the appropriate boarding gate for Paul's outgoing flight.

"Grogan will meet you at BWI," were the only other words that mattered to Paul.

In cases like this, Paul kept any questions he might have to himself. The emissary, he knew, would have no answers.

Napping through the comparatively short flight to Frankfurt hardly compensated Paul for so many sleepless hours in his constantly lighted cage, regularly interrupted by aggressive interrogation, random noise, and revolting music at a very high volume. His captors had wanted to keep him awake, and they did.

The Frankfurt International Flughafen is a great place to kill time if you must. Paul arrived in the evening and was pleased to have several hours before boarding time to Baltimore. First he washed up, shaved, and changed clothes in a rest room. The lavatory attendant, provided with the Deutch Mark coins from Paul's plastic bag, procured materials and assisted Paul in changing the old, unsightly wound dressing on his forehead.

Refreshed and clean, Paul exploited a traveler's check at one of the Flughafen's fine restaurants, where he supplemented his limited and unappetizing, prison-ward fare with a richly satisfying *jaegerschnitzel* dinner.

After disposing of the last flavorful remnants of meat, sauce, and boiled potatoes, Paul remained at his table enjoying his first cup of palatable coffee since before the last operation. The restaurant had no walls and was open to the general airport waiting areas. Still, it was redolent with tempting aromas and permeated by an atmosphere of quiet comfort. Paul sat, relaxing and happily scanning the current international edition of *Time*, when a shadow fell across the page.

"Have a chair, Barney," Paul said without looking up.

"How did you know it was me?" Bernard Rice asked in his customarily quiet, cultivated speech, tinged slightly with an acquired English accent.

Paul smiled while Barney seated himself across the table.

"I've told you before, Barney. If you ever want to make a break for it and disappear, you will have to give up smoking that pipe. Even when it isn't in your mouth, you and everything you have on emits the very distinctive scent of Balkan Sobranije tobacco."

Barney smiled graciously from under his thick, ginger mustache and pale-blue eyes. He had spent much of his adult life on the continent and was something of a Europhile. Today he was wearing a heavy Harris Tweed jacket over a black turtleneck and had just removed a snap-brim, green, Tyrolean hat, which he placed gently on the table next to a tightly rolled, British gentleman's umbrella.

"Maybe I should be asking how you found me here," Paul suggested.

"No problem at all, my friend. Grogan advised me when you

were coming in. I knew how long it was since you had a decent meal. It didn't take much logic to guess I would find you in the first good restaurant you might come to. Beyond that, the bandage on your head sort of flagged you for identification."

"You should have seen what I looked like when I arrived here. Anyway, Sherlock, you've done it again."

"*Nein, danke,*" Barney told the waiter, who had approached to see if he wanted anything.

After the waiter retreated, Barney began speaking clearly but softly with a facial expression that showed no sign of seriousness.

"I thought you'd bought it that night."

"So did I," Paul replied, "and you will never know just how certain of that I was. What did it look like from where you stood?"

"Pretty confusing. I was stumped when I turned around inside the tree line and found you weren't there—nowhere at all. Then all of a sudden there was that stinking APC coming down the embankment.

"I knew the zone was unsafe for loitering, but I stayed long enough to see the APC stop at a point along our track. A half-dozen troops jumped out and started running around like crazy. At first, I thought you might have been shot, but then I could tell they were digging for something. I presumed it was you they pulled out and dragged to the vehicle, but I could not hang back any longer to confirm it."

"Understood," Paul said. Then he told Barney about falling into the snow pit, going under and thinking he was going to die. He omitted any reference to his experiences between then and waking up in the Ministry of Interior prison ward. Paul was still waiting for the right opportunity to sift through those events for what he himself thought about them.

"At least the operation went down all right," Barney said. "After that, I got through to Grogan and let him know what had happened."

"That's good. What did Grogan have to say?"

"You can guess," Barney said with a shrugging gesture. "The decoded cable read, 'Barney, you idiot! Strong message will follow.'"

They both laughed.

"I'm sure neither one of us has heard the last of it," Paul said. "Grogan is meeting me personally at BWI. I expect he will have more than a few choice words about our exploit. Are we going back on the same bird?"

"Mercifully not," Barney came back. "I have some chores to do in Wiesbaden, Bonn, and Munich before my repatriation comes through. I'm on my way to Wiesbaden right now. I'll probably see you in a few weeks."

"My flight leaves in a couple of hours."

"Don't count on it; the atmosphere is kind of thick outside."

Barney, it developed, was a reliable prophet. The weather was consistent with Frankfurt in late January: wet snow, freezing rain, and fog. Boarding was postponed three times until long past midnight, when passengers were able to take seats on the Delta Airlines Boeing 747 and go on waiting impatiently for it to be de-iced again before takeoff.

With all the delays, Paul thought, an eight-hour, non-stop flight should put him at BWI just before seven a.m. Since he was flying from east to west, arrival time would be only a few hours later than the departure time from Frankfurt. The original schedule would have forced Grogan to meet him in the very wee hours. Now Grogan might get a little more sleep, but knowing Grogan's disregard for anyone's convenience, Paul doubted that would make any difference.

Once airborne, Paul wanted to think. He intensely wanted to think about the Vale and what had happened to him there. He started to do that, but fatigue, a moderately full stomach, and the comparative comfort and leg room of his business-class seat overtook him. He fell asleep instead.

About six-and-a-half hours into the flight, the attendants roused all the passengers to complete the necessary U.S. Customs paperwork. Paul finished his declaration forms swiftly and took a turn in the restroom. Then he drew his seat to the upright position and fastened the seat belt to keep the attendants from bothering him.

He was fairly rested now. It was safe to close his eyes and think about the Vale in a way he had not been able to from the moment he had been torn out of it and painfully returned to life.

Closing his eyes this way reminded him of what that had meant in the Vale. There it had locked every sensual impression away from his consciousness, so he might know only the internal working of his spirit in meditation. How different that was from here, with the continuous intrusion of smells, sounds, and the feeling of things, like the inescapable vibrations of the aircraft. Could he attain the clarity of thought he had enjoyed when he closed his eyes in the Vale?

Not in this world, he thought. Grogan had said something like that—the Grogan he knew in the Vale, not the one he was going to meet at BWI. What was it?

Grogan had been saying that, having found grace through faith, people must not think that they are fully locked into self-realization and happiness for life—not in this life. With all of the world's distractions, our very best efforts to focus on Jesus and be ourselves would fail as often as not, but it was the trying that counted.

Look at the saints and martyrs, remembered for their great suffering and sacrifices. They were almost always surrounded by poverty, disease, hatred, and ugliness, but Jesus and the apostles said they are the happiest of all. They were more themselves here than most of us get to be until we come to the Vale or beyond.

Paul wondered why he had been taken to the Vale at all. Does God make mistakes? How could that be?

If Paul looked at linear time alone, it would be easy to say that he had been clinically dead. He was taken away then, but sent back because he was not dead any more. Did that make sense? Maybe it would in a movie script, but not if you reasoned according to simultaneous infinity the way Matt Harriford had explained it. God knew Paul was not finished then, because he knew Paul would be revived. Moreover, he knows when Paul does die.

Funny, wasn't it? Paul now felt so natural and right, blending different tenses when he thought about God. He was forced to conclude that simultaneous infinity was the only way to explain how he spent so much time in the Vale, but so few minutes in the snow pit. As Matt had pointed out, Paul was already in heaven anyway.

Even with simultaneous infinity, or maybe because of it, Paul was having trouble with an obvious paradox. Neither Matt nor Grogan had seemed at all aware that his visit to the Vale would be interrupted. No word they said should have led him to expect anything other than a contiguous completion of his transition to heaven. One of Dr. Trumbull's remarks might be suspect, but nothing else Paul heard in the Vale held a clue to his impending return to earth.

Matt said he had outlived Paul by eight years. Was he talking about eight years from now, or was it from some other date in the future, when Paul would actually die?

Grogan was obviously still alive. Did he know in the Vale what was truly happening to Paul, or did he know Paul to have died at a later date?

Just a minute! What if it did not matter when Paul died? Matt had said it did not. In simultaneous infinity, Paul would be there in the Vale anyway. Matt may be going to die ten or fifteen years in the future, not just eight. *Remember what he said about the relativity of all life on the linear track? Nobody changes position.* Effectively, all Matt said was that Paul had died eight years into Matt's *was* at the time of Matt's own death. If Matt dies eight years into what would have been Paul's *will be* except for Paul's death, it is the same thing. All life in linear time is relative. The same approach would work for Grogan, although Paul had no idea what the linear span might be.

Hold on. Who says Grogan will not die first? The only thing for sure is that he survives beyond Paul's fall in the snow. He could as easily visit Paul in the Vale as Miss Janet did. *Who knows when she died, or even if she has?*

Matt had warned him about this. Paul could not assume anything about God's space and time by looking at what was happening on earth.

All time on earth is linear and relative. God's time is neither one. It makes no difference when you die. Everybody winds up at the same place at the same time. So you spend a day or an eon in the Vale. So what? It does not matter. You still go to meet God where and when he is all at once—all of you.

That was it. Paul knew what had happened. He was back on earth, where time is linear and relative, but his immortal soul was also in the Vale, where nothing is linear or relative. Everyone he met in the Vale expected him to continue his transition to heaven because he does; he was doing that right now. Here, he was confined to a single moment and one place at a time. There, he was not. In God's simultaneous infinity there was no contradiction. He could not be sure, but it seemed likely that, when he finally did die, he might find himself back in the Vale exactly when his memory of it had been interrupted.

Since his return, Paul had never asked himself if his memories of the Vale were real. There were things he still did not understand, but he knew beyond doubt that he had been in the Vale. This was no illusion. Neither was it faith. It was fact.

So, once again, Paul, what do you think? Does God make mistakes?

No.

Now, Paul began to understand. This was no mistake, and that would have a great influence on what he did next.

He could feel the aircraft wheels touching down on the runway.

28

In those days, more than a few people flew long distance without stowed baggage, but they were a measurable minority among those passengers routinely examined by U.S. Customs officials. Paul was among this select group when he arrived that morning from Frankfurt-am-Main. Not needing to wait for checked bags allowed him to proceed with relative speed to one of the customs counters at BWI.

The young, male Customs Officer took Paul's passport and then looked down at his carryon bag.

"Is that all?" he asked.

"That's it," Paul replied.

As if to postpone the matter of inspection, the officer opened and closely examined Paul's passport. Suddenly, his face reflected a flash of recognition. He leaned across the counter and spoke quietly to Paul.

"Sir, could you follow me please."

Paul had been expecting something like this, so he scooped up the little bag and went around the end of the counter to follow the officer into an adjoining corridor. Passengers behind him may have thought that Paul was in deep trouble. Perhaps he was a drug-smuggling suspect being taken to some interior cell for hardboiled customs agents to make a minute examination of his bodily orifices.

About ten yards down the corridor, the officer stopped at an entrance marked Private. Handing Paul his passport, the officer stood aside while Paul passed through and closed the door behind him.

"I ought to fire you both." There was Grogan, sitting behind a gray, government-issue desk in a pigmy chair definitely not his own. Maybe the absence of that powerful totem was contributing to Grogan's irritation.

"Both of us?"

"You and Barney. What a stupid stunt. How could I have sent two clumsy jerks like you to handle so delicate a job?"

"Lighten up, boss. It wasn't all that delicate."

"I'll lighten you up. Anyone who crosses an open meadow next to a river deserves to be buried alive and left behind."

"You have a point," Paul murmured. Grogan, he could see, was not finished thrashing him and would stop only when that distasteful job was done.

"I'm going to make you two immortal. Every operational trainee from now on will study your last job as a perfect example of how not to move through a hostile area. You will become the Laurel and Hardy of covert operations. How do you like that?"

"Thank you," Paul smiled, "we deserve nothing less. And while I'm at it, thanks also for saving my wretched butt from the imprisonment it so richly deserved."

"What else could I do for such an old friend?" Grogan broke into the broadest of grins as he came around the desk to grasp Paul's right hand tightly with both of his. "You don't know what you put us through."

"I can imagine, but tell me anyway."

"Don't ask! You couldn't imagine—and I won't tell you—what I had to give the State Department to do its diplomatic stunts with your host country. And you would never believe what kind of international concessions State traded away to get you back."

"Still, the goons held on to me less than a week. That's got to be a record game, even for you."

"From what I'm told, the only reason it worked so fast this time was that their Foreign Ministry is locked in a bitter, inter-ministerial fight with the Ministry of Interior. The foreign minister just couldn't pass up an opportunity to wave his organizational seniority under Interior's nose. That did the trick for you, Paul. You owe your freedom to the power of bureaucratic envy and spite. Be grateful."

"I am, Grogan, but I am no less thankful to you. Nothing would have happened if you had not gone to the limit for me. Without your crafty deal-making on our end, I would have been lucky to grow old and die in one of the camps. Less lucky and I would have just been shot in some farmer's courtyard and left for the hogs to eat."

"You're welcome, Paul." Grogan went back around the desk, sat down and leaned forward with his elbows propped on the desktop and his fingers laced in front of his chest. Paul was reminded of the time in Okinawa when Grogan had so skillfully manipulated Jason and himself into affirming his authority and doing what he wanted. This was not a good sign.

"Now, you know..." Grogan paused in order to rivet Paul's attention on what would follow. "I would not have come out here to meet you, unless I had something for you that will not wait."

"Work? Do I look like somebody rested and ready to go right back into the field? Check again. Look into my sunken eyes, and I'll bare my teeth. Want to see my bruises? What do you think is under this crummy rag on my scalp? I haven't weighed myself, but I'll bet I've lost twenty pounds in less than a week."

"Come on. I'm not going to be unreasonable. You'll have at least a week for recovery, debriefing, and rebriefing. Give me a break."

"Give *me* a break! I know I owe you my life—this time and a few others—but I'm through with this business. Not just now, but for good."

"You don't mean that." Grogan did not look apprehensive at this point. He truly did not believe what he had heard.

"I do. Trust me, I do."

This time something in Paul's voice and expression got through. Grogan winced like a baseball fan who finds his favorite team has just blown its last chance at the playoffs. He reacted instinctively.

"Wait a minute. I know you're tired. Maybe I should look somewhere else for an operator on this one. If you need some time off, you've got it." Grogan was giving ground fast, trying to convince both Paul and himself that Paul's decision was not final.

Paul felt a huge debt to Grogan, but he had made a commitment from which he could not withdraw.

"You don't understand," Paul said. "It isn't your operation that puts me off, and I don't particularly need a vacation. I made up my mind before I got off the plane."

This was not exactly true, because Paul had not actually thought about his job on the airplane. His resignation just followed quite naturally from the other conclusions he had reached along the way.

"My decision has nothing to do with you or the organization, Grogan. This is the only real job I've ever had—and I love it—but I can't do it any more. I have to go right now."

"Will you at least tell me why?" Grogan asked.

"Maybe someday, but not now. I know my timing doesn't make much sense to you—believe me—but right now I can't articulate what I'm doing, at least not in any way you would understand. If I tried, you'd probably restrain me and send me off to the Walter Reed neuro-psych ward for a few weeks of observation."

At that moment, Paul recalled his conversation with Grogan in the Vale.

"I can honestly promise that you will eventually know the whole story. I just can't talk about it now."

"What can I say?" Grogan asked plaintively.

Paul could tell that his behavior had taken Grogan completely off guard. Still, he could see that Grogan, the cunning manipulator, was not giving up.

"Nothing. Please. Just accept my resignation as of this moment. Admin has my mailing address. Have them send me all the info trash and everything I need to sign."

"Aren't you forgetting the debriefing you owe us for this operation?"

"No. I'll come in this afternoon to write it up, but that will be my final contribution to the organization. I'll turn in my documents and credentials and clear out through security at the same time."

"All right, Paul." Grogan never surrendered easily. Cut off on one flank, he repositioned himself and pressed the attack. "We both know you're getting pretty long-in-the-tooth for field operations. You're overdue for advancement, but to move up you need to come completely out of the field and take a management position. I have been planning for quite a while to offer you an upper-level slot developing and directing field activities from here. If you're ready for that, it's ready for you. Can we just forget this aberration and move on?"

Paul could not remember ever seeing such a conciliatory side to Grogan. He gave a deep sigh,

"I hope you won't think me ungrateful, but I can't turn back now. I want the job you're offering even less than the job I'm giving up."

"You've been here over twenty years. Even if you quit now, you'll be due a pension when you're sixty-two."

"Mail it to me, Grogan." Paul instantly regretted the unfeeling tone of that remark.

"Look," Paul said, trying to help Grogan understand. "Would you want a man on this next operation, or any of them, who did not want to be in control of things? Would you want someone directing operations who did not even want to direct his own life?"

Grogan remained silent, but Paul could tell that he had hit the target with more finality than intended. Now Grogan was questioning the trust and respect he had given Paul for so many years.

Loyalty was the prime virtue for Grogan. He could never tolerate disloyalty, personal or professional. At this moment he probably considered Paul to be guilty of both. Paul knew that Grogan would no longer oppose his resignation.

"Okay," Grogan said, leaning back in the chair and looking at the ceiling with his fingers still together.

Paul wanted to say something more, to at least shake hands before leaving, but Grogan stayed as he was. His last word was said. Anything more would only be hopelessly awkward.

Paul had the comfort of recalling his experience with Grogan in the Vale. He knew that Grogan would finally understand and forgive what he had done. Yet, Grogan had not mentioned it there. In the Vale, Paul supposed, things like that were just not worth talking about.

Paul turned around and left the room. He was uncomfortable, turning his back on the mentor and friend who had just saved his life. This time he simply had to do it.

Unlike many events in Paul's life, this decision offered no lack of alternatives. He had plenty of options, but only one right path to take. Now he was taking it.

29

It was after eight o'clock and some of the stores in the BWI main concourse were open. Paul did not plan to go directly to his apartment, so he invested another traveler's check in a windbreaker jacket to keep himself warm on the wintry Washington streets. All the checks he had signed for would, he knew, be deducted from his final pay.

He caught an airport limo to the nearby light-rail station and rode a train into D.C., arriving at Union Station. The hour was still early and he was hungry, so after stowing his small bag in a temporary locker, he stopped in the food arcade for a breakfast of bagels and cream cheese, which occupied him until around ten o'clock.

Coming out of Union Station onto Pennsylvania Avenue, Paul was thankful for the jacket. Skies were clear, but the morning was sharply cold and windy. He turned right and walked briskly past the J. Edgar Hoover Building on the left toward the National Archives a few blocks away. His purpose that day did not lie in the main offices, so he turned south at Ninth Street and followed the west side of the complex to Constitution Avenue. There he turned left and walked on until he came to the main entrance of the rotunda in the middle of the block. Climbing the steep steps to its impressive, high-pillared porch, he went in.

As he had done so many times before, he planned to make the rotunda his retreat of solitude and thought. On the way there, he had intentionally diverted his thoughts from what lay ahead. Now he hoped to capture some degree of the disembodiment he could command in the Vale by closing his eyes. That was why he stationed himself quietly and comfortably at the rear, well back from the document area where the tourists would be. He was standing not far from the location where Petra had suddenly come back into his life.

Pondering the Vale, he recalled something odd he knew about this building. The rotunda and exhibit hall sort of nestled into the Constitution Avenue side, while the main offices were on Pennsylvania Avenue. Each floor on the main side had a wide, vaulted corridor running east and west at the front of the building. An observer standing in one of those corridors might become curious about the difference between the relatively modest interior space that is visible and the full, two-city-block building seen from the outside.

During his archivist training, Paul had learned what creates that paradox. Beyond those elevators, corridors, and the main rooms to which they gave access lay the bulk of the building's interior, arrayed with many low-ceilinged floors, connected by narrow stairways, where a multitude of documents were catalogued and stored. Effectively, the broad perimeter of a few high-ceilinged floors embraced and concealed much larger spaces with many more floors, where unseen archivists labored to preserve the nation's precious records. Invisible as those inner spaces may have been, they were no less real or important than what one could see from outside. Somehow, thinking about that phenomenon helped him relate to his memory of the Vale and its many remaining mysteries.

He had sorted out quite a few things this morning on the airplane, but now he needed to critically re-examine all of it. What was he being called to do?

Called? Isn't that a little presumptuous?

I don't think so. If God doesn't make mistakes, my experience in the Vale must have had a purpose.

Sure it had a purpose. You were dead. The Vale is where dead people go, unless they wind up in the terminal ward.

But that's what I mean. I was going to be revived. God knows that. So I should not have gone to the Vale just because I was momentarily dead. That would mean God made a mistake, but we know he doesn't make mistakes. Where does that leave me?

Looking for a reason why God did it that way, I guess.

Precisely, so I must have learned something there that God wanted me to know back here.

You tell me. What did you learn?

That's just it. I cannot make it out. Simultaneous infinity was big news to me, but it is not something I would have to go out of this world to conceive. It helps me understand quite a few things about the Bible and my faith in God, but it does not particularly help me do anything in my current linear universe.

What's that about faith in God? Weren't you talking to Grogan about that in the Vale?

Yes, Grogan said that faith in God is not much more than finding out nothing else can make us happy. Also, remember that happiness comes from being ourselves the way God made us. Grogan told me that happiness is the authentic experience of self. That is not being your own self, but being the self God made.

Then identity is the thing. Your true identity, not some false one you made up.

Isn't that obvious?

Hey! You're the one running around with a phony passport.

You're right. That's just it, or part of it, anyway. I have been living under a false identity. Not just the passport, and I don't mean like one of those poor souls in the terminal ward. If I were headed there, I would never have come to in the Vale.

Still, I have been moving in my own direction at my own speed. When you think about it, my phony passports make a pretty good metaphor for the counterfeit path most of my life has followed. I've spent it all in a repressive line of work. I lived in constant fear. If I lost control, things could go fatally bad for me and other people. Remember Jason? That is what I was trying to make Grogan understand this morning. I don't want to do that anymore. I can't, because God has something else for me to do.

There you go being pretentious again. What makes you so special? There are zillions of people carrying phony passports out there. Why would God pick you?

I don't know, but I don't think I should be asking that question. It isn't for me to ask. Remember the prophets? Remember Moses? Most of them started out asking, "Why me, Lord?" or saying, "Not me, Lord. You've got the wrong guy."

Perhaps you're right. But if that's it, what does he want you to do?

I don't know. But I am convinced of this. I have been granted a prophetic vision. Maybe that was the main reason for my untimely trip to the Vale. Maybe that's how some prophets are called. Couldn't that be what's happened to me?

You? A prophet? Get serious.

Look. Prophets are not just people who receive a revelation from God, although I certainly got one in the Vale. They are also people God sends out to do things. Think of Moses, Elijah, Ezekiel, and even St. Paul. Prophetic vision is not only a view of future events. It can also be God's call and command.

What about Isaiah, Daniel, and the Revelation of John the apostle? Might some of the prophets of the Bible have visited the Vale as prematurely as I did? It is always there, you know, and they may have received the same kind of cultural imagery support that I was given.

You think you're as good as those guys?

No. I am not vain enough to put myself in company with biblical prophets, but the fact remains that I came back from the Vale. Souls do not usually travel in that direction. That alone means there is something important going on, and I am about to be up to my neck in it.

If calling what has happened a prophetic vision seems too strong, think of it as a conversion experience. Maybe that is not just a once-in-a-lifetime thing. Maybe some people have lots of them, but if the c-word hangs you up, call them epiphanies or revelations. Some are wholly spiritual, but others may come through God-driven reasoning. I know now that my childhood conversion was real, even if I managed at the time to almost worry myself out of it. My next big epiphany was that night in Texas, when barroom theology and reasoning led me to purely spiritual discoveries about God and myself. That one got away from me, but God brought me back to it in the Philippines with Father Don. Now God has hit me with a major league revelation by cycling my soul through the Vale.

What I experienced and was told in the Vale gives me a certainty about life here and hereafter that most souls cannot achieve in the here and now. At this very moment, some of God's holiest servants on earth are asking questions about God to which I already have some answers. All this must have a purpose, but what is it? Whatever God intends for me, he now has my full attention.

I guess that's something, but what else can you say?

I am not sure, but what happened to me in the Vale was some kind of preparation.

Weren't you being prepared for heaven?

Yes, but this is something more than that, or I would not be here now. I was being prepared for some very specific service to God.

Are you sure of that?

Nothing else makes sense. I had four good sessions with people I have known here. Each of them was in some way dramatically different from the person I knew on earth. Each had some terribly important things to tell me. Some, if not all, of them are still living. Yet, I talked to them there as they are for eternity.

Most of them had changed substantially before they left earth. Think of Matt and Dr. Trumbull. I saw them in the Vale as their true selves, selves even they did not fully know or become when they were here. Except for Miss Janet, I did not know them at all that way before.

Maybe they had no idea I would be coming back here, or maybe they knew. It does not matter. What they said there has brought me to an altogether different spiritual outlook. Was that because I am going to need it? I think so. Before long, I will be given something to do.

What?

Whatever I am told—God will take care of that part. My job is to listen in every way I can: prayer, study, worship, and meditation. I may even be sent to do a little down-to-earth searching for a place and way to serve. Maybe it will be something like the 360-degree assessment I was thinking about just before I was dumped out of the Vale. Any way that may be, I expect the whole process to take whatever remains of my life.

For now, perhaps I should call Father Don to see about some kind of retreat.

Who knows? Maybe Dr. Trumbull's references to systematic, social injustice hold a clue to what God has in store for me.

There you go again. Stop hurrying things. Stop trying to take control.

"Not that, Lord," Paul prayed. "Please help me not to do that."

Paul stretched and walked out of the rotunda.

He paused a moment on the high porch to take a deep breath from the crisp, winter morning. It was almost noon, but for him the day was just beginning.

For the first time it occurred to him to wonder what Petra might think when she found out he was no longer with the organization.

They were still very close and she had not remarried. The thought was a tempting distraction, but he put it on hold. Personal concerns could wait while he gave attention to more immediate priorities.

He needed to prepare for something he could not predict, a life totally different from any he had known or planned. His vision of that new life was still blurred and uncertain. Yet, he was confident and secure, no longer in his own control of things, but in God's control of him. He had learned at least that much in the Vale, but even with that advantage, maintaining his balance would be difficult. He would sometimes fail.

Why? Knowing what he knew now, why couldn't he hold on permanently to the truth he had seen? The fact was he had seen plenty of that truth before he knew about the Vale. He could not unerringly hold on to it then, and he would only be somewhat better at that now. After all, he was still who he was and where he was. He again recalled that paraphrase from Grogan of the Vale—not in *this* life.

Watching the traffic below, he remembered his recent thoughts about false passports. He had often carried them in his former career to support cover-stories and legends that obscured his true identity. This was not the sort of thing most people did, but he now recognized it as a parallel to the double lives everyone built into their souls, schizophrenic facades that clouded reason and camouflaged spiritual truth. The point of this comparison had eluded him in the pain and confusion of coming back to earth, but now he saw what Grogan was talking about.

Just being in earth's universe would always make it impossible for Paul, even with his Vale insight, to fully appreciate his own identity. By God's grace through faith alone, mortals might muddle through, but all would regularly fail to maintain a pure vision of the soul's most urgent need and divinely granted reality.

That, Paul thought, *is why God took me to the Vale, and until this moment, I did not recognize it.* This was not exactly so, he realized. Only now had he begun to explore the most memorable aspect of his voyage. What he had been told in the Vale was important enough, but theological tutoring was not the root outcome that made his visit there so purposeful.

His memory informed him by replaying those desperate moments from the Hungarian Revolution when life and death seemed to depend on his ability to extract meaning from a core of intense radio interference. Maybe the static noise of earth would eventually distort some of his recollection of the Vale, but he hoped he would always remember the absolute identity of his own soul that he had known for every instant he had been there. It was the experience of what he had unwittingly defined for Matt Harriford as completion, something so natural, right, and true that he had barely noticed it at the time. Recalling it now brought him a fleeting, unearthly recreation of the sublime.

Back on earth, a prisoner of the linear and the relative, Paul at last understood. In the Vale he had fully and continuously discovered what Grogan called the authentic experience of self. He ached to be like that again. Now he knew he would.

Author's Note

The Vale is just fiction. I made it up so I could explore a soul's identity in conflict with its human ego, as that might seem to someone outside the world looking back.

Simultaneous infinity is something else. I chose that term to embrace some thoughtful proposals, but it is not new. Immanuel Kant mentioned it. Some skeptics have called it impossible and used that judgment to minimize the powers of God. I cannot prove it, but it is an interesting concept that might reconcile what look like contradictions in Christian Scripture and tradition. Writing about the Vale, I did not have to argue that simultaneous infinity might be. I only had to have some characters say that it is and see how that worked. For me it did.

While I was concentrating on questions of faith, some of my characters seemed to get ahead of me with agendas of their own. Please remember; these are fictional folks. What they say about *how* God does things is pure guesswork. What they say about God's nature and ours speaks, I think, to the heart of Christian faith.

Paul's shadowy organization, cover arrangements, and covert

operations are all factless fabrications. Official policies against homosexuals in the federal government are accurate where they appear in the story, but have significantly moderated since that time.

Some dates are generalized, but the earthly action, other than flashbacks, is set during the Cold War soon after 1980. In the Vale, of course, the time is always now.